M000167205

Praise for Melanie Dickerson

"This second volume in best-seller Dickerson's Dericott Tales series follows two narrators who overcome self-doubt in accepting their physical differences and gain the confidence to love while finding solace in their Christianity . . . Dickerson writes a well-developed and wholesome romance between pleasant characters whose happy ending readers will easily root for."

—*Booklist*

"Dickerson does a nice job of evoking late-14th-century England and has succeeded in crafting a pair of engaging—if sugary-sweet—characters that romance readers will enjoy following. The Christian flavor of the story feels natural and appropriate to the time period."

—*Kirkus Reviews* on *Castle of Refuge*

"*Court of Swans* is a well-crafted escape thriller with plenty of longing glances to break up scenes of sword fighting. Delia is a compelling protagonist because she is able to see the good in people—rarely do you see an obviously wicked stepmother so often given the benefit of the doubt. A perfect pick for fans of period dramas who want a little action mixed into their romance."

—Molly Horan, *Booklist*

"*The Piper's Pursuit* is a lovely tale of adventure, romance, and redemption. Kat and Steffan's righteous quest will have you rooting them on until the very satisfying end!"

—Lorie Langdon, author of *Olivia Twist* and the Doon series

"Christian fiction fans will relish Dickerson's eloquent story."

—*School Library Journal* on *The Orphan's Wish*

"*The Goose Girl*, a little retold fairy tale, sparkles in Dickerson's hands, with endearing characters and a charming setting that will appeal to teens and adults alike."

—RT BOOK REVIEWS, 4$\frac{1}{2}$ STARS, TOP
PICK! ON THE NOBLE SERVANT

"Dickerson is a masterful storyteller with a carefully crafted plot, richly drawn characters, and a detailed setting. The reader is easily pulled into the story."

—CHRISTIAN LIBRARY JOURNAL ON THE NOBLE SERVANT

"[*The Silent Songbird*] will have you jumping out of your seat with anticipation at times. Moderate- to fast-paced, you will not want this book to end. Recommended for all, especially lovers of historical romance."

—RT BOOK REVIEWS, 4 STARS

"A terrific YA crossover medieval romance from the author of *The Golden Braid*."

—LIBRARY JOURNAL ON THE SILENT SONGBIRD

"When it comes to happily-ever-afters, Melanie Dickerson is the undisputed queen of fairy-tale romance, and all I can say is—long live the queen! From start to finish *The Beautiful Pretender* is yet another brilliant gem in her crown, spinning a medieval love story that will steal you away—heart, soul, and sleep!"

—JULIE LESSMAN, AWARD-WINNING AUTHOR OF
THE DAUGHTERS OF BOSTON, WINDS OF CHANGE,
AND HEART OF SAN FRANCISCO SERIES

"Dickerson breathes life into the age-old story of Rapunzel, blending it seamlessly with the other YA novels she has written in this time and place . . . The character development is solid, and she captures religious medieval life splendidly."

—BOOKLIST ON THE GOLDEN BRAID

"Readers who love getting lost in a fairy-tale romance will cheer for Rapunzel's courage as she rises above her overwhelming past. The surprising way Dickerson weaves threads of this enchanting companion novel with those of her other Hagenheim stories is simply delightful."

—JILL WILLIAMSON, CHRISTY AWARD–
WINNING AUTHOR, ON *THE GOLDEN BRAID*

"Dickerson spins a retelling of Robin Hood with emotionally compelling characters, offering hope that love may indeed conquer all as they unite in a shared desire to serve both the Lord and those in need."

—*RT BOOK REVIEWS*, 4$^{1}/2$ STARS, ON *THE
HUNTRESS OF THORNBECK FOREST*

"Melanie Dickerson does it again! Full of danger, intrigue, and romance, this beautifully crafted story [*The Huntress of Thornbeck Forest*] will transport you to another place and time."

—SARAH E. LADD, BESTSELLING AUTHOR
OF THE CORNWALL NOVELS

FORTRESS
of SNOW

Other Books by
Melanie Dickerson

FORTRESS
of SNOW

MELANIE
DICKERSON

THOMAS NELSON
Since 1798

Published in Nashville, Tennessee, by Thomas Nelson. Thomas Nelson is a
registered trademark of HarperCollins Christian Publishing, Inc.

Thomas Nelson titles may be purchased in bulk for educational, business,
fund-raising, or sales promotional use. For information, please email
SpecialMarkets@ThomasNelson.com.

Publisher's Note: This novel is a work of fiction. Names, characters, places,
and incidents are either products of the author's imagination or used
fictitiously. All characters are fictional, and any similarity to people living or
dead is purely coincidental.

Library of Congress Cataloging-in-Publication Data

Names: Dickerson, Melanie, author.
Title: Fortress of snow / Melanie Dickerson.
Description: Nashville, Tennessee : Thomas Nelson, [2022] | Series: The
  Dericott Tales ; 4 | Summary: In medieval England, Mazy tries to find
  her place in the world and meets a friendly knight, Sir Berenger.
Identifiers: LCCN 2022020911 (print) | LCCN 2022020912 (ebook) |
  ISBN
  9780785250807 (hardcover) | ISBN 9780785250814 (epub) | ISBN
  9780785250821
Subjects: CYAC: Love--Fiction. | Knights and knighthood--Fiction. |
  Christian life--Fiction. | Middle Ages--Fiction. | Great
  Britain--History--Medieval period, 1066-1485--Fiction. | LCGFT: Novels.
Classification: LCC PZ7.D5575 Fo 2022 (print) | LCC PZ7.D5575
  (ebook) | DDC [Fic]--dc23
LC record available at https://lccn.loc.gov/2022020911
LC ebook record available at https://lccn.loc.gov/2022020912

Printed in the United States of America

22 23 24 25 26 LSC 10 9 8 7 6 5 4 3 2 1

To Aaron
The one I love
The one who loves me

ONE

ENGLAND

SPRING 1383

MAZY RAN HOME CLUTCHING THE FLOWERS SHE'D GATH-
ered in the meadow where the sheep sometimes grazed. She
hurried through the enormous front door and up the stairs to
her father's bedchamber.

"I picked you some flowers, Father," she called as she ran.
Bathilda, the head house servant, caught her by the arm.

"Don't make so much noise," she hissed in a raspy whisper.
"You're too old to be running around and yelling in sickrooms."

"I'm sorry, but I brought Father these flowers. They will
cheer him."

"It may be too late for that." Bathilda wiped her eyes with
her apron and Mazy noticed the tears on her face.

Still clutching the flowers, she rushed to her father's bedside, ignoring the physician, who sat on a stool with his arms crossed.

"Can you see the flowers, Father? I picked them for you, the blue and pink and yellow ones that you like."

Father barely opened his eyes. "Thank you, my child." His voice was so weak. What had happened? After being deathly ill for weeks, he had rallied earlier that morning, talking and even taking a bit of food. He was getting better.

Now he seemed paler and weaker than ever.

"Father, can I do anything for you?"

"Pray for me."

Mazy took his hand gently in hers and began praying softly under her breath, a rote prayer she'd learned from the priest intermingled with her own pleas for Father's health. When the tears choked off her voice, she prayed silently, *O God, if Father dies, I will be so alone. I don't want him to be in pain any longer, but please, I need him. What will I do if he leaves?*

Mazy's mother had been gone since she was five. Surely God would not take her father as well. Father was her protector and her voice of wisdom. He was such a good father, giving her opportunities to learn anything she set her mind to. She loved him, and he loved her. He was the only person in her life she could talk to, the only person who really listened to her.

The pain in her chest was nearly unbearable. He couldn't die. It hurt so much to think she might never hear his voice again, never talk to him again.

And if he died, what would become of her? She rarely saw her brothers, who no longer lived at home. Her brother John had gone to train as a knight when she was very little, and she had no other family besides her half brother, Warin.

Warin did not care for her, and he would inherit this house when Father died. Would Warin send her away? Where would she go? He would marry her off to the first man who asked for her.

God, please don't take Father. I love him and I need him. Her breath seemed to stop before it reached her chest.

But when she opened her eyes and looked at Father's face, he was so still, his chest no longer rising and falling. Surely nothing terrible had happened while she was praying.

His hand was limp inside hers. She moved away, her flowers dropping onto his chest.

The physician came forward and placed his cheek just above her father's face for the longest time. Then he pinched her father's nose and put his cheek on her father's lips. Finally, he straightened and looked at Mazy. He shook his head.

A sob escaped her throat. She ran out of the room and all the way to her own bedchamber and closed the door.

Painful sobs racked her chest as she tried to stop thinking, to let her mind go blank. But thoughts forced themselves on her, refusing to be pushed away.

"God, I am all alone," she cried into her pillow. "What will I do now?"

She pressed her hand against her chest. It hurt so much. Her father had been her friend. She'd loved him with all her heart, and now God had taken him from her.

The tears poured from her eyes. *Forgive me, God.*

She should not blame God, for He was her only hope, and

the only One who knew what would happen to her now that Father was gone.

Warin arrived the next day with his wife, Edith, and their eighteen-month-old son, Percy. Mazy watched them from her second-floor window as they walked from their horses to the front door.

Warin was a baron now, inheriting that title as well as the only home she'd ever known. He looked quite pleased, a small smile on his thin lips, not sad at all that his father was dead. But perhaps she was wrong to think that, to judge Warin by his expression.

She splashed some water on her face, dabbed her eyes with a cloth, then found her looking glass. Her eyelids were only slightly puffy and red, even though she had been crying all morning. If only her brother John would come home from Bedfordshire, where he was training squires with the Duke of Strachleigh. John would understand her pain, and she would not feel so alone if he were here.

Mazy had only been five years old when he was sent away, and their mother died the winter after John left. Mazy couldn't remember her mother's face, only that she was gentle. She did remember her mother's laugh, though, when Father would tell amusing tales at bedtime. And she remembered her father and mother staring into each other's eyes, smiling and embracing each other. Mazy's life had been rooted and strong in her parents' love.

She had missed John and had longed for him to come home. Once, when he was twelve years old and she was seven, he came for a visit. He knelt in front of her and said, "I will be a noble knight someday, and I will always protect you. If anyone tries to harm you, you must send me word. Understand?"

In awe of her strong and courageous older brother, she'd believed him with all her heart. But that was eight years ago. Did he remember his promise? Was he even at liberty to fulfill it? John had not been able to come home often, and the last time she'd seen him was two years ago. But with her father gone, she needed him now to be her protector.

She knew little about Warin and nothing about his mother, except that when she had died, Warin had gone to live with her family. She had seen him only two or three times in her life.

One memory of him remained with her, one she had recorded in the book of blank pages her father had bound together for her, where she wrote down her thoughts, poems, and things she found interesting. Warin had been about eighteen years old and she was ten. He had cornered her on the staircase when no one else was around. Staring at her, his upper lip curling, he spat out, "Father may like you and your brother best, but I will inherit this house. And when I do, you and John will not be welcome here."

Mazy went straight to her father and told him what Warin said.

"Warin was always cruel and ungrateful," Father said in a growly voice. Then he'd patted Mazy's shoulder. "But don't you worry. I am going to be around for a long time. And I will find you a good husband, someone rich and well able to care for you and give you healthy children."

"But first we will go to new lands and see many sights, Father, remember?"

"Yes, of course," Father said, smiling affectionately. "I shall not forget my promise. I shall take you to see London, to the lakes, to the mountains, to Scotland, and to the Continent." His voice became raspy and full of wonder as he spoke of all the far-off places.

In the meantime Father indulged her every desire to learn whatever skills she fancied, many of which were not considered suitable for a woman—as one of her tutors had argued. But Father had told him to mind his tongue and do as he was hired to do.

She learned archery, how to throw knives and axes, and how to fish and snare a rabbit. She was as good as any man at horseback riding, being able to ride astraddle and sidesaddle. She could play the lute, and read and write in Latin, German, and French.

After his steward died, Father allowed her to keep his books, and she recorded the figures and details of the household, the crops, and the tenants.

Father also indulged her with books, every kind of book, but especially books about all the places he promised to take her. But already her father's indulgences seemed like something in the distant past, now that Father was gone and Warin and his wife and son would be living in her home.

Bathilda burst into her room without knocking. "Come. We must go down and meet the new master of the house. He must be welcomed." She bustled over to Mazy's trunk and pulled out her best dress, a pink-and-blue silk bliaud with embroidered flowers. Before Mazy could say anything, Bathilda was taking her woolen kirtle off over her head and pulling on the fancier one.

"We should cover your hair with a veil, like a proper young lady, and you must be on your best behavior. No running around and turning somersaults like a jongleur."

"I'm sixteen. I know how to behave in company."

"Come, come. Sit and be still." Bathilda arranged her long brown hair quickly, fastening on the veil to cover it.

Mazy started down the stairs with Bathilda, and her stomach did a sickening flip. What would Warin and Edith, whom she had never met, say to her? Was Warin still cruel? Her emotions were still so raw. One unkind word and she'd probably either explode into a rage or dissolve in tears.

She was halfway down the staircase when Warin looked up and saw her.

"Is that you, Mazelina?"

She felt herself bristle at her full name, which she didn't particularly care for. John and her father always called her Mazy. But Warin didn't love her as they did, so perhaps he shouldn't have the privilege of calling her Mazy.

"Yes."

"Edith, this is Mazelina. And, Mazelina, this is my wife, Lady Wexcombe." He smirked at his wife as though she were some prize he had won.

"Good day to you, Warin. Lady Wexcombe." She nodded respectfully at each of them.

Edith stared at her from beneath lowered eyelids but said not a word. She was as thin as Warin was plump, and she wore a pinched expression.

"It seems as though you're still unmarried," Warin said, his attention now on Mazy as his smirk turned into a grimace. "I would have thought Father had found a husband for you before now." Warin raised his brows. "Had he found someone?"

"No."

"Hmm." Warin and Edith exchanged frowns.

Mazy's stomach dropped at the way her half brother and his wife looked at her, the sour downturn of their mouths, the narrowing of their eyes.

If Father had known he would suddenly become sick and die, he would have betrothed her to someone, but he had been in no hurry to marry her off. "There is plenty of time for that. You are not anxious to leave your home and your father, are you?" he would say if she asked about any potential suitors, wondering about her future.

She had happily said no. Why would she want to marry when she had a happy home and a father who loved her?

But now she had no one to care if she lived or died—no father and no husband—no one except her brother John. And she had heard nothing from him in over a year.

The rest of the day went by slowly as she tried to speak politely and kindly with Warin and Edith. She even tried to help with their eighteen-month-old, Percy, but the child mostly cried and only wanted his nurse, adamantly refusing to let Mazy console or entertain him.

The nurse said with an apologetic expression, "His new teeth are coming in. But when he feels better, I'm sure he'll want to play with you."

Mazy smiled and nodded, then went into the small room where her father's body lay in his coffin.

She sat on the stool beside him and whispered, "Father, why did you have to leave me?" She'd been stuck in this little village, in this drafty old castle, her whole life, while John had gone away training and having adventures, learning to fight with the sword—which was the one thing she asked to learn that her father refused to teach her. John even occasionally did heroic deeds, helping to defend castles against would-be conquerors. He wrote few letters, but the ones he did send made his life sound very exciting and valiant.

"Do not worry," Father would tell her. "One day I shall take you to see all of the king's castles and go to all the places your brother has been. We shall have many adventures too."

"When shall we go, Father?"

"Soon, but we have plenty of time. You are still so young."

When she turned sixteen a few months ago, she had pushed him to set out on their journey. "I am not so young now."

"You must wait until the summer. Summer is when men go on journeys."

But when spring came, her father fell ill. And now her adventure with her father, the thing she had looked forward to all her life, was never to be.

As she sat alternately staring at her father's face—because she would never be able to look upon it again—and looking away from it because it hurt too much to see him lifeless, she heard someone come into the room behind her.

"There you are." Warin clasped and unclasped his hands as he came toward her in a strange shuffling gait, as if he couldn't quite decide whether or not he wanted to walk forward. But he finally made it halfway across the room.

Mazy did her best to wipe the tears from her face before he noticed them.

"So, did Father have some potential husbands in mind for you? Someone he was thinking of betrothing you to, perhaps?"

"He never told me of any."

"Surely he must have known you would need someone to provide for you." He placed his hand against his chin, as if he was confused and mulling over this quandary.

He probably thought you would provide for me. You are my brother, after all.

"Perhaps I can find someone suitable, but I must say, I thought Father would have taken care of this."

She wanted to tell him not to trouble himself with finding her a husband, that she would try not to disrupt his life too much or eat too much food, and she could find her own husband among the villagers, perhaps a butcher or baker whose wife had died. But Father said sarcasm in a girl child was extremely rebellious. She did long to say it, though, just to see the look on Warin's puffy face.

"Well, I shall do my best." Warin sighed heavily. He did not progress any farther into the room, did not view Father's body in his coffin, and said nothing to comfort Mazy before walking out.

She hated to admit it, even to herself, but she had been hoping that Warin would show her some compassion. Any half-decent person would have expressed some sympathy at the loss of their father. As a brother, he could have commiserated with her in grief and the prospect of never being able to talk to their father again. Though Father had never seemed very fond of Warin, he was still his father.

Perhaps Warin resented that Father had sent him away after his mother died. Mazy could not remember her father ever saying a kind word about Warin's mother, calling her a cold, selfish woman. Her father's animosity seemed to have spilled over onto Warin, as he rarely spoke of his older son, and when he did, he sounded predisposed against him.

Still, she had thought Warin would have at the very least pretended to mourn the father who was leaving his title and all his worldly possessions to him.

What was to become of her now? Could she trust Warin with her future? Would he match her with a man she could love and have a good life with? Someone who would not mistreat her and would be faithful? She suspected those things were not even a part of his thought process.

Mazy had given no thought to what would happen to her if her father died. He'd always been hearty and strong, despite his age, and she could not imagine him dying. Until he did.

If she could not remain here—and indeed, she could not imagine living with Warin and Edith—perhaps she could go to Bedfordshire, where John was training squires with the Duke of Strachleigh. Would it be possible to stay with him there?

A messenger had been sent to John to tell him of their father's death, but she had heard no word from him. When he came, he would no doubt force Warin to show her some respect and care. She was not some stray dog to be handed off to a new owner, unwanted and soon to be forgotten.

John would make everything right.

John still had not arrived three days later, and so they determined to hold the funeral. The priest said they could not wait any longer or the body would start to stink. Just before the service was to start, a missive came from John.

> I regret that I cannot come to my father's funeral. My duties prevent me from traveling at this time, and I am sure that his life and good name will be honored by the priest and he will be buried in the crypt in the churchyard, as was his wish.
>
> Sir John of Wexcombe,
> Knight in King Richard's
> service

Mazy felt a sting in her chest that her brother did not even mention her, and even more hurt that he was not coming. Why would his benefactor, the Duke of Strachleigh, not release him from his duties for a few days to attend his father's funeral?

She stood in the cold rain outside the family crypt, and in

spite of the rain making everyone miserable, the priest seemed determined to say everything he'd intended to say as her father's body was laid to rest inside.

Warin and his wife stood together with their child's nurse, who did her best to comfort and amuse young Percy. Mazy's little nephew cried and screamed and fought to get down out of the nurse's arms.

Mazy let her tears flow, for how could anyone decipher her tears from the rain?

Every day Warin had spoken to her about the need for her to marry. Did he think of anything else? For someone who had never said more than a few words to her before, he seemed quite concerned about her future. But he was not concerned for her welfare, only for how to get rid of her at the best price.

The day after the funeral, he began listing potential husbands. He was sure to settle upon one soon, and though she didn't feel ready to get married, she had always known it was inevitable. But what kind of man would he be?

"The Earl of Brimley's wife died a few months ago," Warin said to her one morning, a week after her father's death. "If he is looking for another, you could hardly do better. He is very wealthy and might be willing to marry you with no money at all. If he wishes for more children, he might even pay a bride price."

"How old is the Earl of Brimley?"

"I don't know, perhaps fifty or sixty, but all the better for you. He will die and might leave you an inheritance, and then you can marry again."

Mazy let her mouth fall open, then choked out, "I would rather not marry someone quite so old."

Warin waved his hand as if swatting at a gnat. "You are not so squeamish, are you? You are an orphan now and must put away childish notions of true love and all that. I shall write to him directly."

Her father had been dead only seven days. She was still trying to accustom herself to the idea that he was gone. How could she endure her half brother's incessant, callous way of throwing up men to her? And now he was writing to the Earl of Brimley, a man as old as her father, perhaps older.

But what choice did she have? She had to endure it, would have to marry, for Warin obviously did not wish to let her live in her own home—his home now—even long enough for her to get used to being without her father.

She'd imagined that one day she would marry a baron, like her father. She'd live in a castle with her children around her and would not send her sons off to be knights. Instead, she'd have tutors at home to teach them the skills to become a knight. Her daughters would learn to read and whatever else they desired to know. Her husband would be so wealthy that her children would never have to worry about making their own way in the world, and she'd be very happy.

Now that Father was gone, she began to wonder if any of her hopes and plans would come true. Would she end up the wife of a cruel husband, someone who would not care what she thought or desired? Someone who disregarded her feelings? Or, even worse, would she end up alone and in poverty, barely able to survive, with no one to protect her or help her when she was in need?

She mustn't think the worst. Father always encouraged her to think hopeful thoughts, to be confident that all would turn out well.

John could help her. He'd told her that if someone tried to harm her, she was to send him word. He would make sure she was not alone and unprotected. John would help her find a good husband, someone who would treat her well and make sure she was well provided for.

If John would not come to her, then she would go to him.

She went into her room and wrote a note for Warin saying that she was going to Strachleigh to visit John. She would find someone to accompany her on her journey, then pack her bags with clothes and essentials.

If her father could not take her to see new and interesting places, she would take herself.

Two

BERENGER RELISHED BEING IN STRACHLEIGH WITH HIS SIS-
ter, who was married to the Duke of Strachleigh. And it was in
the duke's service that Berenger was able to train other young men
as he had been trained. Strachleigh, whom Berenger had called
Sir Geoffrey before he gained the title of duke, and who himself
was an excellent swordsman, kept too busy with his duties and
his large estate to help with the young men who had come to be
trained to fight and serve with courage, integrity, and chivalry.

Berenger only wished his assistant was not Sir John of
Wexcombe.

Just when Berenger was certain the man was not so bad and
actually had some good qualities, he would do something such
as what he had done that morning.

They were sitting down to eat their morning meal, breaking their fast with some of the servants in the room next to the
kitchen, when John suddenly stood up and threw his porridge.

The wooden bowl hit the wall and broke in pieces, splattering mush on the wall and floor.

The women servants gasped or cried out, while Berenger's hand instinctively went to his dagger handle in his belt. Ready to spring from the bench, he watched Sir John as he looked around the small room that was crowded with people, a tense expression on his face.

Finally, while everyone stared at him in dumbfounded silence, he spoke in a much louder voice than was necessary. "This porridge tastes like dog dung." He glared at anyone who dared to look at him. His voice increased in volume with every word. "You can eat it if you want, but I'm not eating an animal's excrement."

He stalked toward the door, grabbing two handfuls of bread rolls as he went. "Having to survive off bread and water. A fine way to treat a knight."

As he left, he slammed the door behind him.

The servants glanced around with wide eyes and went back to eating.

Truly, the porridge was nearly the same as every day. Sir John must have been angry about something else. Berenger never knew what kind of attitude he was going to wake up with. Sir John was unpredictable and volatile, but he had noticed it was always someone under him, someone with less power and authority, on whom John took out his ill temper.

Berenger ate most of his porridge, dumping the last bit in the slop bucket, then put his bowl on the table. He nodded to the cook's helper, who was collecting the bowls. The young man looked surprised at even that small gesture of politeness and acknowledgment, and he nodded back. Berenger took some bread and smeared butter on it, then took a bite as he went on his way, ready to begin the day's training exercises.

Perhaps Sir John was upset about his father's death. Berenger couldn't understand why he had not gone to the funeral.

Berenger had been standing nearby when the messenger came with the news that Sir John's father had died suddenly of an illness. Berenger expressed his sorrow for Sir John's loss. Then he explained that he understood because his own father had died only two years before.

Sir John had looked upset at first, even breathing hard and looking as if he would cry. But then his expression changed as a muscle twitched in his cheek.

"I suppose you got wronged, just as I did. We were sent away from home while our oldest brothers enjoyed an easy life and inherited everything. We have to slave and fight and work and hope that a war or a battle breaks out so we can distinguish ourselves enough to garner the king's favor, or we will never have our own property or enough wealth to do anything with our lives. We will never be anything more than soldiers and guards without some great luck or good fortune."

It was true, more or less, although Berenger believed he could distinguish himself regardless of whether war broke out.

"When do you need to leave so you can be present for the funeral?"

"I'm not going."

"Where is your home?"

"Not far from Lode."

"You can get there in one day if you ride hard."

"Why should I? My father is the only reason to go home, and now he's dead. There's nothing else for me there. My half brother will be the lord of the manor now."

"Don't you have younger siblings?"

"A sister."

"How old is she?"

"I don't know. Fifteen or sixteen."

"I'm sure she would like to see you, especially now."

"Why don't you go to the funeral?"

"He's not my father." Berenger felt his face growing warm, but he reminded himself that Sir John had just found out he lost his father. "Listen, Sir John, I know this is a hard time. You can take the rest of the day if you want. I can take care of whatever needs to be done."

Sir John nodded and walked away.

Berenger might have excused him by saying he was one of those men who hated to show emotion, who held everything inside, but he knew that was not true from the way he behaved sometimes, like today when he threw his porridge bowl across the room.

John had returned to his duties the next morning, but Berenger wasn't sure he wanted him training knights, with his volatile temper. And yet, with or without his help, it was time to begin the squires' training for the day.

He finished his buttered bread as he walked across the castle bailey to the stables, where the half dozen young pages and squires were supposed to be waiting. It was a cool spring morning, cool enough for three layers of clothing, with a cold rain beginning to fall. A few of the knights in training were beginning to shiver.

Sir John was nowhere in sight.

"Get inside the stable," Berenger ordered.

The young knights-in-training looked surprised and grateful as they headed into the relatively warm, dry building. Then they spent the next three hours practicing saddling and unsaddling their horses.

"This is a skill you will need no matter where you go," Berenger said. "And in a battle or siege situation, you may not have a squire to do it for you. You will need to be able to saddle your horse as quickly as possible."

The squires were very diligent to practice. They were a good lot who obeyed orders and worked hard. But Sir John was constantly complaining about them. For Berenger, it was harder to overlook Sir John's constant criticisms of the squires than his terrible temper.

"Help me, please!"

A servant boy who looked about eight years old, his voice high and desperate, his eyes wide, was running across the bailey.

Berenger went toward him. "What is the matter?"

The boy said, "My mother hit her head and she's bleeding. Please. Come with me."

"Where is she?"

The boy turned around and ran toward a small servants' barracks behind the castle.

Berenger never would have thought about going into the

barracks where the female servants lived. He was a knight, after all, and he adhered to the strict code of conduct that all knights were sworn to, but the boy looked so desperate.

Berenger went to the door and peeked inside the gloomy interior.

"Come, come," the boy said, motioning with his hand.

"I'm coming in," Berenger announced, unable to see if anyone was inside.

His eyes adjusted to the dim light and he followed the boy over to a low bed where a woman lay, her eyes closed. Blood matted her hair on one side.

"I tried to wake her," the boy said. "She won't wake up."

Berenger knelt and placed a hand over her lips and nose to see if he could feel any breath. He waited, but there was none that he could tell. Meanwhile, the boy had lifted his mother's hand and was holding it in both of his, his eyes fixed on Berenger.

"We need to find a healer." Berenger stood and hurried from the sad sight.

The boy followed him.

"What happened to her?" Berenger asked the boy as he hurried along. "How did she get the wound to her head?"

"Margaret, one of the other servants, said she fell and hit her head on a rock. She helped her back here to rest, but when Margaret left, Mother fell asleep and now she won't wake up."

"What is your name?"

"Roger, sir."

"Where is your father, Roger, and your brothers and sisters?"

"My father is dead, and I don't have brothers or sisters."

His heart sank. The poor boy. But Berenger's sister, Delia, would make sure the boy was taken care of. She was good and kind to her servants. For that reason the boy was more fortunate than most would be in his situation.

He finally located the woman they called the healer. She hurried with him back to the woman's side. But after she had listened with her ear against the woman's chest, then against the woman's lips and nose, she shook her head sadly.

"I'm sorry," she said, "but your mother has gone to be with Jesus and the angels."

Little Roger's face was sober as he stared down at his mother.

"I am very sorry," Berenger said, placing a hand on the boy's shoulder.

"Where will I go?" The woebegone high pitch of the boy's voice sent a pain straight to his heart.

"Do not worry. You will stay here at Strachleigh Castle. Lady Delia will ensure you are taken care of."

The boy sat down and let his head rest on his dead mother's shoulder. He patted her cheek and closed his eyes.

Knights did not cry, but Berenger had to blink fast to clear the wetness from his eyes, remembering his own mother's death when he was hardly older than Roger. The death of any boy's mother was a pain that boy never forgot.

"Can you stay with him a few minutes," Berenger asked the healer, "while I go inform Lady Delia? I'm sure she'll send someone to comfort him." If he knew his sister, she would come herself.

"Of course." The woman patted the boy's shoulder with her wrinkled hand, pulling up a stool to sit beside him.

Berenger hurried out.

He climbed up the hill to the castle, thinking of how he might spend some time with the boy in the days to come, take him fishing in the stream or teach him to use a bow and shoot. He did not want the child to feel he was abandoned and forgotten.

Mazy started on her great adventure early in the morning after telling only a few of the older servants that she was going away and leaving the note for Warin. It would probably only take one day of travel to reach John, but she had never been that far from home in her life.

She mounted her horse and whispered, "God, please give us Your favor and protection."

She rode to the end of the lane that led to her father's castle, where a young man from the village was waiting for her.

She'd hired Piers, the son of one of the older servants, to travel with her. He was one of the few people in the village who owned a donkey that could be spared from the fields, since it was planting time. She had not dared to take a horse for Piers, knowing Warin would be angry she took a horse for herself. After all, everything belonged to Warin now.

Piers was young and strong from working in the fields, but he did not have the regal, confident bearing of a knight, or even one of her father's guards. He walked with a slight stoop in his shoulders, though he was only twenty-three years old, and he had a strange, slow gait. She worried he would not appear able to defend her should robbers attack.

It was only a one-day trip, she told herself. They would be safe enough.

"I have a long knife," Piers assured her. "It's quite sharp."

Mazy had brought her knives as well. Keeping them close to her gave her comfort.

Her father had told her more than once, "Men are not to be trusted alone with a fair maiden, especially one as fair as you."

"You only say that because I am your daughter." She knew that all the fairest maidens in stories and ballads had gold or raven hair and were pale as milk. But her hair was brown and her skin was rather tan from all the time she spent outdoors in the sun.

"No." He shook his head and looked very grave. "It is true, and you must be careful because of your beauty. You are young and innocent and do not know what men are capable of. You must promise me never to allow yourself to be alone with any of the guards."

He had warned her about the guards, but not the male servants or their tenants. She thought it was because none of them had the confidence to even raise their eyes in her presence. For this reason, and because she knew Piers a little better than the other tenants, she was certain he would never harm her.

She had been careful to take only the small amount of jewelry her mother had specifically left her, and she brought only what belongings she could fit into two saddlebags. She had also brought some coins that her father had given her over the years.

Leaving the books behind was the hardest. Her heart ached as she gazed at them one last time. But they were too heavy and cumbersome, so she took only her Psalter.

Rain began to fall as soon as they started out. At first, Piers's donkey kept up with the pace Mazy's horse set, but after an hour, he became so sluggish that Mazy had to force her mare to slow down.

Soon the donkey began to bray. Then he stopped.

"Let's get off the road," Piers said, a raindrop sliding down the bridge of his nose, then clinging to the tip, refusing to fall. "He may just need to graze a little."

They huddled under a stand of trees while the animals cropped some green grass at the edge of a field. At this pace, they surely would not reach their destination that day.

But she was on an adventure, she reminded herself. She tried not to focus on the fact that she was here with Piers and not her father, that her father would not be able to show her all the places he had spoken of. No, instead she would think about how she was escaping Warin and the dreadful future he was devising for her.

Around her was only a meadow, some trees, wildflowers, and a road, but she had never seen them before. They were new sights, and she could at least appreciate that.

"Thank goodness it's not very cold today," Piers said, wiping the rain from his face with his wet hand, succeeding only in removing the larger drops of water.

"Yes." But the rain dripping from her hair, soaking her clothing, and running down her neck was most unpleasant. The wet clothing chafed her skin and made her shiver.

Perhaps she should have worn as many layers as Piers seemed to have on. A shirt was peeking above his laced-up tunic, a thin cloak over that, and another thicker cloak over all, with two hoods covering his head, and that was only what she was able to see. Meanwhile, she had only a thin linen underdress, a sleeveless summer bliaud that laced up the sides, and a rather thin cloak, the hood of which was plastered to her head, soaked through.

When Piers was able to coax his donkey back on the road, they continued on their way, struggling to dodge the muddiest parts of the road.

They would have to stop and spend the night somewhere. The thought made her stomach sink a little. It would be all right, she told herself. She wanted to travel, and travelers must accept the difficulties of the road.

Whenever they encountered other travelers, Mazy studied them to see how they were dealing with the rain. A couple of men rode past them on large warhorses. They could be knights, as they wore expensive-looking clothing, rode like they were accustomed to being in the saddle, and had swords strapped on their backs. They wore hoods but looked as if the rain did not bother them at all. When she looked closer, she saw that their cloaks appeared to be made of waxed wool, as they were shedding water like a duck's feathers.

That was what she needed. Perhaps she could find someone at Strachleigh who could teach her how to wax her cloak.

They met a few people walking with sticks or staffs, with packs slung over their backs. One old woman was so bent over, the hump in her back was higher than her head. What was so important that she needed to travel in this rain? But the woman did not even glance at them, so focused as she was on the road just in front of her feet.

How many different people there were in the world! People who did things and knew things and worked at things Mazy had never thought of before. Her life had always been so isolated at her father's castle, although she'd learned many things from the servants and her tutors.

"Thank you, Father," she whispered under her breath.

And now she was going to be with her John. No doubt he would have many more interesting things to teach her that he'd learned in his training. She especially hoped he'd teach her how to wield a sword, which she'd always thought was the noblest way to defend oneself.

THREE

THE SUN WAS GOING DOWN ON THE SECOND DAY OF HER journey when Mazy and Piers arrived at a village. They'd slept the night before on the soggy ground, too tired to go on.

"Pardon me," she said to the first woman she encountered on the little village's only street. "If you please, can you tell me the name of this village?"

"This be Strachleigh village, miss," she said.

Her heart rose at the news. Praise be to God.

"Strachleigh Castle is just beyond that bend at the end of the street," the woman went on. "They will not turn you away if you need a place to rest from your travels."

"Thank you." Mazy's voice was wispy as the breath rushed from her.

"You look as though you could use a rest," the woman said with a smile.

Mazy reached up to smooth down her hair, wishing she had

brought a looking glass with her. Her clothes had finally dried, though it had taken a good part of the day. She felt herself blush as a few people stopped to stare at them, as had happened at most of the villages they had passed through.

"God speed you on your travels." The woman smiled, letting them go on their way.

Mazy's heart beat hard as she imagined John seeing her for the first time in two years. How would he greet her? Would he run to her and embrace her? No, he had never been very demonstrative.

And he had not come to Father's funeral. Perhaps he would not even be pleased to see her.

No, she would not think like that. Of course he would be pleased. He loved her.

Around the bend a castle of gray stone with several towers, a curtain wall, and a large gatehouse came into view. The castle itself was massive, resting on a rise above the village, surrounded by groups of trees and a meadow.

They walked across a wooden bridge that spanned a dry trench to the gatehouse, and a guard stepped out and greeted them.

"We are here to see my brother. I am Mazelina of Wexcombe and my brother is Sir John of Wexcombe."

The young soldier's brows went up. He pointed. "I don't know the whereabouts of Sir John, but the knights' quarters are in that stone building there."

"Thank you." Mazy nodded to the soldier, and he stared after her.

The back of her neck prickled as she walked toward the

knights' quarters. Was this something she shouldn't be doing? She glanced at Piers, but he wore the same slack, unbothered expression he always did.

She would find John, and he would know what to do and where she might stay. He could help her figure out what to do about Warin trying to marry her off to someone ancient and undesirable. She had to marry, of course, but John could find someone who was not vicious or cruel.

As she drew nearer to the knights' barracks, she saw three men come and stand outside, talking quietly to each other.

The tallest one had brown hair and a strong chin, broad shoulders, and a kind expression on his face. In the moment when his eyes met hers, she was quite sure he was the handsomest man she had ever seen.

"Do you need help?" the tall knight asked as she approached, glancing from her to Piers and back to her.

"I am looking for my brother, Sir John of Wexcombe. Do you know where he is?"

"You are his sister, then?"

"I am."

"I shall fetch him for you. Wait here." He turned to go, then spun around. "And I am Sir Berenger of Dericott." He smiled as if amused at himself for forgetting to introduce himself.

"I am pleased to make your acquaintance, Sir Berenger." She smiled back and wished she had not come through a rainstorm, slept on the ground, then traveled all day in the sun.

While they were talking, one of the other knights went into the barracks and came out with her brother right behind him.

John was easily recognizable by his wide forehead and sharp blue eyes, but he had grown a dark mustache and beard since she'd last seen him.

"John, it's Mazy." She smiled.

"What are you doing here?" He walked toward her, his eyes widening.

"I came to visit you." She closed the gap between them and embraced him.

He was quite awkward as he put an arm around her and squeezed, somehow getting her neck caught against his collarbone and choking her for a moment. But she didn't care. She had found her brother, the one who called her "Mazy" and "Maze Queen" and "Leap Hare" because he said she jumped around like a hare in the spring. Now that Father was gone, he was the only person who cared for her. But she couldn't think about that now. She'd start crying in front of all of these men.

"What are you doing traveling so far by yourself?" He glanced at Piers.

"The farmer Alan's son, Piers, accompanied me."

By the way John looked Piers up and down, he was not impressed with him.

Piers mutely bowed to John.

"Did anyone try to harm you? Were you robbed?"

"No, of course not." She shook her head, almost laughing. "We encountered no robbers nor any nefarious men along the way. We are only tired and hungry after being wet for too long and—"

"Warin is a knave for letting you come all this way alone.

What was he thinking, letting you put yourself in harm's way?" His expression was fierce, his eyes turning cold and hard.

"Warin did not let me come. I left without telling him. I wanted to see you."

"He did not come and find you and take you back home, did he? He is a scoundrel." John's face clouded even more. "I should run him through with my sword for that."

Her heart rose into her throat. She had created a difficult situation for both of her brothers. But she could not stay there. Surely John would understand.

"Nothing bad happened. I am well, and I suppose I am at fault for putting myself in danger, if I was in danger."

"He let you wander away. Any number of dangers could have befallen you, alone on the open roads with no one to protect you but this villager."

While her brother ranted, the other knights shifted their feet and didn't look directly at her or John, except for the handsome one, Sir Berenger. He stared first at John, then at her. Then he spoke up.

"Don't you think we should find somewhere for the lady to sleep tonight? Your sister looks tired."

John said something under his breath.

"I'm sure Lady Delia will be happy to help," Sir Berenger said. "Let us go and speak with her, shall we?"

"Thank you, that is very kind." She wanted to take her brother's arm, but the stiff way he held himself dissuaded her. Was he angry with her? Perhaps she should have thought more about a plan instead of impetuously setting out to visit John. She could have written to him, could have asked Warin for an escort, could have been more thoughtful.

But she was here, she had made it safely, and she had found her brother. And how much her brother loved her! So much that he was angry at the thought of harm coming to her. Still, she wished he would not carry on so.

She wanted to talk to him, to hear about his life at Strachleigh Castle, to tell him about how broken her heart was at their father's death. She wanted him to have a good excuse for not coming to the funeral and the burial, wanted to hear him say how sorry he was that he had not been there to comfort her.

Instead, they walked in silence toward the castle, Sir Berenger in the lead. As they reached the castle kitchens, Sir Berenger asked, "Are you hungry?" He looked at both Mazy and Piers, while her brother completely ignored the humble farmer's son.

"We have not eaten very much today." Her empty stomach twisted at that very moment. All the walking and riding, with little food to eat, had at times made her dizzy.

"Go to the kitchen and get some food," Sir Berenger said, "and I will fetch you when I find my sister, Lady Delia."

"Thank you."

His sister? Was the duchess Sir Berenger's sister?

He entered the kitchen ahead of her, asked the kitchen servants to provide food for her and Piers, and then slipped out again. John must have gone with him.

The cook quickly gathered some leftover pasties, bread, butter, and cold meat and placed it all before them while one of the kitchen servants, a young woman, asked her name.

"Mazelina. But my family calls me Mazy."

"Where did you travel from?"

"Wexcombe," Piers said, his mouth full.

"How far away is that?"

"It's a day's ride on a good horse," Mazy said, "but it took us two days."

"I've never been anywhere." The servant girl sighed and sat down across from Mazy on the bench, then propped her chin in her hands, her elbows on the table. She probably would not have spoken and behaved so familiarly if she knew Mazy was a baron's daughter, but Mazy was glad. She liked that the girl was talking to her.

"This is my first journey." Mazy was beginning to feel stronger and more hopeful now that she was eating.

"Everyone tells me I'm fortunate because I live in Strachleigh, with a kind master and an impressive castle. What do you think? Did you see anything very interesting on your journey?" asked the servant girl.

"I think England is very beautiful. I saw wildflowers I've never seen before, lovely trees and streams, and a few villages, but honestly, I did not see anything to compare with Strachleigh Castle. Even though I have not seen all of it yet, I can already tell that my father's castle is small in comparison."

Mazy instantly regretted letting it slip that her father owned a castle. She hoped the servant girl wouldn't stop talking to her now.

"Your father has a castle?" The girl's eyes, which were already larger than most, grew wide and round.

"My father was a baron, but he died." She made the statement as blandly as she could, as though he'd been dead for years, hoping to keep the tears from springing to her eyes.

"Oh. My father is dead too."

"Martha, why are you talking that poor girl's ears to death?" Cook said. "She's tired from her journey."

"I don't mind. It's good to have someone my age to talk to." Mazy smiled at her new friend.

The door creaked open, revealing Sir Berenger and John standing there.

"My sister wishes to see you," Sir Berenger said.

She went with the two men, marveling at how much more muscular her brother had become, though he was shorter and less muscular than Sir Berenger, and the way he carried himself was different, less confident.

"But first, my sister wishes to provide a bath for you, if you like, and she is having some clothing brought to your room."

Sir Berenger led her to the castle and to the room where she would be sleeping. When he left, John patted the top of her head like one might pat a hunting hound. That bit of affection warmed her heart. Perhaps he wasn't angry with her after all.

"I'll let you take your bath, Maze Queen," her brother said. "I'll see you tomorrow."

"All right. Thank you, John."

How good it was to have a kind brother who cared about her.

Beside her was a tub of water big enough for her to sit in. Mazy took off her clothes and stepped into the tub, sinking down, the water embracing her with soothing warmth. She leaned back and closed her eyes.

Mazy startled awake. The servant girl—Martha, if she remembered correctly—was coming toward her with a bucket.

"Some water to warm your bath," Martha said.

"I was so tired I must have drifted off to sleep," Mazy said, sitting up.

"I brought you some liquid soap, called 'shampooing,' for your hair. May I help you?"

"Thank you."

Martha poured water over Mazy's head while she leaned forward. "My mistress says it comes from the Far East where spices are from. She even lets the house servants wash our hair with it because she says it keeps the lice away. Have you ever used it before?"

"No, never. It smells good." She should probably open her eyes so she didn't fall asleep again, but it was so relaxing to have someone else wash her hair, kneading her scalp with her fingers.

But all too soon her bathwater started to cool and Martha was helping her out, giving her a cloth to dry herself, then drying her hair with another.

How good it was to feel clean and warm and dry. Martha helped her put on a long chemise, then a lovely pink bliaud with multicolored embroidery—birds and flowers and trees across the bodice and on the wide hem. She gave her a belt of the same colors and braided her damp hair quickly into two braids, twisting them into a knot on the back of her head.

"Now you are fit to see the queen of England, I would think." Martha smiled at her.

"Thank you so much. Your Lady Delia must be so kind."

"Oh yes, she is." Martha nodded vigorously. "And now I shall take you to her."

Martha led her to a stone staircase and they started up.

How fortunate that John had a friend like Sir Berenger and a mistress like Lady Delia. He had not been so fortunate when he was a child, as he had told her tales of harsh treatment at the hands of other knights and lords under whose tutelage he was being trained. The injustice of it still stung her.

"Here is her solar. Fare well, miss."

"Thank you, Martha."

Mazy opened the door to find a cozy room filled with many pillows, cushioned chairs and benches, and a beautiful young woman sitting by a window holding a baby on her lap.

"Please come and sit near," the woman said. "You must be Mazy, Sir John's sister. I am Lady Delia."

Mazy bowed and curtsied. "My lady, I am very pleased to meet you and so thankful for your kind hospitality. I shall return the dress tomorrow."

"Please keep it as a gift from me, for all your brother does here, his service to the squires, and his protection. My husband was also a knight and a guard once."

"That is very generous. I thank you."

"And please allow me to say how sorry I am to hear of your father's death."

She said the words so kindly, with so much sincerity in her voice, that tears instantly sprang to Mazy's eyes. Unable to speak, Mazy nodded.

So few people had even acknowledged her pain that she had

pushed it to the back of her mind as much as possible. But it was still fresh, the sorrow of never being able to talk to her father again. She blinked away the tears.

The baby's eyes were closed as he slept against his mother's chest.

"Your baby is very handsome. A boy?"

"Yes. He is a joy to us. I never knew how wonderful it would feel to be a mother." She smiled and her face was radiant.

Would Mazy be married soon to someone who would make her a mother? In a year or two she could be holding her own baby.

That thought made her heart skip a beat.

"I know you are exhausted from your journey. Please take the bedchamber where you took your bath, if that is suitable to you. You may stay as long as you like."

"You are so kind. Thank you."

Truly, this must have been the right decision to come here to John and see at least something else of the world beyond the place where she had grown up. Tomorrow she would speak to him about what they should do to find her a husband.

She wondered why Warin had not sent men after her. Perhaps he had and the guards had somehow missed her on the road. No doubt he was furious with her for running away. But John would not allow him to do her any harm. John would make sure she was safe and well.

FOUR

BERENGER DIRECTED THE SQUIRES AS THEY PRACTICED
their archery. Sir John's sister stood nearby. After watching them
for a while, she walked toward them and pointed to an extra
longbow lying on the ground.

"May I try?"

A few of the squires turned to stare, open-mouthed, while
others grinned in amusement.

"Of course." He doubted she could even pull the string back,
but she might as well be allowed to try.

Mazy, as Sir John called her, was sixteen, so she was still
very young, and she seemed oblivious to her own beauty. Sir John
could sometimes be rather heartless, but he had made it clear to
the other men that she was his sister and therefore under his
protection. That was the only thing keeping some of the guards,

and even knights, from approaching her and making lascivious offers.

She picked up the bow and two arrows, nocked one of the arrows to the string, and aimed at the closest target—a wooden shield with a circle painted on it.

Two of the squires snickered behind their hands.

Mazy pulled back the arrow, her elbow at the perfect height, and shot. It hit the center of the target. Before he even saw her nock the next arrow or pull back on the string, she had shot the second arrow, which hit directly beside her first arrow.

A couple of whistles came from the squires. Some of the boys' mouths hung open, while others yelled and expressed disbelief and jealousy.

"How did you learn to shoot like that?" Berenger retrieved her arrows, handing them to her.

"My father's guards taught me." She laughed. "I did not like sewing so I learned other things instead."

"What else do you know how to do?"

"I can throw a knife pretty well, and I know how to track a deer, how to fish, and how to snare a rabbit."

This young woman was the most interesting one he had ever encountered.

He retrieved some throwing knives, the ones he used in training the squires, and said, "Show me."

She took three of them and threw them in quick succession, sticking the points of all three near the center of the wooden target. The squires all whooped and whistled.

"That is very impressive." Berenger couldn't help smiling.

"What is going on?"

Sir John's voice was rather loud and tense as he came walking up behind them.

"Your sister is showing us her archery and knife-throwing skills. Did you know she was practically a knight herself?"

Sir John said nothing, did not even move, as he stared at Berenger. With that look he often had, his eyelids drooping and his face expressionless, Berenger couldn't tell if he was angry, glad, or sad.

Berenger retrieved the knives. "Show him." Berenger handed the knives to her.

Mazy threw each one, taking a little more care and time, and each one stuck near the center of the target. She picked up the bow and arrows and did just as well with those.

Sir John shook his head. "At least no man can ever take advantage of you."

Mazy's smile was as bright as the noonday sun at her brother's words.

"Is there anything you don't know how to do?" Berenger asked.

"I never learned to sword fight. The sword is a bit heavy for me, and Father wouldn't let his guards train me."

"We could get you a lighter wooden sword like the squires start out practicing with." Berenger expected her brother to fetch her a sword, but instead he started talking to her in a low voice.

Berenger did not want to interfere when Sir John was talking to his sister, so he ordered the squires to get back to practicing their archery skills.

Mazy had never had the opportunity before to show off her archery and knife-throwing skills. It was quite satisfying to hear the squires, though they were only boys, teasing each other by saying, "She's better than you are."

When John came over to her, she decided this was her chance to talk to him about her future.

"You should be careful about spending time out here with these boys, especially when the guards are around." John spoke in a low voice, with no emotion at all, a sharp contrast to his angry ranting of the day before. "Some of them are not very noble toward women."

"I will be careful." She believed she was safe as long as Sir Berenger was around, but decided not to tell her brother that.

"I don't know what you plan to do," her brother began, "but I won't be at Strachleigh forever."

"I know. That is what I wanted to talk to you about."

"And you haven't heard from Warin? It's his responsibility to take care of you. He inherited everything," John said sullenly.

"I haven't heard from him, but I don't trust him to find a husband for me, which was all he seemed interested in doing for me."

"You'll have to marry."

"Yes, I know." She wanted to say that she was hoping John would help her find a husband, but something stopped her.

"You are too young to find a husband on your own, but not too young to marry," John went on. "Warin should be helping you. He's older and knows more rich noblemen. He didn't spend his life training. He went to balls and feasts and took his ease."

Mazy let out a slow breath. John sounded bitter, and he obviously wasn't eager to help her.

"I don't trust Warin," she said again.

John turned to the side and spit on the ground. Finally he said, "I don't know what to tell you. I'm just a knight."

Mazy's heart sank at hearing John's words. It hurt that John was not willing to help her, clearly more focused on his own pain than her predicament. But she also felt relief at knowing that she would not be married off right away.

Her future seemed more uncertain than ever.

During the next couple of weeks, Mazy spent her time with the squires and knights, watching them, learning what she could. Often Sir Berenger included her in the squires' training. John, however, mostly ignored her, which she understood, to a point. He had a job to do, after all.

Piers had left the day after they arrived, and she had told him not to keep her whereabouts a secret from Warin if it meant he would be punished. She was surprised Warin still had not sent men to find her and make sure she was safe.

She hoped John would send word to Warin that he was taking over responsibility for finding her a husband, but given his attitude, that seemed unlikely. And Mazy was afraid that asking John to write to Warin would make him angry. She was disappointed that John had not treated her the way she'd imagined. But he was her brother, and she still believed he cared for her.

She felt safe as long as Sir Berenger was nearby. She'd heard about the compassionate way he treated the little boy who had recently lost his mother, and she'd seen the way he treated women, even the lowliest of the servant girls, with great courtesy and deference. He never offended her with the wolfish glances that other men often gave her, especially when they thought she wasn't looking.

One day Mazy came upon the squires having their jousting lessons. Seated on their horses, one after the other they charged at a small wooden shield that hung from a tree. She'd heard one of the boys say it was easier than tilting at a quintain, which had a revolving arm. If a squire didn't spur his horse to move quickly enough after hitting the target, the sandbag on the other end would spin around and hit him in the head.

"Would you like to take a turn?" Sir Berenger asked.

"Me?"

"Why not? These lances are a lot smaller and lighter than a knight's lance. They're just for practice, so there's not much danger, as long as you don't fall off your horse or slam your lance point into the ground."

His smile was neither challenging nor insulting.

One of the squires said, "You can't let a girl practice jousting!"

"She'll only hurt herself!" another called out.

"Let her try," said a third. "She's better at knife-throwing than you are."

The boys laughed as Sir Berenger ignored them and helped Mazy mount the seasoned warhorse and handed her a lance.

"Just don't let the tip touch the ground. If you lose your grip or you can't hold it up, throw it down, away from the horse, so he doesn't trip on it."

Mazy nodded. Sir Berenger fixed the end of the blunted lance against her shoulder.

"This is the vamplate," he said, pointing to the metal plate that was like a shield for her hand. "It will help you keep a firm hold on the lance and keep your hand from sliding forward—or the back end of the lance from hurting your shoulder—when you strike the target."

Mazy nodded.

"If you're ready, just give the horse his head."

Mazy urged the horse forward with her heels against his sides while loosening her hold on the reins. The horse sprang ahead and trotted toward the wooden target, which hung from a tree.

Mazy tilted the lance tip up, balancing the end of the lance under her armpit, but it was too little, too late. The tip passed just below the target.

Mazy's stomach sank. Had she proved the taunting boys right? That a girl should not practice tilting with squires?

When she and her horse circled around and came back, a couple of boys snickered, but most of them watched with a hint of respect in their expressions. After all, she hadn't dropped the lance or fallen off her horse.

"Try again," Sir Berenger said. "Aim your lance now, before you start toward the target."

Mazy followed his advice and raised the tip, eyeing the target in the distance. Then she urged the horse forward and trotted toward the shield.

As she neared the target, she aimed for the center and hit it with a loud *thwack* and a jolt to her hand, arm, and shoulder. The jolt was not hard enough to cause pain, and a triumphant breath bloomed inside her chest.

Some of the squires whooped as her horse circled around and carried her back.

"Well done!" Sir Berenger greeted her. "Would you like to go again?"

She shook her head.

"Why not? You didn't hurt yourself, did you?"

"No. I enjoyed it. Thank you for letting me try."

"Are you sure you're all right?"

"Yes, I'm very well. I just wouldn't want the boys to hate me for being better at jousting than they are." She said this with a smile at the boys standing near enough to hear her.

The boys scoffed and protested, but good-naturedly, and she handed off her lance to the servant who was assisting Sir Berenger.

Sir Berenger smiled and said, "You did very well."

"Thank you."

He helped her down from the tall horse's back, one hand on

either side of her waist, before assisting the next squire preparing to take his turn at tilting.

Mazy observed the practice the rest of the afternoon, but she found herself mainly watching Sir Berenger. She kept remembering how he had smiled at her, the way the dappled sunlight filtered through the leaves of the trees and shone on his brown hair.

Could there be a handsomer or more gallant knight than Sir Berenger? She didn't think so. But how horrified her brother would be if he knew she was watching his fellow knight and thinking about him as often as she did. She needed to put him out of her thoughts. He was her friend, and her brother's friend, and nothing more.

Mazy had been at Strachleigh Castle for over two weeks. Lady Delia did not seem to expect anything in return for her gracious hospitality, but Mazy tried to think of ways she might be helpful anyway. As the mistress of a great estate, Lady Delia had a great many responsibilities, in addition to her duties as a new mother who nursed her own child instead of employing a nurse, as most great ladies did.

As she sat watching the knights and squires at their jousting training, a messenger rode up the castle mount on his horse. As he drew nearer, she recognized him as one of Warin's men.

She braced herself. What kind of message might Warin be sending? Had he found a husband for her? Was he demanding she come back to Wexcombe? Or was he only trying to discover if she was alive and well?

But compassionate concern was not one of Warin's known traits.

The guard dismounted and made his way forward. He caught sight of her, recognition altering his expression, and asked, "Where is Sir John? I have a missive for him."

"Is it from our brother, Warin?"

"It is. From the Baron of Wexcombe."

"I shall take it to him."

"My instructions were to give it only into the hand of Sir John."

How annoying men could be. "Come with me, then."

She led the way to the knights' barracks and asked one of the men standing outside to look and see if John was there, but he came out shaking his head.

"He is here somewhere," Mazy said to the guard and went to look in the kitchen.

He wasn't there either, but when she came back, she saw John striding across the bailey toward the guard.

"Sir John of Wexcombe?" the guard inquired.

"I am he."

The guard handed John the rolled-up piece of parchment that was sealed with her father's—now Warin's—seal and colored ribbons.

John broke it open, unrolled it, and stared. Then he violently smashed it between his hands.

"Warin dares to damage my sister's reputation?" His voice started out at a normal volume but rose precipitously until the last word was shouted at a throat-searing pitch.

The guard took two steps back.

John glanced around and caught sight of her several feet

away. "Our brother refuses to do his duty by you. Look at this." He shook the parchment at her, still clutched in his tight fist.

Mazy's heart sank like a stone at seeing John so upset. Out of the corner of her eye she saw Sir Berenger and a few other men coming toward them.

John glared at her and threw the parchment on the ground, stalked away a few steps, stopped, then turned toward her.

"Why did you come here? Why couldn't you stay at home where you belonged? Am I your keeper? Are you my responsibility?" His finger repeatedly stabbed his own chest.

Mazy's cheeks burned as she picked up the parchment and straightened it out, reading it silently and quickly.

My dear brother, Sir John,

Your sister, Mazelina, has left her home and all protection and ventured out into the world on her own with a poor farmer's son, and I know not what may have befallen her on the way. Therefore, I no longer consider her to be my responsibility. I wish to inform you that I, the Baron Wexcombe, will no longer search for a suitable marriage for her, nor will I acknowledge her as my sister, as I cannot vouch for her virtue. Do with her as you will, as I consider her your responsibility now, not mine.

Respectfully,
Baron Wexcombe

Mazy felt sick, as if she might lose her breakfast. John was furious, and Warin had disowned her and would refuse to use his influence, or provide any dowry, to procure her a husband. And how dare he insinuate that she had lost her virtue! She'd done nothing wrong, but he would cause her to lose her good name and reputation. She would no longer be known as the virtuous only daughter of the Baron Wexcombe, and she could never make a good match now.

O God, help me. I am ruined.

FIVE

SURELY WARIN COULD NOT BE SERIOUS ABOUT DISOWNING her. And why was John looking at her with that furious expression? This was Warin's doing, his shirking of his responsibility. He must know that she had done nothing wrong, not with Piers, nor with anyone else.

"Was I wrong to want to come here and see you?" Mazy tried to speak in a quiet voice, well aware of all the knights and squires looking on.

"You came here without any protection besides that whey-faced ploughman, Piers. And you traveled alone with him. Did you not think of your reputation? You never should have come. How can I be responsible for you? I'm a knight, not a nursemaid."

"I left Warin a message saying where I was going, and Piers is one of Father's tenants, a respectful farmer's son who would never make advances toward me. Nothing happened to me on the way here. We were not attacked, and no one came near me. I only came here because I thought you might help me find a suitable husband, since Warin wanted to marry me off to whoever would pay the most money."

"You should have married whomever Warin told you to marry."

John's words were like a knife in her heart. Her mind whirled, a tangle of painful thoughts. John was angry with her, he did not care about her, and he would not help her.

John spun on his heel, glaring at everyone in earshot. "This is not a miracle play. What are you staring at?" Then he turned and stalked away, his hands fisted by his sides.

Sir Berenger came toward her. "What does the missive say? Is it so bad?"

His manner was so kind, so gentle, so opposite of John's that she handed him the parchment to let him read it for himself. It only took him a moment. When he lowered it, his brows were drawing together.

"I can hardly believe . . ." He gazed at her. "This is wrong. This is very wrong. Lord Wexcombe has no right to accuse you of doing something wrong or to assume your reputation was damaged. Sir John and I shall go to him and force him to change his mind."

It was kind of him to say, but . . . "I did nothing wrong, but you cannot force him to change his mind. He only wanted to get rid of me, and now he has found a way. And there's nothing either of us can do." The terrible ache in her chest that she'd felt for days after her father died was back. *O God, I wish my father had not died. I miss him so much.*

"Did Warin harm you? Is that why you left home after your father died?"

"No. But he does not care about me at all. He found an old man for me to marry, older than my father, so I came here to escape that fate and to see John. I missed him, and I thought he might be able to help me." Tears, which were always close to the surface since her father died, started to leak out. Mazy covered her face. "I was foolish. John is right. I never should have left home."

"You did nothing wrong. This is not your fault. Warin is being selfish and unreasonable. What you did was not bad; you just weren't thinking about the dangers. But Warin also did not send anyone after you or send word to your brother to see if you were safe. No, he did this for his own benefit, not because you had done something wrong." Sir Berenger's eyes were intense, his brows drawn together in a look of sincerity and concern.

It was a relief that Sir Berenger did not think she had done something terrible, but it was painful to think that Warin would cast her aside her so quickly, ruining her future. Could he hate her so much?

Also painful was the memory of John saying, "You never should have come." His words stabbed through her chest like a knife. Not only did Warin want nothing else to do with her, but even John, her beloved brother whose love she had been so sure of, blamed her for Warin casting her off.

Everyone else had wandered away, as it was time for the midday meal, but Sir Berenger remained with her.

"I'm sorry Sir John was so angry. I'm sure he did not mean what he said."

Mazy nodded, even though she was not so sure. How could he say such things if he did not mean them?

"Come. Let us go and get some food. And later Sir John, the duke, and myself will write Lord Wexcombe a letter persuading him to change his mind."

Sir Berenger was so kind. She went with him, even though she just wanted to be alone. She did not wish him to know how broken she felt.

She and Sir Berenger went into the kitchen where the servants and guards ate, and everyone turned to stare at her. When she sat down, they went back to serving the meal.

John did not come in while she ate, and another one of the knights came to Sir Berenger to ask for his help.

"Forgive me," he said. "I have to take care of this."

"Of course." She nodded to him. When he was gone, she excused herself and went to her room.

She was on her own now. She could no longer count on her brothers to take care of her or make sure she married well. Now that she was without Warin's protection and wealth, she had to stop taking the charity of the duke and duchess. Even though Lady Delia had said she was happy to show her hospitality for the sake of her brother and what he meant to their household, Mazy was beginning to realize it was just a way for the lady to show compassion. John seemed to do the bare minimum. It was Sir Berenger who went beyond his duties to help and serve.

Disowned. Abandoned. Alone.

As she lay across her bed, the words from Warin's letter ran through her mind. "Father," she whispered, desperately missing her father, longing to speak to him and hear his voice again.

God had let him die when she needed him, when God knew that Warin would not care for her and would cast her off. He could have healed her father, but He chose not to.

"God, why?" she whispered as she buried her face in her pillow, tears seeping from her eyes.

She had a place to sleep, but for how long?

Several of the servants who had gone to work for her father were orphans, some as young as nine. They'd had nowhere else to go, so her father had brought them into his household to work. Was that what Mazy needed to do? Become a servant to earn her food and a bed? But Mazy had not learned the skills of taking care of a household. Her skills at archery and knife-throwing would not get her a position as a servant, and she was a woman, so she could not be hired as a guard.

But she would do what she had to do, and she would not feel sorry for herself. Her servant Bathilda, who was more of a mother than a servant, had taught her to disdain self-pity, had pointed it out in Mazy whenever she saw it.

"You don't want to be like the little girl," Bathilda had said, "who cried because she wanted a wolf for a pet, to keep her from being lonely. She was inconsolable until the mother went out to look for a wolf cub to bring back home to her and was eaten by the wolf cubs' mother. Then the girl was truly alone."

Mazy wanted to say that the child was more foolish and

indulged than self-pitying, but she was too afraid Bathilda would smack her hand for being impertinent.

Whenever Bathilda saw Mazy get tears in her eyes, she would say, "No self-pity. Remember the girl who cried for a pet wolf."

Mazy vowed to be strong, and she would not complain or feel sorry for herself. She would look for things she could thank God for.

That vow would surely be easier to make than to keep.

Berenger went looking for Sir John, tramping through the forest to the rock outcropping where Sir John was wont to go when he took a notion to drink strong spirits.

And sure enough, when he reached the place and got close enough to see through the dense trees, Sir John was there, pacing one way, then spinning on his heel and pacing back the other way. In his hand was a flask like the one the alewife in the village used to contain her strongest drink.

Sir John took a sip from it, then muttered to himself as he paced.

Berenger would much rather turn around and go back to the castle, lose himself in his duties, and leave Sir John to his own vice. But he was here for Mazy. She needed someone to advocate for her, since her oldest brother had abandoned her.

"Sir John."

He froze and snapped his head in Berenger's direction.

"I hope you don't mind, but I wanted to talk to you."

"What about? My blighted, cursed family?"

The words were extreme, but then, Sir John often spoke in such extremes. "Your sister is very upset about what her brother did. I'm sure she would like to hear a few words of comfort from you."

Sir John took another drink from his flask before speaking. "She never should have left home, should have married whomever Warin found for her. It was foolish, and now she has no prospects, no way of making a good marriage."

"Not because of what she did but because Warin chose to react the way he did. He is the one at fault. Your sister only wanted to see you, her brother. She had lost her father and was grieving. I'm sure Warin had no sympathy for her."

Indeed, if Sir John had gone to her when their father died, she would not have had to come looking for him. He bore some of the responsibility for her predicament. But if Berenger said that to him, Sir John would only become enraged and refuse to cooperate.

"You have the opportunity now to show her that she is not alone in the world," Berenger said, trying to phrase it as positively as possible. "Family cares for family, and brothers must care for their siblings." Berenger had learned this lesson well when he and his siblings had been locked in the Tower of London, falsely accused and even sentenced to death.

How would Sir John react to his lecture? He waited to see if the knight would be angry and start yelling.

He did not speak for several moments, before finally saying, in a very mild voice, "Mazy is a good girl. I will take care of her. Brothers must take care of their sisters."

The man possessed two opposite temperaments, and this was the Sir John that Berenger liked—mild and agreeable.

"Warin is the one who caused all this. He is the one who should pay for ruining my sister and casting her off. And I shall be watching for a way to make him pay."

And this was the Sir John who made everyone uncomfortable with his aggressive anger and bitterness. But at least he wasn't yelling.

"You missed the midday meal," Berenger reminded him. "Why don't you come back with me and get some food? We will be doing more jousting practice this afternoon. That's always amusing to watch, is it not?"

Sir John sometimes ridiculed the young squires' uncoordinated attempts at tilting with their undersized lances. Berenger did not approve of that, but at least it might make Sir John come back with him and not drink himself into a stupor.

"I'll be there shortly," Sir John said and sat down on a boulder with both hands wrapped around his flask.

Berenger walked away. He'd done what he could. Hopefully Sir John would remember what he'd said about taking care of siblings.

There were many things in Sir Berenger's life that he was glad about, and one of them was that he and his siblings had banded together and fought against those who were trying to destroy them. His greatest fear had been that he would not be able to save his brothers and sister when their enemies attacked them. He'd not been there to save his own father, and consequently, his father had been murdered in a most cowardly way.

And he had not been a good enough fighter to save his oldest brother, Edwin, from losing his arm to a guard's sword. And that was a regret he would carry with him always.

Berenger loved his brothers and sister more than anything or anyone. He hated not being able to do his duty to save those under his protection. To save the needy and innocent seemed the highest calling for any man, especially a knight.

Now he needed to ensure, if he possibly could, that Sir John understood that his highest calling was taking care of his sister, Mazy. She was an innocent young woman with a kind heart, and Berenger couldn't bear to think of anything bad happening to her.

"I would like to do something to help your household."

Mazy stood before Lady Delia and prayed silently that she would understand. She needed something to take her mind off of her anxious thoughts, grieving her father's death and worrying what would become of her now that Warin had cast her off. And she needed to repay Lady Delia's kindness and earn her keep.

"Something to help the household?"

"Some kind of job that I could do. I'm not good at sewing, but I know I could do something—cooking or cleaning or taking care of the sheep or . . ."

Lady Delia's mouth fell open, her knitted brows making her look slightly horrified. "But why? You are the daughter of Baron Wexcombe. You do not need to do any work of that sort."

"My father is dead and my older brother, the new baron, has disowned me." The words made the tears flood her eyes.

She did not want to cry in front of the duchess. She could not bear to let the lady think she was trying to manipulate her into feeling pity for her. But as hard as she tried to blink them away, scold them away, think about something else, the tears would not stop. She kept her head down to hide her face from Lady Delia's view.

"Disowned you? What do you mean? Surely he could not have done that."

"He wrote a letter to my brother, Sir John, and said that he would no longer provide for me or help me find a husband because I left home and came here in the company of a farmer's son, who was only with me to act as my guard. So I wanted to know if I might do something for you to earn my food and shelter."

"Perhaps my husband can reason with Lord Wexcombe, persuade him to change his mind."

"I thank you for kindly wanting to help me. But I am not sure I can trust Warin to find a husband for me, even if he does accept me back home." Truly, she had never trusted Warin, and she would certainly never trust him now.

"You poor child." Lady Delia's voice was soft and kind. "But how can I ask you to work?"

"I want to work." She spoke quickly, trying to remember the speech she had practiced to persuade Lady Delia. "I am used to training with my father's guards, going hunting and fishing. And I took care of my father—reading to him, since his eyesight had dimmed, and playing games with him and writing his letters for him. I also did his books, listing the expenses and income and accounting for livestock and crops. He lost his steward a few years ago, so I took on those tasks. I do not mind working. I don't like being idle."

Just then Lady Delia's baby began to cry from his crib a few feet away.

"Shall I get him for you?" Mazy asked.

"Yes, if you would like. He's probably hungry."

Mazy bent and carefully picked up the baby from his crib. This was one domestic task she knew a little about. She had often visited with a couple of the servants who had babies, enjoying holding and cuddling the newborns.

She handed the baby to Lady Delia, who smiled at the crying child.

"Do you mind if I feed him? You are welcome to stay if it does not bother you."

"I don't mind. I have seen a woman nursing a child before." She felt rather proud that she was so worldly and experienced.

Lady Delia unlaced the bodice of her dress. "Do you mind turning the key in the lock?" She nodded at the door.

Mazy locked the door so no one could come in and disturb the duchess while she fed her baby.

"I am so very sorry that your brother did that to you. But you will always be welcome here, and if I can do anything . . . I will ask my husband to speak to the baron anyway, or at least send him a letter, if that is all right with you. No one should be able to take away a child's birthright. You are the rightful daughter of a baron and he should not be able to say otherwise."

"Thank you. But Sir John will be my guardian now. I shall be well enough." She wanted to be loyal to John, but she wasn't sure she actually believed her words.

They sat in peaceful silence as the baby nursed, Lady Delia cradling him in her arms.

"And I shall think about what you said, about finding an occupation for you, and discuss it with my husband."

"I do truly appreciate that. I know my skills are strange for a woman, but I will do whatever seems good to you and His Grace."

Mazy was not sure what would become of her or what her future looked like, but she was determined not to let Warin ruin her. She was actually glad she was no longer dependent on Warin for anything. She would take care of herself.

Six

Mazy took a walk along the river. Her mind was on her father, and she prayed aloud, but very quietly, as if she were speaking directly to God. Her priest had told her she could pray that way, and she often did when she went on walks, but very quietly so no one would hear her and think she was moonstruck or addle-brained.

"God, help me remember happy times and be thankful. Like the time Father took me on a quest for orange grisette mushrooms in the forest. He could have sent a servant to pick them, but instead he took me."

Certainly Father had not done these kinds of things with either Warin or John. She actually felt sorry for them. They hadn't been loved and cared for the way she had, had not had the experiences with Father that she'd had. Did that have something to do with the way they treated her now?

She stared at the river, the sunlight on the water sparking like two flints, but only where the light filtered through the leaves.

"Thank You, God, that Father spent time with me and taught me things and let me learn what I wished to, like music instead of embroidery, and knife-throwing instead of sewing. He could have told me that was only for boys to learn, but he didn't. And I'm thankful for that. He was my father, but he was also my friend, someone I could talk to. I'm thankful for that as well."

"Is that you, Mazy?"

Roger, the newly orphaned boy, was sitting on the riverbank with Sir Berenger. They were each holding a long, thin pole at one end with the other end in the water.

"Good morning, Roger. Are you catching any fish?"

Sir Berenger had a soft heart toward the boy, as she'd seen him spending time with him before. He'd been with Roger when his mother died, or so Lady Delia had said.

Mazy felt a kinship with the boy, as they had both lost their only remaining parent.

"Not yet, but one just nibbled on my pole." The boy's eyes were wide and he was smiling.

Sir Berenger motioned her closer. "Come and sit with us."

Would she be intruding on their time together? Roger showed no signs of wanting her to leave, so Mazy joined them.

"Sir Berenger taught me how to make a trap for the fish using a basket," Roger gushed. "Have we caught a fish in the basket yet?"

Sir Berenger's voice was low and gentle. "Not yet. Catching fish is about being patient more than anything else."

Roger lowered his voice to match Sir Berenger's as he

explained to Mazy, "We also have these poles with hooks on the end." Roger lifted his pole out of the water to show her. "Mine has a worm on it. Fish like worms. A fish will swim up and bite the worm, and then I'll catch him on my hook."

"That's very clever," Mazy said. "I hope you catch a big one."

Roger chattered on for a few minutes, then said, "I think there's a fish in the trap."

Sir Berenger lifted the straw basket out of the water and showed Roger that it was empty. Mazy studied it, trying to see if it was different from the traps her father's guard had taught her to make. It was similar, with an open end for the fish to swim into with the current, the other end closed so it couldn't swim out. The basket was secured to the bank by a thin rope.

While Roger was busy looking for more worms to put on his hook, Mazy said, "Your sister is letting me help her with her baby. I mostly watch him when he sleeps and wait for him to wake up, and I play with him when Lady Delia is busy. He is the most adorable baby I've ever seen."

"He is a handsome little boy, but since he is my first nephew, I am probably not the best judge."

"He is very good-natured as well, and so rarely cries. The duke and duchess seem like excellent parents."

"They are good people. But you know you are not obligated to help my sister."

"I want to be responsible for myself now. Besides, I am well aware that the little bit of help I give them does not make up for their generosity."

"Strachleigh and I are planning to pay a visit to your brother, the Baron Wexcombe, in the next day or two."

Mazy's chest and shoulders felt heavy as she stared out at the river. She let out a long breath. "Lady Delia told me. I do appreciate your help, but I don't have much hope that he will listen."

"Perhaps he will give you a dowry at least, since you are staying here at Strachleigh. He must know that your honor is safe here."

"Perhaps he will. If anyone can persuade him to change his mind, I'm sure it is you and the Duke of Strachleigh." Mazy stood up and brushed off her skirt. "I should go finish my walk. I don't want to intrude."

"You're not intruding," Sir Berenger said. "You can stay."

"Thank you, but I'll be back this way."

"Come back and see how many fish we've caught," Roger said.

"I will."

How good it was to see the boy looking happy. Sir Berenger was so kind.

Mazy went on her way, talking to God and telling Him both the sad things that were on her mind as well as the things she was thankful for. It made her feel better to shed a few tears and to remember her many blessings.

After an hour or so, she turned to go back to the riverbank. Just thinking of seeing Sir Berenger again lifted her spirits.

Berenger thought about how sad Mazy had looked when he mentioned trying to get the baron to change his mind. She certainly did not have the protective and loving brothers she deserved. Sir John was not a particularly kind or generous man, but his main failing was his angry temperament. And Lord Wexcombe had proved himself to be selfish and cruel.

As he leaned down to check the fish trap, he saw her returning along the river's edge.

"Mazy, I caught a fish! Look!" Roger held up his pole to show the fish dangling from the end. "And we caught two more in the basket trap." He turned to Berenger. "Can I go show the boys? James said he would help me clean them."

"Go and show off your fish." Berenger ruffled the boy's hair.

Roger took his catch and ran away.

"You have made him very happy today," Mazy said. "It's so kind of you to teach him to fish."

Berenger smiled at her praise and lay back against a folded-up cloak. "He's a good boy. I'm glad I had time today to spend with him. Can you sit and talk with me?" He squinted up at her against the light that came through the trees.

Mazy sat on the grass and started picking the tiny wildflowers that were all around her.

"Who were you talking to when Roger and I first saw you?" He couldn't resist asking.

"No one." She stared at the flower between her fingers. "That is, I was praying. I like to pray out loud when I walk. You probably think that is strange."

"Not at all. Everyone prays. I pray out loud, too, sometimes."

They sat quietly for a few moments, then Berenger started telling her a funny story about what had happened during sword-fighting practice the day before. And that led to Mazy telling him about when she first learned how to throw knives.

He was so comfortable talking to Mazy. She may have been old enough to marry, but she had such an innocence about her. At the same time, she could speak intelligently about so many subjects. He found himself enjoying their conversation and wishing they could talk for the rest of the day. She was so different from her brothers. Delia had already grown quite fond of her, and he had as well, truth be told.

"The sun is so high, it's probably past noon," Mazy said as they lounged on the ground by the river. She wanted to give him a way out, to go back to the castle if he didn't want to stay there talking to her.

"Looks like it."

He didn't seem eager to go anywhere. His head was propped on his arms as he gazed up at the leaves on the tree above them.

"My sister says you're very good with my nephew. She says you have helped her a lot."

"She is being kind." Mazy felt herself blushing. "Truthfully, I know only a little about babies. Sometimes I rock him in my arms to get him to go to sleep. It doesn't usually work." Mazy laughed and Sir Berenger smiled.

"Are you always so modest?"

"I am not being modest. I am just very honest." She told the truth even when it made her look foolish. She couldn't seem to help it.

"Honesty is a good character trait."

"One of my father's servants once told me that I didn't always have to be so honest, and that when I get married, I should not tell my husband the truth all the time. But that doesn't sound wise to me."

"I don't think your husband will see your honesty as a fault, unless he is very unwise himself."

"If I ever find a husband."

"You are fair and lovely, and therefore will have many men vying for your hand in marriage."

Sir Berenger thought she was fair and lovely?

Mazy's heart did a flip inside her chest. But he was only being kind, like his sister.

"I think it unlikely that I shall ever marry."

"I am sure you will marry. And Lord Wexcombe may change his mind about helping you."

"Do you know whom you shall marry?" Mazy wasn't sure why she asked that. Was it impertinent? Would he be embarrassed? She wasn't even sure she wanted to know. She had a sinking feeling in her stomach to think of him marrying.

"I don't. But I hope, someday, I shall have something to offer a lady."

That left Mazy out, since she was no longer a lady.

Sir Berenger was a knight, and he no doubt aspired to much more. His father had been an earl, and his older brother, Gerard, had married the Princess of Montciel, a small kingdom on the

Continent. Sir Berenger would not be content to live in a small house with a woman who was no one.

What was she thinking? Of course he did not think of her as a possible wife, so how could it matter? He was Lady Delia's brother and John's fellow knight. He was someone who let her practice archery with the squires he was training. That was all.

But he was so very noble, and handsome too.

"I suppose we should go get some food." Sir Berenger got up from the ground and stretched. "It must be well past midday."

Mazy agreed, and they walked together through the woods toward the castle, chatting about Roger, about caring for his nephew, and about whether a woman could ever be a knight.

It was good that he did not think of her as a possible wife because that made their friendship all the more comfortable, though it did hurt just a bit, deep inside, that Sir Berenger did not think of her that way. And yet, she could hold close the words he had said—"You are fair and lovely, and therefore will have many men vying for your hand in marriage."

That must mean something. But perhaps he was only being kind.

SEVEN

BERENGER AND THE DUKE TOOK TWO GUARDS WITH THEM as they set out on the journey to speak to Baron Wexcombe.

Poor Mazy. She was such an intelligent young woman, not to mention kindhearted, enjoyable to talk to, and fair of face and form. It was a shame she had such selfish brothers as Sir John and Baron Wexcombe, and even more of a shame that her father had died.

The journey would hopefully be a pleasant one, especially if the weather remained good. As his brother-in-law, Strachleigh was more friend than master. He treated Berenger as an equal, even though he was a duke and Berenger might never be more than a knight.

Although Mazy probably did not want to rely on the charity of his sister and Strachleigh, at least she never would have to feel as if she had no place to go.

He truly hoped, for her sake, however, that her brother would decide not to cast her off.

When they reached Castle Wexcombe, they were welcomed with cold formality by the baron and his wife.

"We have come on behalf of your sister, Mazy," Strachleigh said.

The baron frowned. "My sister who ran away from home with only a common ploughman? Who traveled for two days before reaching you?"

Strachleigh's mouth tightened but he made no reply.

"She ran away from my protection and from the marriage that I was trying to arrange for her with the Earl of Brimley. She refused my provision, and I owe her nothing."

A sudden thought came to him and Berenger asked, "Did you make an arrangement with this Earl of Brimley? Does he wish to marry Mazy?" If an agreement had been made, Mazy might yet have to marry this Earl of Brimley. His heart was in his throat as he waited for Baron Wexcombe to answer.

"As a matter of fact, the earl has already married someone else."

Berenger was surprised at the depth of his relief.

"Is there another reason you have refused to take responsibility for her future and well-being?" Strachleigh looked incredulous, as if he couldn't believe a brother would treat his sister this way. Certainly Strachleigh adhered to a noble code of conduct and morality that would forbid such a thing.

"For two days she was alone with a poor ploughman's son.

Anything could have happened. She could have done anything, and anything could have been done to her."

Berenger was almost ready to shove his fist in the man's face. "A loyal tenant of your father's was with her for her protection, nothing more. They both say that nothing untoward occurred between them, nor did your sister meet anyone else on the road. It is very unchivalrous of you, not to mention cold and un-feeling, to accuse your sister and endanger her reputation this way."

"I have no way of knowing whether what they say is true. How can I provide a husband for her when I cannot vouch for her virtue?"

"That is preposterous." Berenger wanted to fight the man. It was on the tip of his tongue to offer to battle the man any way he preferred—sword, archery, jousting—as Mazy's champion, but it would be too unfair, as the man obviously had never trained to fight. He was as soft and bloated as a bullfrog.

"Baron Wexcombe," Strachleigh said calmly, "we ask that you would reinstate Mazy's birthright. If you do not wish to offer a dowry, I am prepared to—"

"No, I will not reinstate her. She is rebellious and unwilling to do as she is told. Her reputation is beyond repair, besides the fact that she was indulged by my father to such an extent as to be unuseful as a wife. I wash my hands of her forever. I will not change my mind."

You don't deserve her as a sister, Berenger was thinking. *She is too good for you if you cannot see her worth.* Berenger's hands clenched into fists as he struggled to control himself. At least Strachleigh was calm.

"It is unfortunate you feel that way. A young woman whose own brother and the head of her family rejects her is often mistreated and left to the vices of evil men. You are still willing to cast her off?"

"I am. She has made her own choice. And she has a brother, the son of her mother, who can be responsible for her."

Again, Berenger struggled not to challenge the man to a sword fight.

Without staying any longer, he and Strachleigh took their leave of the coldhearted baron and his stone-faced wife and returned home.

Mazy glanced up at the sky. It was overcast, but the clouds did not look especially rainy.

After her last outing, when a badger hissed at her, she decided to take a walking stick with her before she went into the woods.

She thought about the conversation she'd had with Sir Berenger the day before, when he told her that he and the duke had been unsuccessful in convincing Warin that he should not disown her.

"You are not to blame," Sir Berenger had said, gazing intently into her eyes as they talked behind the kitchen. "The baron is a hard-hearted man. Selfishness, no doubt, is his motive for not wishing to do right by you."

Mazy hadn't realized just how much she had been hoping Warin would give heed to the duke's and Sir Berenger's pleas to not abandon her. Her heart was heavy.

"I am grateful to you and the duke for trying. It was very kind and generous of you to take the time to go to him."

"I cannot believe that man is your brother." Sir Berenger huffed out a breath and ran his hand through his hair.

"Half brother. I did not spend any time with him, as he was nearly an adult when I was born. He lived at his mother's estate that she inherited and left to him. My father and he did not have a very good relationship. I think Warin resented John and me because my father seemed to prefer us—and our mother. Father spoke of Warin as petty and small-minded and rarely saw him. So I suppose Warin has his reasons for casting me off."

"But none of that is your doing. He should be a man and do his duty to his sister."

"All will be well. And I know I must forgive Warin, but I could never trust him again. But all is well. My priest always said, 'God has a plan and a purpose for everyone and everything.'"

But Sir Berenger still seemed almost distraught. "You know my sister and Strachleigh will always have a place for you here. You will not be completely destitute. You know this?"

"Yes, of course." Mazy had smiled and reassured him. But she was less sure after she let herself feel the rejection and the weight of her half brother's abandonment.

Lady Delia and the duke were good and kind, and yes, she knew she would always have food and a place to sleep at Strachleigh, but she wanted her own life. She'd imagined traveling with Father, then marrying a baron or some other wealthy person. But now she would probably never be able to travel, and her chances of marrying well were almost nonexistent. She would need to find some other plan for her life.

She was heading toward the small stand of trees next to the stable to look for a good-sized stick when she heard someone crying. Stepping around the side of the stable, she came upon Roger sitting with his back against the wooden building, his head down and almost resting on his knees.

"Roger? Are you hurt?"

He quickly scrubbed his face with his hands and sniffed. "No."

"It's all right. I was about to go for a walk. Would you want to go with me?"

He shook his head, then wiped his nose on his sleeve.

Mazy picked a leaf off a low-hanging branch and studied it, tracing the veins with her fingernail. "Is there anything you want to talk to me about?"

Roger shook his head, then after a short pause, he said, "Do you like music?"

"Yes. Do you?"

"I heard a song once on Midsummer's Eve that was about a boy who gave a flower to a girl and she wore it in her hair. Do you know that song?"

"I know the very one."

"I know that song too."

They both turned to find Sir Berenger standing a few feet behind Mazy. He strode forward, joining them.

"I was just thinking," Roger said, sniffing again, his face

dried but his eyelashes still dark and wet, "I would sure like to hear that song again. I wonder when the duke will hire some players to come back to Strachleigh."

"I could play it for you if I had a lute."

Sir Berenger and Roger both stared at her.

"You can play the lute?" Sir Berenger asked.

"I can."

"Delia has a lute. I'll borrow it from her if you will play a song for us."

"Would you?" Roger asked excitedly.

"Of course." She would probably not get to go on her solitary walk today, as playing a lute always drew a crowd, but it would be worth it if it distracted Roger from his unhappy thoughts.

A few minutes later Sir Berenger was striding toward them with a beautiful lute, painted with brightly colored flowers. And sure enough, there was already a small crowd following him.

Sir Berenger found a stump for her to sit on. She sat and started strumming, reminding herself of how the song went. Was she brave enough to play and sing, too, with all these people around her, especially in front of Sir Berenger?

"I will play the song, but you all have to help me sing it. Roger? That means you."

The boy smiled. "I will help!"

Mazy started to play the song and then to sing. Several people in the crowd joined in. Some knew slightly different words to the song, but it sounded quite nice, Mazy thought. The best part was the way Roger looked—so happy and content as they all sang the song he had requested.

When the song was over—or, rather, when no one could remember any more of the verses—Mazy asked, "Does anyone else know how to play an instrument?"

Sir Berenger had such a guilty look on his face that she asked, "Do you know an instrument, Sir Berenger?"

"I play the pipe, but I'm not very good at it."

"Go get it! You must play with me." Mazy and the rest of the crowd, which had grown quite large, began shouting for Sir Berenger to get his pipe.

He good-naturedly gave in, and a few minutes later he came back with a pipe, which looked very small in his large hand.

"What shall we play now?" Sir Berenger leaned close to ask her.

"Do you know the song about the shepherdess, the wolf, and the friar?"

"I think I remember."

He stood quite close to her and they began to play. Everyone knew the words and joined in the song. Roger even clapped his hands in rhythm.

When that was finished, Sir Berenger asked Roger to pick the next song. He chose "The Stork and the Swan," and soon they were playing and singing again.

Sir Berenger's eyes stayed connected to hers as they played. It felt as if they were the only two people there, even though they were surrounded by a crowd.

After four or five songs the stable master ordered the grooms back to work, and several of the house servants went back to the castle.

"I should be getting back, too, to help Lady Delia."

"I'll walk with you," Sir Berenger said.

As they walked up the hill together, Mazy was highly aware of his taller, stronger frame beside her. How charming he had looked, his fingers on the little pipe, playing along with her.

"You amaze me, Mazy."

Mazy's breath caught in her throat as she waited for him to explain.

"You are a woman of many talents and skills. And you made Roger very glad, singing all his favorite songs."

"You also made him glad."

They found Lady Delia in the solar, and Mazy handed the lute back to her. The tips of Mazy's fingers were red and raw, as she had not played in a long time, so she curled her fingers inside her hand so they wouldn't see.

Lady Delia smiled. "You impress me with your skills."

"Is there nothing you cannot do?" Sir Berenger was gazing at her with a look that made her warm inside.

"You are very good with the pipe." She tried to deflect his praise.

He lowered his voice. "Roger will never forget today, because of you."

"And you. He adores you, and you are so patient with him."

Lady Delia smiled as she looked back and forth between Mazy and Sir Berenger.

"Mazy, you are welcome to borrow the lute whenever you like. It belonged to my husband's father, but he never learned to play it."

Sir Berenger and Lady Delia hardly looked like brother and sister, as he was dark from the sun and his brown hair had a chestnut tint, while Delia had pale skin and very dark, almost black hair. But they had similar natures and temperaments.

Sir Berenger's gaze lingered on Mazy, but then he said, "I should go. I'm sure the squires are wondering where I am. If I'm not around to keep them in line, they will run off to the river or go off trapping hares."

They told him fare well, and she watched him go. He was so gentle and kind, and so very handsome.

Surely Sir Berenger did not think about her as often as she thought about him. But would it not be wonderful if he did?

She sighed.

EIGHT

BERENGER SAT IN HIS FAVORITE SPOT AT A BEND IN THE river that shared both its banks with open meadows, where the sun shimmered on the water every hour of the day.

He stared back and forth between the gently flowing water and the missive that had come, inviting him to join with the Duke of Rudhall in traveling to Prussia to vanquish some Teutonic Knights who were trying to take over the castles and lands of a Prussian nobleman.

After being knighted by King Richard, Berenger had come to Strachleigh to help his brother-in-law establish a loyal set of guards after taking the estate over from his treacherous uncle. He'd already stayed longer than he'd intended to, as Strachleigh had asked him to help train his squires.

As a knight and third son of an earl, he would have nothing unless he distinguished himself. And the last thing he wanted was to be seen as a do-nothing with no ambition.

So now that this opportunity was presenting itself . . .

Berenger read again the section of the letter that promised him "recognition with King Richard himself for your service to his allies in Prussia."

If Berenger returned victorious from Prussia, perhaps the king would grant him lands, a castle, and maybe even a title. He could marry a lady of his choosing then, could settle into life in his own castle, have children, and, Lord willing, never have to fight again.

Not that he minded fighting, if it was for a good cause. And he considered fighting against tyranny to be a very good cause.

Someone, or something, was coming through the underbrush behind him.

Mazy emerged into the clearing. She caught sight of him and stopped. "I didn't know anyone was here. I'll go."

"Come over and sit." He brushed the flat rock clean beside him.

She did so, tucking her feet under her and hugging her knees over her skirt. "I was just out for a walk."

"At least it's not raining. I was beginning to wonder if it would ever stop."

"I know. It rains so often here."

"My brother Gerard says it doesn't rain as much in Montciel, where he lives now. But they have very harsh winters."

"What's it like to have so many brothers? Lady Delia told me there are seven brothers in your family."

"It is good. I love all my brothers. Although Merek is the one with the most volatile temperament. He likes to tell others what to do, and he can get very angry when people don't do what he wants them to."

"Like John?"

"A little." But Merek never made ridiculous accusations the way Sir John sometimes did, blaming others for his own faults, or becoming furious over a small thing like scorched porridge. And Berenger had seen Merek more than once go out of his way to help someone when he thought no one would notice. He was fiercely protective of Delia, their younger brothers, and anyone else who might be in a weak state and unable to defend themselves. He never backed away from a fight.

"I know John loves me, but sometimes . . ." Mazy shook her head. "I don't understand why he gets so angry and yells so much."

Berenger wasn't sure what to say. Finally he said, "I am sure he wishes he was better able to take care of you. But you are safe here, as long as you wish to stay."

Mazy nodded and smiled, but her eyes were sad.

They were quiet for a few moments, then Mazy pointed at the parchment in his hand. "Did you get some news from one of your brothers?"

"This? No. It's an invitation from the Duke of Rudhall to go to Prussia with an army he is gathering. I'd be fighting against the Teutonic Knights."

"Prussia. That is a long way from here, is it not?"

"It is, but . . . this is what I've been preparing for all my life."

"Are you going?"

"Yes, I think I am."

"Will John go too?"

"I don't know. He hasn't said."

"So he was also invited?" She chewed on her bottom lip.

"Yes, all the knights were, but even if he decides to go, you are welcome to stay here at Strachleigh as long as you like, and you will be protected and cared for here."

"Thank you. You and your sister are so kind."

She was putting on a brave face. Truly, he thought she might be better off if Sir John did go to Prussia with him. His sister and her husband would watch over Mazy, perhaps even help her make a good match, but Sir John? Berenger was not at all sure Sir John would go out of his way to do anything for her.

"I will be sad to see you go." Mazy did not look at him when she said the words. She stared out at the river instead.

Mazy was a good girl, and quite beautiful. If he were not about to go away . . . But he had nothing to offer her anyway. Besides, sixteen was a bit young, in his opinion, though girls younger than sixteen were married all the time, to men much older than Berenger.

Someday he'd find the right woman to marry, someone who was a good match for him, someone who would appreciate and even love him. He would not accept anything less. And if he was honest with himself, he also hoped she would be someone he could rescue.

When he was a young boy, he'd dreamed of rescuing a damsel in distress, a woman locked in a tower by an ogre or a dragon, or a princess oppressed by her enemies. Of course, ogres and dragons did not exist, except the human ones who oppressed or abused others. He'd even struggled not to be jealous of Gerard, who actually had rescued a princess, helped her defeat her enemies, and then married her.

Deep in his heart, Berenger still hoped to experience the thrill of rescuing that fair maiden in need of his help.

Perhaps he would find her in Prussia.

Mazy watched Sir Berenger and a few other knights and soldiers leave at dawn several days later. Sir Berenger sat tall in the saddle on his enormous warhorse, leading the way as they rode to join the others traveling toward their mission in Prussia.

She had to hurry back to her room so no one would see her face and guess what she was feeling and thinking.

Why did her chest ache with unshed tears? After all, John had not gone with them, preferring to stay and protect Strachleigh.

"Someone has to defend England, in case there's another rebellion or an invasion." John had sniffed and then spat on the ground beside him with that now-familiar look of his, his head lifting high, his eyes half-closed. She had come to associate that heavy-lidded expression with a pretense of indifference. But what her brother was really thinking or feeling, she had no idea.

Secretly she had hoped her brother would say something like, "I can't go because I must protect my sister." But if he was staying for her sake, he wasn't saying so.

As she lay hugging her pillow to her chest, missing her father for at least the hundredth time that week, she let her thoughts go to Sir Berenger.

The handsome knight had been a genuine friend to her, always talking honestly and openly with her, but he had never seemed to look at her as anything but a friend, the sister of his fellow knight, and his sister Delia's helper.

Mazy tended to stay away from the other guards, careful not to be alone with them. In addition to her father's long-ago warning, there was something about the way they looked at her, a slyness in their expressions. But Sir Berenger was different. He had made her feel protected, as if he cared about her. Now that he was leaving, Strachleigh would feel very different.

Life was strange and intimidating now that her father was gone and Warin had disowned her. And her hopes and expectations about John had proved to be unfounded. He rarely even spoke to her, and he certainly didn't speak to her about her future or what he might do to help her. She no longer expected him to help her find a husband.

She hated feeling that she needed her brother's help, especially since he was so reluctant to give it. And she could certainly protect herself. After all, she knew how to shoot an arrow and throw a knife better than most of the squires training to be knights.

She could defend herself, if need be, and she could procure food for herself, with her knowledge of traps and tracking and fishing. She even knew which mushrooms in the forest were edible and which were poisonous.

But now that Sir Berenger was leaving, perhaps for more

than a year, the thought of him being killed in battle was a deep pain she could actually feel, something she had to reject and expel from her mind or it would overwhelm her.

She would see him again. In her spirit she was sure of it.

"I've decided to join the king's guards in London," John said, "and you can come with me, if you don't wish to stay here."

Mazy stared at John with her mouth open. "Why?"

John blew out an irritated breath. "Do you think I can achieve anything while sitting here in Bedfordshire, training squires? I can never be recognized by the king here. I could die and never be noticed, a pauper living out of an outbuilding on someone else's estate."

John overstated everything.

"I'm a knight! Do you expect me to do nothing with my skills?"

"You may do as you wish, of course. I am sure you know best." John's anger had taught her to speak blandly to him. He had said he wanted to stay in order to protect Strachleigh, but she decided it best not to point that out.

John let out a long, slow breath, as though his pique of temper had passed.

"I am leaving in two days, as I've been offered a position as a captain in the guard at the Tower of London." He finally looked her in the eye. "You may come with me, if you like, or you may stay here," he repeated.

What would she do if he left Strachleigh? She'd only come here because of John.

"As you know, Warin has disowned me, so you are my only family." She said the last words with a bit of disgust creeping into her voice.

"You're not going back to Warin, then?"

"That is not an option."

"Well, then?" John frowned at her, folding his arms over his chest.

She should probably think about it before making a decision. But what real choice did she have? It felt too strange to stay at Strachleigh, living off the generosity of people who were not her family and owed her nothing. Besides, she'd so desperately wanted to see more of England, and if she went with her brother, she'd finally get to see London and all its sights.

"I would like to go with you, if you don't mind."

"I asked you to come, didn't I?" Then he added, "You're my sister. And I can keep an eye on you if you come to London."

Perhaps he truly did care about her.

"I have always wanted to see London."

John was no longer looking at her. Instead, he was staring at the group of guards who were gathering near the stable.

"Just be sure you're packed and ready in two days. We leave at dawn."

"I will be ready."

He was already walking away, calling out to one of the other men, who waved him over.

So she was to leave Strachleigh. Truly, she would miss Lady

Delia and her sweet baby. She and the duke had been so generous to her already, more than she deserved. Yes, she had been helping with the baby, but Lady Delia did not truly need her. Mazy felt as if she was in the way more often than she was truly helping.

She was grateful, and she knew she was safe here, but she should go with her brother.

But would she ever see Sir Berenger again?

Nine

London was as loud and smoky and crowded as Mazy had imagined.

What she could not have imagined was how enormous the king's Palace of Westminster was. Neither could she have imagined how tall St. Paul's Cathedral was, nor how beautiful, taking her breath away and bringing tears to her eyes.

She exclaimed to John about how beautiful St. Paul's was, but he started talking to one of the other knights while she was in midsentence. After that she simply stared, thinking how she would describe each building in her mind, and tried to keep up with her brother and not become separated in the endless swarms of people in the streets.

She was not sure what she would do now that she was in London, but she hoped to find some way of making money. John had told her that a guard captain's salary was minimal. His real hope was that he would gain attention by doing something grand, like thwarting a plot to assassinate the king or some other such service that would obligate the king to reward him.

"We will have to find a place for you to live near the Tower. I will stay with you when I can, but when I'm not there, you might have to defend yourself. Do you think you can do that? Could you kill a man with your knife if he was trying to harm you?"

"Of course. I can do anything I have to do."

"Good. That's what I like to hear from my Maze Queen."

They slept that first night at an inn called the Green Dragon. The next day she and John went in search of more permanent lodgings for her. They found a set of rooms over an alehouse called the Swan, very near to the Tower of London.

"You couldn't find a better place," the Swan's owner said. "My last tenant drank so much he lost his job as a clerk and couldn't pay."

"My sister and I are wanting a quiet place, very safe and private. Though I warn you . . ." John stuck his finger in the proprietor's face. "My sister is the best knife thrower you've ever seen. Anyone trying to harass her will find himself stabbed through. She has very good aim. Or if he gets too close, he could get his throat—" John drew his finger across his neck.

"I doubt it not." The man raised his brows and nodded. "But you'll find this place safe and quiet. My daughter and I live on the middle level, and you and your sister will be at the top of the stairs. Besides my daughter and me, there's no one else here, no other tenants." He held out the key.

"And no other key?"

"This be the only key."

John glanced around before finally saying, "I reckon we'll take it."

Mazy sighed in relief. She dared not give her opinion—John had made it clear that he would make the decision—but she was glad they had found a place so she could get some rest. There had been so much noise in the inn where they'd stayed the night before that she'd barely slept.

She and John carried their meager possessions up the stairs to their rooms, where there were two straw mattresses on the floor.

"We're not sleeping on those." John kicked the mattresses into the corner of the room. "Dirty things. We'll go out and find some clean straw tomorrow."

They laid their blankets on the floor. Thankfully it was a warm night. They did not even build a fire in the fireplace before falling asleep.

The next morning John told her, "I'm going to the Tower of London to check in with my commander. You can go to the market and buy some food." He handed her a few coins. "Don't talk to anyone. London has too many bad characters."

"And you will return soon?"

"I don't know how long this will take. But I'll be back before nightfall."

Mazy nodded.

Shortly after her brother left, she put on one of her older dresses, which shouldn't attract attention, and set out to find the market.

At the bottom of the stairs she found herself in the back of the alehouse. Despite the early hour, she could already hear men's voices around the partition in the main room. Opening the door to the outside, she slipped out into the narrow alley. Turning to the left, then left again, she was in the street at the front of the Swan.

The sun was shining, but dimly, through a thin layer of clouds. Still, it was good to be in the great town of London. She was awed by the number of people moving about, along with horses and donkeys and carts of all description. The street was dirt but it was hard-packed.

She saw the daughter of the owner of the alehouse, whom she'd been introduced to the night before, standing in the doorway of the Swan.

"Good morning," Mazy said to her. "Can you tell me where I should go to find bread and cheese?"

"There's a small market that way." The young maiden—Mazy couldn't remember her name—pointed down the street. "But it's easy to get lost if you don't know the way. I'll show you. Come."

The maiden hurried down the street in her bare feet, carefully dodging a pile of horse manure as she went. "What is your name?" the maiden asked.

"Mazelina, but I am called Mazy."

"Mazy. I like that. My name is Roesia Sadler, but you can call me Ro."

"Thank you, Ro, for helping me. This is my first time in London."

"First time, eh? Is it just you and your brother? Is he a knight?"

"Yes, just us two, and yes, he is a knight."

"Who was your father?"

"The Baron Wexcombe. He died. My older brother is the baron now. But he disowned me." Perhaps she shouldn't have told her that. She had only just met this girl.

"When did your father die?"

"Two months ago." The sadness caused a sharp intake of breath. "I've been living with my brother John since then."

"Two months. I'm sorry. If my father died I'd be all alone. My mother died when I was a baby, my father never remarried, and I don't have any brothers or sisters, nor even any aunts or uncles."

Mazy nodded. "My mother is dead too." They smiled at each other, and Mazy's heart swelled. Perhaps Ro would be her first London friend.

They arrived at the market and Ro showed her the best vendors for bread, cheese, dried fruit, and nuts.

"You should buy some of these pasties. They are the best."

Mazy bought some, although the fried fruit pies looked very greasy.

On their way back to the alehouse, Ro asked, "How old are you?"

"Sixteen."

"I'm sixteen too!"

"My brother John is twenty-one, and my older brother is twenty-four."

"I would have had an older sister, but she died before I was born. Were you ever married or betrothed? You said your father was a baron."

"No, never married or betrothed." Mazy almost mentioned Sir Berenger, but that would be strange. He was not even a marriage prospect. He was also not her brother nor any relation to her. She missed him, though, and prayed for him every day, that God would keep him safe, give him great success in his quest, and bring him back to England quickly.

"You probably shouldn't tell anyone that you have only your brother, especially if he is to be away a lot."

"Why?"

"You might attract the attention of someone nefarious. But I'm sure you will be well. I don't want to frighten you the way my father frightens me." Ro rolled her eyes heavenward. "He treats me like a little child, like there's a wolf around every corner, waiting to eat me."

"I'm sure he only wants to keep you safe."

Ro showed her around the streets between the marketplace and the Swan, pointing out various shops and places of interest, sprinkling in lots of advice about where to go, what to do, and what not to do in the busy town of London. Mazy felt more and more as if God in His goodness was blessing her with a great friend.

"What did you do to get your brother to disown you?" Ro's green eyes looked at her sharply.

Mazy decided she could trust Ro, so she said, "My oldest brother was trying to marry me off to a very old man, so I ran away to see John, who was living nearby. One of my father's tenants accompanied me, and my brother cast me off for being in his company. But nothing happened. Nothing at all. I think he just didn't want to be responsible for me."

Ro shook her head and slammed her fist into her palm. "It is unfair the way men treat us."

"I don't need him. I can defend myself."

"My father said you can throw knives."

"And I can shoot a bow as well as most men."

"Lovely!" Ro laughed. "Will you teach me?"

"Of course."

"I like you, Mazy. You're not afraid of anything, are you?"

"I try not to be."

"That is good. We shall be great friends, you and I." Ro smiled and slipped her arm through Mazy's.

When they reached the alehouse, Ro squeezed her hand. "I have to go help my father or he will be angry, but I will come up to your room when I can. If I can sneak away from Father." She whispered the last part and hurried into the alehouse.

A man's voice shouted from inside. Mazy's heart skipped a beat and she listened outside the door. She was fairly certain the voice was Ro's father's, but she could not make out the words.

Mazy peeked in the door. Ro's father waved his hand and she scurried into the back of the alehouse. Her father suddenly caught sight of Mazy, an ugly scowl on his face.

"Ro was helping me," Mazy said, taking a step inside the doorway. There were only two other men inside, but they were both staring at her. "It was my fault. I didn't know the way to the market."

The scowl on his face softened as he said, "Very well. But she has work to do now."

Mazy hurried out and around the back of the half-timber

and plaster building. She went in through the back door, and there was Ro, picking up a large burlap bag.

"You are so brave," Ro whispered, a big smile on her face. "But don't call me Ro in front of my father. He hates it when people call me that."

"Oh, I'm sorry."

"No, it's all right. I have to go."

Mazy nodded and headed up the stairs to her room.

When she reached the door, she remembered she'd forgotten to lock it. Her brother would be furious with her if he knew. She thought of the men downstairs in the alehouse. Did they know she lived here? Anyone could come into the back door and walk up the stairs.

She went inside and set her basket on the floor. With her hand in her skirt pocket, clutching the handle of her knife, she listened as she went into both of their rooms, checking to make sure no one was there. When she had made certain she was alone, she locked the door with the key.

She was not used to locking doors. She'd never done that before, not at her father's house, nor at Strachleigh Castle, but this was London. She would have to be more careful.

Mazy had cleaned the rooms as best she could, borrowing a broom from Ro's father, promising to get her own broom as soon as possible. The food had taken almost all the money John had given her, and it would not last very long. She had some money of her own, but she saw how fast money went when she had to buy all their own food.

She needed a way to make money. She hated sewing, so she didn't think she could make money that way. Was there something else she could do?

She'd helped Lady Delia with her baby. Was there anyone in London who would pay her to watch their children? No doubt it would have to be a wealthy person. But she knew no one in London besides Ro.

She remembered the women in the market who were selling bread and other foods. Could she bake bread? She had never been allowed to help in the kitchen at home, but she'd seen Cook making bread at least a hundred times. There was no oven here in their rooms. But perhaps Ro's father would allow her to use his oven.

She cleaned, ate, and took a nap on the floor, and still John had not come back. He said he'd return by nightfall. She stared out the window as the sunlight grew dimmer and dimmer. Some men came and lit the tall lamps along the street, but there was still no sign of John.

A knock came at the door. Mazy hurried to it. "Who is there?"

"It's me."

John sounded grumpy, and Mazy hurried to unlock the door.

He came inside and she smelled strong drink. Was it only the ale from below?

"How was your day? Did you speak with your commander?"

"I start work tomorrow. Did you have any problems?"

"No, all was well. The alehouse owner's daughter helped me. What is his name? I forgot."

"Thomas Sadler."

"His daughter is my age and she took me to the market. I bought some food. Are you hungry?"

"What do you have?"

Mazy showed him. He picked up a plum pasty and took a bite.

He spit it out into his hand. "Too greasy."

Mazy hurried to bring him the slop bucket, and he threw the offending pasty into it.

"Sorry. But there's cheese and bread, and dried fruit and nuts."

He nibbled at the food, then lay down on his blanket. "You didn't find us any beds, I see."

Mazy bit her lip. Did he not remember that he said the two of them would go and find some clean straw for their beds?

"What did you do all day?" she asked him. "I thought you would help me—"

"I do what I have to do, when I need to do it." John raised his voice but did not look at her. "I can't do everything. Do you think I want to be a guard? I should have gone with Sir Berenger to Prussia. Instead, I stayed here to take care of you."

Mazy's stomach twisted. Did he blame her for not going to Prussia to fight? He never said she was the reason he'd stayed.

After waiting for him all day, she suddenly felt quite sad that he was there.

She went to the window and stared out at the people still

milling about on the street, fewer than in the daytime, but she was surprised at how many there were. Where were they going? What did they do to make money? There were more men than women, and she saw no young women her own age. No doubt they were at home, safe with their families.

John's breathing was loud and steady; he was already asleep.

Perhaps he'd been cross with her because he was tired. Or because he'd been drinking.

Perhaps she should have stayed in Strachleigh. But at least she wasn't in Wexcombe with Warin, who didn't care if she lived or died.

Mazy was here in London, and she would not feel sorry for herself. Even if John was neglectful of her, she would survive somehow. She could and she would.

T EN

JOHN LEFT BEFORE THE SUN WAS UP THE NEXT MORNING. Mazy arose, ate the last of the food she had bought, and went down the stairs. She wanted to explore London, but she also needed to buy more food.

From the light of the lit candle in a wall sconce at the bottom of the stairs, she could see a room with a few burlap bags, bulging and full, resting against one wall. If there were so many nefarious people in London, why did Sadler not keep the back door locked?

Mazy stood there, not making any sound, listening. She hoped to hear Ro's voice.

After waiting a few minutes without seeing or hearing her new friend, Mazy went out the back door and into the street.

She patted the key in her pocket, happy she had remembered to lock her door this time, then slipped her hand inside her other pocket, where she kept one of her throwing knives. If anyone tried to attack her, she was ready.

Mazy was careful to notice the streets she went down. She could easily imagine herself getting lost, so she paid close attention.

The Tower of London was a good marker for her, as the White Tower was the tallest building near the alehouse, just south of her new home. She could also see the spire on the top of St. Paul's Cathedral. The cathedral was easily visible from wherever she walked, as the church was built upon the highest hill in London. Her father had told her it had taken three hundred years to build. She longed to go inside it, as John had been in a hurry when they arrived and did not let her go in. It didn't look terribly far. It would probably take her less than half an hour to walk there.

As she walked the streets Mazy noted all the colorful signs, passing the Green Dragon where they had slept their first night in London, its wooden sign carved and painted with a dragon breathing fire. She saw other signs for the Sword and Shield, the Ram's Head, the Hammer, the White Knight, and the Rooster. Mazy loved them all.

When she finally arrived at St. Paul's Cathedral, she strained her neck looking up at the breathtaking structure, its intricately carved facades and tall spire. Finally, when she'd taken in the outside, she covered her head with her shawl and entered.

It was so quiet she could hardly believe she was still in London. The ceilings were incredibly high, and the stained-glass windows were colorful scenes of people and animals, recognizable stories she had read to her father from the Bible. She took in every beautiful colored glass window, every carving, every statue and bust and crucifix, the painted frescoes, the arches, the polished floors. They all seemed to fill her spirit until her feet were barely touching the floor.

The hush was reverent. Everything about the cathedral made her heartbeat slow down, her breathing deepen. As she slowly proceeded farther in, Mazy placed a small coin in the box for the poor and genuflected before the crucifix, making the sign of the cross. She walked all the way to the chancel and knelt, bowing her head. She whispered a prayer beside a few other women who were kneeling there.

How incredible that man could make such a magnificent structure. It must surely be the power of God working through those who built this cathedral, for even Strachleigh Castle paled in comparison, a mere house next to this glorious homage to the God of heaven.

After Mazy had prayed for a while and lit a candle, she walked slowly around the nave, taking a longer look at everything—the ceiling, the windows, the statues. She understood why men became priests, so they could work and live in awe-inspiring places like this, worshipping and serving God, always mindful of His majesty because of the majesty surrounding them.

When more people came in, Mazy decided to depart, but she hoped to return again soon, and often.

Back on the street and feeling more confident that she would not get lost, since she could see the White Tower across from her home, she explored some of the streets near St. Paul's Cathedral.

She happened upon a marketplace that was much larger than the one near the Swan. John had forgotten to leave her more money when he left, so she had taken her own coin purse to purchase a stool or a bench to sit on, and perhaps even a couple of mattresses, though she knew not how she would carry them back home.

She tried to find what she needed, but there were so many people, more people than she had ever seen in her life. The smell of raw fish, smoked meat, and unwashed bodies, along with the sounds of shouting and people haggling over prices, overwhelmed her.

A woman brushed against Mazy's side.

"Pardon me," Mazy said. The woman said nothing, did not even turn to look at her, and continued on her way.

Other people bumped into her until Mazy learned to stop asking for pardon and longed for wide-open spaces. The walkways between the market stalls were too narrow to pass through without occasionally touching someone, and Mazy seemed to be the only one who tried hard to avoid it.

A man's shoulder hit her in the back. He turned, scowled at her, then walked on.

Perhaps she should have stayed in the cathedral where she'd felt so peaceful just half an hour before. But she needed things for their new home. What would John think if she did nothing all day while he was out guarding the king?

A man was coming toward her with a load on his back so big that it stuck out on both sides. Mazy tried to move out of his way, but there were so many people that she was trapped. When the man passed her, his pack of goods hit her in the head and scraped her arm.

Her throat seemed to be closing up, preventing her from getting a deep breath. She had to get away.

Mazy turned and fled to the closest opening, then the next and the next, until she was finally out of the marketplace and on a less crowded street.

She put a hand to her head. It was not bleeding, nor was her arm. She went to a building nearby and leaned against the wall to catch her breath.

"What's the matter?"

A man was grinning at her from a few feet away, his mouth full of broken and missing teeth.

"Where are you from, girl?" he demanded. "Not from London, I'd wager."

He was old enough to be her father, but he looked her up and down, a sneering grin on his lips.

"Good day, sir," she said, starting to walk away from him.

"What's your hurry? Tarry with me a while. I'll buy you some food from the inn."

He was following her. She could hear his voice getting closer.

"I do not want anything. Good day."

"Oh, come, come. I won't hurt you." He touched her shoulder.

Mazy spun around to face him. Her heart beat so hard she could scarcely draw breath. Her hand clutched the knife in her pocket.

"I just want to buy you something to eat. You look hungry." He laid his hand on her shoulder.

Mazy whipped out her knife and unsheathed it. She pointed it at his face.

"Get away from me. Now."

The man's expression went from smiling to dark and tense.

"Get away from me, I said." Mazy kept her voice gruff to force away the trembling. She took two steps back.

People were starting to stare at them, but no one seemed interested in helping her. They just kept walking.

"You little witch," the man said. "Threatening me with a knife?"

Mazy kept backing away. The man did not move.

She wanted to turn and run, but the man would surely chase her. What if he caught her?

"Go on. Get," he told her, waving his hand at her. "But if I see you again, I'll take that knife and use it on you." He spat on the ground, then stared with hate in his black eyes.

Mazy shuddered, a chill snaking across her shoulders.

Just then several people who didn't seem to notice their stand-off began to walk between them. Mazy backed away quickly, even though she bumped into people as she did. Finally, when she couldn't see the man for all the people, she sheathed her knife and broke into a run.

She dodged people and animals and carts until her chest hurt and she couldn't run anymore. No one seemed to be chasing her, but she continued walking in the direction of the White Tower, now following alongside the river.

The Thames was the widest river Mazy had ever encountered, much wider than the small rivers near her home and

Strachleigh. But it was also filthy. Trash floated in it, and it was so dark and murky it looked nothing like the sparkling waters she was used to. But thinking about the river instead of her frightening encounter helped her heartbeat to slow and her breathing to return to normal.

She'd never been so frightened in her whole life. She'd also never pointed her knife at a person before, but she knew she'd done the right thing.

Her hands were still shaking a bit, her knees weak. She didn't want to think about what he might have done if she had not had her knife in her pocket.

She kept walking, kept moving. Had he singled her out because she looked vulnerable, standing there propped against the wall of that building? Ro had said something about certain parts of London being dangerous. Had she wandered, unaware, onto an unsafe street?

Now she just wanted to get home and lock the door. She did not feel safe anymore, and she kept seeing that man's ugly face, with his snaggled teeth and his messy, unkempt hair and beard.

Finally she reached a familiar street and hurried to the alehouse. She went around the narrow alley to the back door, and it suddenly seemed dark and sinister. Anyone could hide there and wait for her. Anyone could jump out at her.

She took her knife out of her pocket and held it at the ready as she moved forward, her eyes wide, listening for any sign that someone was near. Carefully she opened the door and looked inside. No one was in the back room. She climbed the stairs and unlocked her door and went inside. She locked it again and sighed.

She finally sheathed her knife and held it close to her chest. Would she ever feel safe again?

For the rest of the day she sat by the window, waiting for John to come home. She watched all the people passing by on the street below, trying to see how she might detect which men were kind and trustworthy, like Sir Berenger, and which were frightening, like the man she'd encountered that morning.

She went downstairs a few times to see if Ro was there, but she never found her. And now it was dark.

She wanted nothing more than to tell her brother what had happened, how she had been so terrified and had drawn her knife on a man. Hungry and teary-eyed, Mazy lay on her blanket and fell asleep.

Mazy had just awakened when a knock came at the door. "It's me, Ro," the voice said on the other side.

Mazy opened the door. "Good morning."

"I brought some sweet bread rolls I made. I'm sorry I didn't come and see you yesterday. My father kept me too busy. Our servant was sick, but she's better today."

Mazy invited her inside and they ate the warm rolls while sitting on the floor, as she had no stools or benches. Then Mazy told Ro the story of the previous day.

"You are brave to pull a knife on a man like that, and it is good that you did. You were right to defend yourself."

"I was so afraid. I'm not sure I could have cut him unless he attacked me or tried to hurt me. The truth is, he might have been able to take the knife from me as he threatened."

"No, no, you would have fought him off, I'm sure of it." Ro looked and sounded excited, as if Mazy had done something important. "You would have cut him. That man thought you were easy prey, but you proved your worth to him. You are a Londoner already!" Ro whooped and started twirling in place, a celebratory dance.

Mazy laughed. They both twirled around for a moment. Then Mazy said seriously, "Why did he choose me to attack?"

Ro looked thoughtful, placing a hand on her hip and staring at Mazy. "It was probably because you were alone, or maybe it was your wide-eyed look. You have to look tougher, get a meaner look in your eye, like this." Ro squinted and stared with a cold look.

Mazy wasn't at all sure she could look as tough as Ro did. But perhaps she could pretend when she was around strange men. When they stared at her, she could give them a cold, hard, squinty look. Mazy practiced it with Ro.

"Perfect!" Ro cried.

Next, Ro looked through Mazy's clothing, separating her dresses into two piles. "Don't wear these, not unless you want everyone to think you grew up on a farm."

"Ro, I was thinking, I need a way to provide for myself, but I don't know how to sew or do anything that would make me a good servant. Do you think I could learn to make something that I could sell? I was thinking of baking bread to sell at the market, but I don't have an oven."

"You could borrow Father's oven when the alehouse is not busy."

"Do you think he would allow it? I don't want to get in his way."

"He only uses the oven for bread, and only twice a day, just before midday and again before suppertime, when we have the most customers."

"If we sold bread at the market, we would only need the oven early in the morning."

Ro's eyes widened. "That's perfect! Let's go ask him."

They went downstairs and told Ro's father about their plan to bake bread and sell it in the market.

He scowled at Ro. "If you can do your other work and that too, then you can do it. But the alehouse comes first."

"Yes, Father."

"I will help her," Mazy added.

"The profits of what you sell at the market you can share between you," he said, "but I'll not be paying you for helping Ro with her work in the alehouse." He pointed a finger at Mazy.

"I understand. Thank you, sir."

He looked at her as if she were daft, then he shook his head and walked away.

Mazy had never imagined selling bread in a marketplace, and certainly never imagined working in an alehouse, but she had also never felt so hopeful. And, strangely, she felt . . . strong.

Warin had not destroyed her life by casting her off. And though John had all but abandoned her in London, she would not be dependent on him for provision. And even though she was an orphan, she was not completely alone. No, she had a friend in Ro, she was a Londoner now, and she would take care of herself.

Someday she did hope she could marry a good, kind man who loved her and whom she could respect and love in return, someone who would make her feel safe. Then she would not be alone and would not have to brandish a knife at every ruffian in London. Someday. But he would have to be an exceptional man indeed to compete with Sir Berenger, with whom she would inevitably compare him.

However, should this exceptional man never come to her, she could provide for and protect herself.

John did not come home until the next night. He smelled of strong drink and he hardly spoke.

"Look, Mazy, I'm not going to be able to come back here every night. I have to sleep most nights at the knights' barracks at the Tower."

"Oh." Her stomach sank, but at least he was telling her and being honest.

"I can try to get you a position at the castle, but it will be as a servant, and you're not accustomed to that work. But at least if you worked in the castle or at the Tower, you could stay with the other servants at night and you'd be safe."

"I'm safe here. I can lock the door."

"You think you're safe here?"

Truthfully, she wasn't sure, especially after her encounter

with the man outside the market. But she found herself saying, "And I think I've thought of a way to earn money, baking bread with Ro in her father's kitchen and selling it at the market."

John pulled on his chin and stared at the wall before saying, "That sounds like a good idea."

She still wanted to tell him about pulling her knife on the man who threatened to attack her, but she was not sure she should. He might try to force her to work at the castle or the Tower, and Mazy could think of nothing she'd be very good at there. Besides, she felt much better about how she handled the man after telling Ro about it. No, she would not accept John's offer. She would stay here at the alehouse, and she would find a way to provide for herself.

Her brother lay down and was snoring within moments.

ELEVEN

TWO YEARS LATER
LATE SUMMER 1385

BERENGER WALKED THROUGH THE STREETS OF LONDON leading his horse by the bridle. It was good to see London Town after such a long time, after so much had happened.

The last time he was here, he was being held in the Tower of London, awaiting his execution, along with his brothers. He felt a strange sensation at being here again, even after being fully exonerated and his family enjoying once again the good graces of the king.

He was also seeing this great, historic English town for the first time since going to war in a foreign land and experiencing battles, hardships, and triumphs. He'd come through relatively unscathed, with only a few small scars to show for the arrows that had grazed him and where a sword point had gotten past his own blade.

Other men had not been so fortunate, and he often prayed for those who had been permanently maimed, as well as for the souls from both sides who were killed.

The sun was actually shining today after the last few days of nothing but drizzling rain. And though Berenger was not sure what would happen, he felt uplifted by the prospect of this day's encounter with King Richard, who had summoned him to the king's apartments at the Tower of London.

"Your exploits and bravery have been brought to my attention," the missive from the king read, "by both your commanders and the Prussian nobles. I wish to commend you in person for your great deeds."

Being noticed for his "great deeds" by the king of England was good in itself, but the king was also quite generous with those who found favor with him, often awarding them land and castles. He was also known to create a title for those with whom he was pleased.

As he made his way toward the Tower of London, Berenger came upon a small market. He handed his horse's reins to his squire and went in to purchase some food.

Almost immediately, a young woman caught his eye as she threw her head back and laughed. He knew that face, and he knew that laugh. Delia had told him she had gone to London with Sir John not long after he left for Prussia, but could it really be her?

"Mazy!"

He called out to her and she turned her face toward him. Her eyes went wide and a smile spread over her entire countenance.

Mazy hurried out of the stall and threw her arms around him. But only for a moment. She stepped back, and Berenger saw her blush, as if the impulsive embrace embarrassed her.

"Sir Berenger. You are back from Prussia."

"I am. And you are in London."

"It is so good to see you. I prayed for you many times. Because of the fighting. Your battles with the Teutonic Knights, of course."

"Thank you for your prayers."

"I am so glad you are well. Let me introduce you to my friend, Roesia Sadler." She turned and waved her hand at the red-haired woman selling two loaves of bread to a woman.

"Is this Sir Berenger?" Roesia said, looking from him to Mazy and back to him.

"Yes, this is John's friend, Sir Berenger of Dericott."

"I am pleased to make your acquaintance, miss."

"You may call me Ro." She was smiling from ear to ear, while her eyes examined him from head to toe.

"Delia said Sir John is now a guard captain at the Tower of London." He could hardly take his eyes off Mazy. It had been two years, and she was pretty as ever, even more so now that she possessed a bit more maturity in her expressions and confidence in her manner.

"John was a guard captain at the Tower, but now he is one of the king's personal guards. He follows the king wherever he goes."

"And you?" He leaned closer to Mazy so no one else passing by might hear. "Are you staying somewhere safe, with safe people?"

Mazy smiled, showing white teeth, her eyes sparkling. He'd never noticed before how delicate her brows were. Had her eyelashes always been so thick and dark?

"I am living on the top floor of Ro's father's alehouse, the Swan. I am quite safe."

Berenger nodded. "I am glad."

"Have you been to visit your sister in Strachleigh? I know she missed you very much. We send each other letters, and she writes of you often."

"I did. I went there as well to see my brother at Dericott. Delia is well. Did you know she is having her second child soon?"

"Yes, she wrote to tell me. She is such a good mother. Her children are so very blessed."

"I quite agree. And she told me that you are well, but she did not say what you were doing."

"Oh yes, Ro and I started out baking bread and selling it here, but now we sell many other things, as you can see." She stepped back and showed him fruit pasties, various kinds of bread, goat-hair scarves, woven hoods, embroidered belts, and even wrought leather shoes.

"Did you make all this?"

"No, we get most of our wares from women who live outside of London and who entrust us to sell them, then we give them most of the money. We can get a better price for them here in London, so everyone benefits."

"I am very impressed."

She was not the shy young woman he had known at Strachleigh. But even then, she had been eager to help, to learn, and to be independent.

Sir John must have to stay alert to protect such a beautiful, sweet-tempered sister as Mazy.

Mazy could hardly believe Sir Berenger was right there in front of her. He had changed a bit, as his face was fuller, he had a short beard now, and his brown hair was longer. But he was just as handsome as ever, and more so, and the gentle expression on his face gave her the same warm feeling inside.

Ro's eyes were wide and so was her smile as she stared at him.

Ro had once asked her, "Is there any man alive that you would marry? If you had to get married tomorrow, who would you choose?"

Sir Berenger instantly came to her mind. In fact, there was no man in the world she would marry—no one except Sir Berenger. Unfortunately, she admitted this to Ro, and now Ro would probably say something to embarrass her.

But Mazy knew she was foolish to think of Sir Berenger. He only saw her as John's little sister, and he would marry a lady of noble birth. He would never want to marry her.

Truly, she had not realized how rare he was—a good man who was brave but kindhearted and thoughtful—until she had come to London and seen that most men were nothing like Sir

Berenger. The men she encountered every day were many things, but kind and generous, gentle and helpful were not usually qualities they possessed. Sir Berenger was all those things, and the longer his absence, the more she felt it. In fact, she had begun to think she was probably remembering him as better than he actually was.

"Lady Delia told me that your army was victorious."

"We were. I am on my way now to see the king. He summoned me to the Tower of London."

"Oh! That sounds very promising. He will reward you for your service."

"I am not sure what he intends. We shall see."

She wanted to ask him more intimate questions about how he felt during his first time fighting a battle. He must have many thoughts and feelings about it, and she wanted to know them all. But it had been two years since they'd seen each other, and she felt a bit of awkwardness between them that had not been there when he left.

"Are you in London to stay?" Ro asked, leaning forward eagerly.

"I am not sure. It depends on what the king wishes and where he sends me."

"I hope you can stay a little while," Mazy said. "Perhaps you and John can come for a meal. I can cook now. I will cook for you." It might be less awkward if her brother came with him, but John rarely came for a visit, even when she sent word, inviting him.

"Mazy is an excellent cook," Ro said.

"I am sure she is. But does your brother not live with you?"

"No, he sleeps at the knights' barracks. I see him only occasionally."

"So you live with your friend and her family?"

Mazy exchanged a glance with Ro. Then she leaned close to Sir Berenger and whispered, "I live alone."

His eyes widened. He opened his mouth, and she was sure he was about to tell her that it was too dangerous for a young woman to live alone, so she quickly added, "But Ro and her father live below me."

"You are sure you're safe?" he asked.

"You know how capable I am with a knife," Mazy said, giving him an arch look.

Oh no. Was she flirting? She'd be mortified if she thought he saw her as a flirtatious woman.

"I know you are, but . . . a young woman living alone? It is unheard of. I can't imagine why Sir John would . . . That is . . ."

He was trying not to criticize her brother, she could tell.

If she were being completely honest, she did not wish to live alone. But it was not so bad. She enjoyed some time by herself after being around people all day. She could do what she wanted with her evenings, and she did not enjoy her brother's company. When he did come for a visit, he was often drunk and irritable. Sometimes he yelled at her or accused her of being the reason he had not gone to Prussia with Sir Berenger and the others, and therefore he'd probably never have an opportunity to distinguish himself and be rewarded with an estate or a title.

When he said this to her, she felt horrible, her stomach sinking to her toes. But after she thought about it, after he had gone, she realized his decision not to go to Prussia had nothing to do with her.

No, Mazy did not wish her brother to live with her. She was better off by herself.

"I suppose I will see Sir John today when I go to the Tower."

"I think you will. He is always with the king."

He nodded, then stared thoughtfully at the ground for a moment before saying, "And if you are ever in trouble, you can send for your brother, I suppose?"

"I can."

"Have you ever had any trouble?"

"Nothing I couldn't take care of myself."

"Truly?"

"Truly." She rather liked that he worried about her. She wouldn't want him to worry overmuch, but knowing he was a little bit worried was oddly comforting.

Mazy smiled at him. And sighed, as he talked to Ro about their wares. He was so handsome, and even after war, he had not lost his humble and easy manner of talking and behaving.

He stayed a bit longer, buying several items from her stall, even things she was sure he did not need. And that was how she knew: he was the same kind, generous, good-hearted Sir Berenger that she remembered. Battle had given him a few extra scars on his hands and one faint scar on his cheekbone, but it had not taken the goodness out of him.

"Fare well, Miss Mazy," he said with a gentle smile. "I shall not leave London without coming back for a visit."

"You had better not. We are old friends, are we not?"

"Of course. And I shall bring Sir John with me, if I'm able."

"Fare well, Sir Berenger."

When he had walked away, Ro grabbed her arm and squeezed it so hard Mazy gave a weak cry, making her loosen her grip.

"Mazy, he is the best-looking man I've ever seen." She was still staring after him as he walked away. "Oh heavens." She let go of Mazy's arm and fanned herself with her hands.

He was very handsome, but something inside Mazy wanted to tell Ro to stop looking at him like that. He was not just good-looking; he was good. And that was far more important and desirable than his outward appearance.

"Now I understand why you talked about him so much." Ro patted her heart. "He belongs to you, of course, but if he didn't . . ."

"He doesn't *belong* to me."

"I don't know. He seemed very happy to see you and very concerned for your safety. And he didn't exactly push you away when you threw your arms around him."

"Was that bad? I am so impulsive sometimes." Mazy put her hands to her cheeks, which were hot as she remembered how she had reacted to seeing him. They'd never embraced like that before. Had she embarrassed herself?

"He didn't seem to mind."

"But he doesn't think about me in a romantic way, I know he doesn't. He thinks of me only as John's little sister and as a friend."

"Well, things can change. You're beautiful, Mazy. I'm sure he noticed."

"But he's a knight and I'm no one."

Ro's expression changed from flighty excitement to a more somber look. She even sighed as she raised her brows at Mazy. "There is still hope. I know knights usually marry women from titled families, but perhaps the king might force the baron to give you a dowry, if you asked him."

"No, that's not even a possibility. And don't let me stir up hope for something that can never be. Sir Berenger will have much higher ambitions than marrying me. He is the son of an earl, a knight who went to fight battles and will have found great favor with powerful men, including the king. I must be content with being Sir Berenger's friend."

Certainly she wanted what was best for him, and if that was for him to marry someone who would give him wealth and power, then may God make it happen.

Berenger made his way to the Tower of London, where he had been told to meet the king at the king's apartments.

His heart was full at seeing Mazy looking so well and prosperous, but a moment later his stomach churned at the thought that Sir John did not seem to be looking after his sister. Thankfully she had her friend's father living in the same house. He must surely provide a measure of protection for her.

At least, Berenger hoped so. He suspected things had not always been smooth and easy since she'd come to London. Strangely, he felt sorrow and guilt over not being there for her, wishing he could have saved her from whatever dangers or loneliness she may have faced.

He'd thought about Mazy many times since he'd left Strachleigh. He was grateful that his sister gave him occasional updates on her, saying she was in London and that she was well. Though he had known her for only two months at Strachleigh, she was his friend, and he felt as if he had let her down.

Perhaps that was only his boyish longing to rescue a damsel in distress, since he hadn't exactly rescued any damsels in Prussia.

His thoughts eventually shifted to his meeting with King Richard. Would the king offer him some kind of reward for his service to the king's allies? He knew that more than one nobleman had written glowing praise of him in letters to King Richard. Or would the king only reiterate the praise and ask him to serve in his guard?

The king was quite young, only eighteen years old, but he had already had to stop a revolt, during which, everyone agreed, he had acted quite bravely. But he was inexperienced and had occasionally acted with unexpected capriciousness, abruptly changing his mind about quite serious matters.

Anything could happen.

Berenger was allowed into the entryway of the king's personal rooms. He did not have to wait very long before he was ushered into a rather small room where King Richard sat at the opposite end.

Berenger's heart beat hard as King Richard summoned him. "Come closer, Sir Berenger."

He hadn't seen the king since he was knighted, which was

not long after Berenger and his brothers were tried and convicted of murder, then absolved of the crime.

Memories of the terrible day of the trial came back to his mind, of King Richard surrounded by his advisers and members of his court. The king was hardly more than a boy at that time, only fourteen, and it had been obvious to Berenger and his brothers that King Richard was being influenced against them. Berenger would never forget the look on the young king's face. His eyes were wide, his cheeks were pale, and he put Berenger in mind of Isaac when his father, Abraham, was about to lay him on the altar of sacrifice.

But the king was older now. His cheeks had filled out a bit, and his gaze was more direct.

"Allow me to welcome you back to England."

"Thank you, my king. It is good to be home."

"I have been told of many courageous acts you performed in Prussia. Your bravery and integrity have been told to me in some detail by the Margrave of Thornbeck, the prince of Prussia, and other noblemen who witnessed your great fighting skills."

"I am honored to have done my duty as a knight in your service."

"It is my pleasure to commend you, and I wish to reward you."

There was silence after this declaration. Berenger held his breath, waiting.

"My will is to grant you something in appreciation of your service. But while I decide what to offer you, I'd like to have you serve in my personal guard, and I'd like to put you in charge, as

I am in need of a commander who is loyal to me. You are loyal, are you not?"

"I am completely loyal to you, my king, as I have no other king except God in heaven."

"Very good. Then I shall expect you to take your place with my guard while I determine how best to reward you for your courage and loyalty."

"Yes, Your Grace. I am ever your humble servant."

The king then sent him to discuss the details with his chancellor.

This was good. He had the promise of a reward, but would it be of the magnitude that Berenger had always hoped for? For good or ill, he would be staying in London with the king for the immediate future. Though he did not relish having to work with the volatile Sir John again.

Twelve

Mazy wished she had asked Sir Berenger to come and tell her what the king said in his meeting with him. She was alone today in the market selling their goods, as Ro had to help her father in the alehouse for the day. The day had been busy, which made the time go by faster, with many of Mazy's regular customers not only buying goods but also staying to converse for a bit.

She saw Martin Fisher waving at her from the other side of the market, coming her way. Mazy smiled, but she wished Ro were there to help her keep a bit of distance between her and the young man who came nearly every day to buy bread from her. "Good afternoon, Miss Mazy."

"Good day to you, Martin," she said.

"May I say, you look particularly beautiful today."

"You may say it, but as you know, it makes me uncomfortable."

She smiled, as she was partly in jest. Martin seemed harmless enough.

Although he had hinted several times that he wanted to marry her. She always told him, as gently as she could, that she was not interested in him. But he came so often that she now considered him a friend.

Martin leaned close to her and spoke in a low voice. "Would it make you uncomfortable if we were married?" He sank to his knees in front of her. "Mazy, I would be most honored if you would marry me and share all my worldly possessions. My father is dead, and I have very good apartments next to my father's inn. I could take care of you and you would never have to work again."

"Martin, you know how I feel." Mazy shook her head gently as she stared down at the kneeling man's earnest face. "You seem like a very good sort of man, Martin, but I . . ." What could she tell him besides the truth? "I am not in love with you, and I do not wish to marry you."

"I shall come here every day and impress on you how much I love you and all that you will gain by marrying me. I shall inspire you to love me."

"That is very flattering, but I am not ready to marry." In truth, her mind went to Sir Berenger, which was the utmost foolishness. She suddenly realized that the biggest reason she couldn't marry Martin Fisher was because Sir Berenger existed in the world.

"I shall not give up. I vow that I shall never love another but you, my lovely Mazy." He stood, grabbed her hand, and kissed it.

"You should not pledge yourself to me, Martin. You will find a good woman who will be glad to marry a good man like you, but I will not change my mind. I am too independent for marriage."

"I shall change your mind."

"No, I don't think you will."

She had to ignore him while she waited on customers. Before he left, he vowed to come back the next day. The entire encounter made her feel unsettled.

Now it was late in the day, and Mazy sat down on an upended bucket to rest her feet. She let out a deep breath and nibbled on a roll of bread and a bit of cheese.

Selling things was not what she wanted to do with the rest of her life. It was an interesting way to make a living, and Mazy was grateful for that. But even with all the friends she'd made, she felt as if there must be more to life, something more enjoyable that she could do to provide for herself.

Sometimes she wondered what her life would have been like if she'd stayed at home and let Warin marry her off. She might be married to a baron or a landed knight, or perhaps even an earl or viscount. Would she have a child or two by now? Would she have liked being a wife and mother and taking care of a home? Probably, but she wasn't sure that life would have completely satisfied her. She craved independence, the respect of other people, the knowledge that she could protect and provide for herself. And perhaps the most enjoyable thing about selling goods at the market was knowing that she was helping the women, mostly poor widows, who trusted her to sell their goods.

She did not mind working. Besides, it was likely that she

would have been forced into a loveless marriage. She might very well be unhappy or even mistreated and abused, so she could not regret the way things had turned out.

Martin Fisher did not inspire love in her, and she didn't think he ever would. But perhaps someday she would get an offer of marriage from someone she could love. It would be good to be loved, to belong to someone. She would not care if he was not wealthy, as long as he loved her.

But her thoughts went back to Sir Berenger. Until she saw someone better, he would always be her idea of an ideal man.

She didn't want to dwell on that, so she distracted herself by watching the people walking through the marketplace. She was accustomed now to the crowds of people that had so overwhelmed her when she first came to London. Some walked briskly and purposefully, while others were so loaded down with oversized packs on their backs that they could barely amble along. Most of her customers were old men and women with lines on their faces and sagging skin buying food for themselves and their families. All around her, every day, people were milling about as they searched for a specific item, sometimes not finding it and hurrying away, no doubt headed for one of the larger markets.

Mazy drank the water from her flask, which now tasted warm and stale. She'd have to draw more from the community well.

A man on horseback caught her eye. It was Sir Berenger.

He dismounted, left his horse at the outskirts of the market with his squire, and started toward her.

Her heart skipped a beat. Was her hair askew? She reached up to try to smooth it down. As was the custom for younger women, she left it partially uncovered by the short scarf that tied it up. At least she had worn her prettiest dress today, one of the ones she had taken from home more than two years ago.

"Have you received good news from the king?" she asked him. "I am sure he was very pleased with you."

"Yes, he wishes to reward me for my service, but he has not decided exactly how."

"Oh. Well, that sounds encouraging."

"I cannot complain. He wants me to stay and be his guard commander, at least for now."

"That is wonderful! Although I know you shall be busy, I will be very glad to see you when you're able. Have you seen John yet?"

"No, but I'm sure I shall."

How would her brother like being under Sir Berenger's authority? She hoped he would not be too disagreeable about it, as they were once equals. Her brother could be so resentful of authority or anyone with power over him.

"I will be able to keep an eye on you now and make sure you're staying safe." Sir Berenger was gazing intently into her eyes.

"That is very kind of you," Mazy said, refusing to let his words or his intense look fluster her. He only cared for her as his sister's friend.

"Are you almost finished for the day?" Sir Berenger asked.

"I can be finished now. I just have to pack up my things." Mazy wished Ro was there to help her.

Sir Berenger was quick to step around the front of the stall, loading her wares into bags and tying them down on the back of her horse. The work was done very quickly with his help.

"I would like to buy you supper at the inn around the corner."

"Oh. That is very kind. I just have two stops to make first." They led their horses by their bridles through the streets until they came to a tiny wattle-and-daub house, half-hidden by a much larger three-story home down a side street.

Mazy knocked on the door and a little boy opened it, dressed only in a ragged oversized shirt.

"Can you take this to your mother?" Mazy handed him a bag of the leftover food from her stall—bread and pasties, mostly.

The little boy took it from her hand and turned and yelled, "Mama! Mazy brought bread!"

Mazy walked back to Sir Berenger, smiling inside at the little one's enthusiasm.

"Oh, Mazy! Thank you," the mother called out from the doorway.

Mazy turned and said, "You are very welcome. I hope you all are in good health."

"Thank you, thank you! Yes, yes. How are you?"

"Very well." Mazy could see the woman staring past her at Sir Berenger, who was holding their horses. She waved fare well to the woman and hurried away.

"Who was that?" Sir Berenger asked.

"Althea. She is a widow with seven children. I often bring

her my leftover bread and pasties. I don't like to sell day-old goods, so . . ." She shrugged.

"That is very kind of you. I'm sure you are helping her a great deal."

"It makes me happy to think that I am."

When she glanced up at him a few moments later, Sir Berenger was still looking at her with a strangely intense but gentle look, as if he wanted to say something but couldn't quite speak.

Afraid she would be embarrassed by what he might say, she said, "Now I need to lock up the rest of the things in the back room of the alehouse where I live. It is not far."

Finally he spoke. "You impress me very much with your generosity."

"Because I give away food that I cannot sell? That is not so generous."

"How do you even know that woman?"

"It is a long story."

"Tell me." His head was bent close to hers.

"I saw her walking through the market one day with all her children. I could tell the children were hungry by the way they looked at the pasties I had on display, so I gave them some food and asked their names. I found out that one of her children was sick and she was looking for some remedy for her. So I asked where she lived and went there the next day to look in on the child and to take them some more food. Now I go every few days. I have two other widows I give leftover food to as well. There are a lot of poor people in London."

"I can imagine." Sir Berenger's brows drew together, and they walked in silence until she reached home.

She unlocked the back door with a key, remembering why they had started locking the door, how she had found a robber there one day after finishing at the market.

Once inside, they unloaded the packs from her horse's back and left them in the storage space and locked the door again. She then installed her horse at the livery stable next door.

"I suppose I should tell Ro and her father that I am going somewhere with you so she won't be worried if I'm a little late."

"Of course."

They went around the front of the alehouse and he waited for her while she went inside the Swan.

Mazy searched the smoky alehouse for Ro before catching a glimpse of her bending over a barrel of ale. Thomas Sadler was standing close to his daughter and caught sight of Mazy.

"You're back."

Mazy approached and said, "I'm going out again. I didn't want you to worry about me, but I'm going to the Sword and Shield for supper."

"Why?" Ro straightened with lightning speed, staring hard at her. "Who with?"

"If you must know . . ." Mazy lowered her voice. "I am going with Sir Berenger."

"Oh, Mazy, that's so exciting!" Ro spoke so loudly that it seemed the whole room stopped what they were doing to turn and stare at them.

"Keep your voice down. He's right outside," Mazy whispered, her cheeks starting to burn.

"How can you expect me not to be excited?" Ro squeezed her arm and let out a strangled squeal.

"Roesia, you're embarrassing yourself and Mazy," her father said gruffly.

"You have to tell me everything that happens," Ro gushed, ignoring her father.

"Nothing will happen. He's a friend, that is all, and he is a man of honor and integrity."

"Promise me you will tell me everything or I won't let you go."

"There will be nothing to tell, but very well. I will tell you if there is anything to tell. Now let me go. He's waiting."

Ro squealed under her breath, her attempt at curbing her enthusiasm, but she let go of Mazy's arm.

Mazy hurried out, her stomach doing flips, but it was only because of Ro's foolishness. Sir Berenger was her friend, and they were only going to eat supper.

She hoped no one she knew was there. She didn't want to answer their questions about the handsome knight she was eating with.

Sir Berenger led the way back down the street to the Sword and Shield. Inside, they found a place at a table, and the innkeeper's daughter brought them cups of ale, bowls of stew, bread, and a dish of butter.

"I'm very curious," Mazy said as they began to eat. "What was it like to see the king?"

"It was a little strange." His eyes clouded over.

"How so?"

"Well, I was remembering the last time I saw him, a few years ago, when my brothers and I were falsely accused of treason. The king was present at our trial. It was a very bad time, a lot of bad memories. But all is well now. The king was pleasant enough."

"I would be so frightened to speak to the king."

"He is very young, an ordinary-looking eighteen-year-old."

"Were his apartments very luxurious?"

"Not especially, what little I saw."

They ate in silence, and then Sir Berenger said, "How have you fared the last two years? My sister wrote a bit to me— information she got from your letters to her—but mostly just to say that you were in good health and were safe and happy. Tell me about your life here in London. You must have many tales, working in the market as you do and seeing so many people."

"I will, but you also have to tell me about what you've been doing the last two years."

"Very well. But you start."

She wanted to tease him about making her speak first, but he was so handsome—the hard lines of his jaw and chin, the short beard, the clear blue of his eyes—that she needed to hurry and distract herself, as her heart was starting to beat so hard it was stealing her breath. He had a tiny scar on his jawline, another along his cheekbone, but the scars only made her want to wrap her arms around him.

She swallowed the lump in her throat, and the first story that came to mind was the one she'd thought about only moments before.

"I always carry two knives in my pockets, just in case I need them. One day I came home from selling bread in the market, and as soon as I walked in the back of the alehouse and closed the door, a man jumped out of the shadows. He must have been hiding behind a bag of flour. He grabbed me by the neck and said, 'Give me your money.'

"I hold a knife in my hand when I walk through the dark alley behind the alehouse, so I stabbed him in the arm with it. He let go and I ran out the door and around the front and told Ro's father what happened. He got a few men who were in the alehouse to go after the man. They found him in the alley. He was crying and holding his arm where I had wounded him."

Sir Berenger listened to her story without once taking his eyes off her. Now that she was finished, he let out a burst of air, as if he'd been holding his breath, and said, "Well done."

"The men and Ro's father threatened him, saying they would beat him and cut off his hand if he ever spoke to me again or if they caught him stealing. But to be honest, I did feel a bit bad for stabbing him."

"Why? You were only defending yourself."

"Yes, I know, and I would do it again. I know I have to defend myself. But I did pray that his wound would not turn putrid."

"Did you ever see him again?"

"I thought I did, once, but he turned and went in the other direction when he saw me."

Sir Berenger raised his brows and grinned. "He didn't want to get stabbed again."

"I suppose not." Mazy couldn't help but feel the approval of Sir Berenger's big smile. She smiled back.

"Did anything like that ever happen again?"

"No more of my stories now. It's your turn. You have to tell me a tale about your travels and battles."

"My travels and battles, eh?" He looked up at the ceiling, as if he was pondering which story to tell. "I once encountered an old man who challenged me to a duel. I was riding along a road in Germany after getting separated from the rest of my troop, trying to catch up. An old man was walking along with a staff in his hand, which was wrapped in a ragged wool cloak. When he saw me, he held up his staff and yelled, 'Stop!'

"I stopped my horse, thinking he needed help. But when I did, he pulled out a sword—a very well-made sword, like a knight would carry—and said, 'Give me your horse.'

"'I'm not giving you my horse,' I said.

"'Then you will die by the sword.' He came at me, swinging his blade. I had no choice but to dismount and fight him. I tried not to hurt him. It was obvious he had had some training, but he was old and slow, and I disarmed him quickly.

"I asked him, 'Who are you, and why are you trying to take my horse?' He couldn't give me a satisfactory answer. He just told me that he was with King Richard the Lionheart when he went on his crusade to the Holy Land, which of course was not possible. It was clear that his mind was addled. He never did tell me who he was, but I put him on my horse and took him to the next village, where he said his sister lived."

He gave her an endearingly humble half frown.

"That is an interesting story. You must have had a lot of exciting adventures. What were Germany and Prussia like? And you have crossed the sea! What was that like?"

"Oh no," he said. "It is your turn again. I want to know if you have any more tales like your first one."

"There have been a few, perhaps. But we started locking the back door of the alehouse after that. A few men have tried to take my money in the marketplace, but they never got anything. I raised the hue and cry once or twice. There was one incident, when I had only been here two days, but I frightened him away with my knife."

Sir Berenger lowered his brows and stared at her with a sober look.

"It doesn't sound to me like London is a safe place at all for a young woman."

"Nothing truly bad has happened. In fact, no one has tried to rob me in quite a long time. Perhaps it's because they call me the 'Knife Girl.'"

"Who calls you the Knife Girl?"

"A lot of people in the market. Word got around, I suppose, that I carry a knife and that I'm not afraid to defend myself with it." She smiled, feeling rather proud of herself.

"I like that you defend yourself. Knife Girl. I like that." He smiled and crossed his arms over his chest. "You always were brave and independent."

Mazy laughed and shook her head, enjoying his praise and attention more than she wanted him to know.

The woman who had brought them their food now came again, swaying her hips, and took their bowls. She pinned her gaze on Sir Berenger and said, "Is there anything else I can get you, love?" The way she stood so close to Sir Berenger, almost touching his leg, her hand on her outthrust hip, made Mazy's mouth fall open. The brazen woman smiled down at him, a suggestive look on her face.

"We thank you, but we are finished." He quickly averted his eyes from her.

"I can fetch you more ale, or a sweetmeat, perhaps?" She leaned down, and her shirt fell open, exposing the tops of her breasts.

Sir Berenger kept his gaze on the table. "No, we are finished," he repeated. His eyes met Mazy's. "Shall we go?"

Mazy stood and hurried toward the door, still shocked at the woman's behavior and suddenly wanting to laugh at how ridiculous it was.

When they were outside, Mazy decided not to tease him about the woman. Sir Berenger fetched his horse and they walked back to the Swan.

"I never thought much about how women in London face so many dangers. That is, until Delia said you were here."

"You were worried about me?" Was she flirting—the way she smiled at him, the tone of her question? Was she as bad as that woman at the Sword and Shield? She suddenly knew how that woman felt—longing for Sir Berenger's approval and attention. Well, she would not let herself hope. She was being foolish, much too foolish, to hope for anything more than friendship.

"I was worried, but I thought Sir John was looking after you. It sounds as if he hasn't been looking after you at all. It sounds as if you've been on your own for the last two years." His voice was quiet but deep, almost tender. There was no longer even a hint of a smile on his face, and his gaze was intent on her. "I'm sorry you had no one to watch over you."

"I do have someone. I have Ro and her father, and strangers have intervened on my behalf. But mostly I take care of myself."

"I know. And God, no doubt, is watching over you, helping you. But . . . would you mind if I came and checked in on you from time to time? And if you ever need anything, anything at all, I will come to your aid. Of that you can be sure."

"That is very kind of you. But I have John. I can always send word to him if I need help." She didn't know why she said that, why she refused his offer of help. Except that she was afraid. And for some reason she almost felt angry that he was so adamant about offering his help. What could he do, after all, if she were being attacked? And why was he so eager to take responsibility for her welfare? She was not his responsibility.

"Of course. But in the event of an emergency, if you need me, I am not far, at least for now. I am sorry for all the evil men who have tried to hurt you."

"None of that was your fault. They did not succeed, and it increased my confidence when I was able to defend myself." She lifted her shoulders, realizing the truth of her statement. She didn't need him or any man.

Where was this defiance coming from? Sir Berenger was only being kind.

He smiled again, that sweet, gentle smile of his. "You impress me, Mazy. Knife Girl. And what is it Sir John calls you? Maze Queen?"

"He always had pet names for me." When she was a child, she thought it meant he cared for her. Now she no longer believed he did. A brother who loved his sister did not ignore her the way John ignored her.

"Will you unlock the door," he asked, "just so I can make sure no one is lurking inside, waiting to attack you?"

"Very well, but if the door is locked . . ."

"I promise I will go as soon as I've seen that all is well. Humor me."

Mazy unlocked the door. Sir Berenger went in first, looking into the corners of the small room, then going to the bottom of the stairs and gazing up the staircase.

"See? All is well. No one is here."

Sir Berenger gave her a crooked smile, staring for a moment before saying, "Fare well, Mazy, and stay safe."

"I shall, if God so wills."

Sir Berenger hesitated, but then he turned to leave.

"Fare well," Mazy said, suddenly noticing the way the muscles in his back rippled against his shirt. She felt a shiver across her own shoulders, her feelings for him almost overwhelming her.

Pushing those feelings aside, she said, "Thank you for supper."

"I shall see you soon," he said over his shoulder. "Don't forget to lock the door."

With that, he closed the door and she locked it. But the sound of the key clicking in the lock was the last she heard before Ro burst in from the main room of the alehouse.

THIRTEEN

"WHAT HAPPENED? WHAT DID HE SAY? DID YOU KISS him?"

"Of course not." Mazy shook her head and rolled her eyes to the ceiling. "We ate supper at the Sword and Shield—"

"Yes?" Ro clasped her hands together.

"He walked me home—"

"Yes?" Ro jumped up and down.

"And he left. That was all."

"But what did he say? Does he want to see you again? Did he touch your hand or your arm or your shoulder?"

"No. He didn't touch me at all. I told you, he thinks of me as John's sister."

"Well, did he say he would see you again?"

"He wants to look in on me, he said. I probably shouldn't have, but I told him the story of why some people call me Knife Girl."

"Oh, I hope you emphasized the danger you have been in and told him that you need him to watch over you."

Mazy huffed out a breath. "I told him the truth, of how I have saved myself more than once with my knives."

Ro looked as if she was about to scold her, but then her face lit up again with her most beaming of smiles as she grabbed Mazy's arms. "But he does want to see you again? I know he will fall in love with you. How could he not? You are everything a man wants in a wife—sweet, demure, and beautiful."

"Sweet and demure?" Mazy made a gagging sound. "I can't afford to let people think I'm sweet and demure."

"Well, you are sweet, and that's what you want Sir Berenger to see."

Mazy shook her head. "You make me laugh, you know that?"

Ro went on talking about Sir Berenger until Mazy said, "I'm tired. I'm going to bed."

Ro followed her up the two flights of stairs to Mazy's rooms, talking without taking a breath.

"Good night, Ro." Mazy smiled and kissed Ro's cheek before slipping inside and closing the door.

She loved Ro, but sometimes her enthusiasm was over-whelming.

She took a deep breath and her thoughts went to Sir Berenger, to the way he looked, to his smile, to the gentle way he had about him, and yet she had no doubt that he could be quite fierce when the situation called for it. He was a knight, after all.

Sir Berenger was good. So good. *God, why could You not make more men like him?*

Berenger could not stop thinking about Mazy as he carried out his duties the next two days, duties that, more often than not, required him to stand still and watch—and there was very little to watch.

He did have to make sure the king's guards did their duty, stayed sober while they were working, and were loyal to the king.

He was getting to know Sir John again. His old friend had changed in the two years they had not seen each other, and not for the better. Sir John drank to excess more than he used to, and he complained about everything. He cursed the weather; he cursed the food; he cursed himself, even, on occasion. His language was foul, even when he wasn't drinking.

He could hardly believe this man and Mazy were related.

Sir John did speak fondly of Mazy, but even when he had time away from his duties, he did not go and visit his sister. Instead, he seemed intent on drinking and carousing with the female servants.

As his commander, Berenger was responsible for ensuring Sir John was alert and unencumbered when he was on duty, but he also felt the need to speak to him about what he did when he was not on duty. After all, he was a knight in the service of the king and queen, and a knight pledged to behave in an honorable way at all times.

When he was finally finished making sure the next watch of guards was in place, which included Sir John at his post just outside the king's apartments at the Tower of London, where he awaited a delegation that was set to arrive by boat, Berenger went to speak to Sir John.

"Fine day today," Berenger said as he approached Sir John.

"Too hot for my taste," Sir John said, shifting his weight onto his other foot as he nodded at Berenger.

"I saw Mazy yesterday."

Sir John raised his brows.

"She was well and spoke fondly of you."

"I haven't had a lot of time to go and see her, but when I do, she's always well."

"We are very blessed to have wonderful sisters, you and I. Very fortunate indeed that they are safe and healthy."

Sir John stared at the ground and said nothing.

"When we are brought up as you and I were, training to become fighters, we find brothers everywhere we go."

"I suppose that's true." But still he did not look Berenger in the eye.

"We forge a family through our common skills and experiences and loyalties."

Sir John seemed to be listening, standing as still as a stone with his head cocked to one side.

"As knights, we also have a duty to look out for our brothers, to treat women well, and to make sure our families are taken care of. You know that, as you brought your sister here with you when she was cast off. And I know about how you defended your brother in arms, Sir Lucius, when he was attacked in town a few weeks ago."

Sir John glanced up and nodded.

One of the knights, Sir Lucius, had refused to pay for his drinks, and the alehouse owner and his son tried to throw him out. Or struck him. The reports Berenger had heard conflicted with each other. But Sir John had defended his friend with his sword—although the alehouse owner and his son had no weapons. At least Sir John had not harmed them, only threatened them.

"I couldn't let Sir Lucius be beaten just because he was drunk."

"You are a loyal friend. And I'm glad your sister has you to care for her. It is a noble thing to care for one's family."

Sir John raised his head and gazed up at the clouds.

"It's also a knight's duty to treat women as he would want men to treat his sister. I have been told that some of the guards here are wont to carouse with women on nights when they're not on duty. Of course, I am not their priest, but I think if we who are knights could put in a word here and there, letting them know that such behavior is not becoming of the king's personal guards, they might change their ways."

Sir John cleared his throat, made a sound like "Hmm," then said, "They might."

If Sir John realized what Berenger was doing—hinting about his own behavior under the guise of asking for his help to change the other men's behavior—he did not let on.

He spoke a few minutes more with Sir John about inconsequential matters, then went to take his rest after being up since before dawn.

If he were honest with himself, he wanted nothing more than to go to the small market where he knew Mazy would be and see her, talk to her, maybe even take her to supper again. But that would not be wise. He did not want to behave in an unseemly way with any woman, but especially with Mazy, whom he knew to be a good-hearted maiden of pure motives and behavior. There was no woman alive he respected and admired more than Mazy and Delia.

So no, he would not visit her again so soon, but he would also not ignore her the way John did.

The leaves had started falling from the trees, and the feel of winter was in the air. Then, three days after Sir Berenger visited Mazy, the weather turned considerably colder.

Mazy and Ro wrapped themselves in blankets while selling rolls and loaves of bread to the people who came to their booth. They even sold some leather flasks and wrought leather saddlebags that morning to a man who said he was going on a long journey. "Before winter sets in," he'd said.

The woman and her husband who made the leather goods,

who were both lame and couldn't walk, would benefit greatly from the sales.

It had been a good morning.

"Do you think Sir Berenger will come to visit you today?" Ro gave Mazy a sly smile.

"No, I do not. And it is not right for you to insinuate things about him. He truly is just a good man, Ro, who feels a very disinterested kind of care for me, as he would for an old family friend. If I were ninety years old, he'd feel the same and show the same kindness."

"Ninety years old, eh?" Ro raised her eyebrows. "He is a man, isn't he? He has eyes, doesn't he?"

"Ro . . ." Mazy put a warning in both her tone and the narrowed gaze she gave her friend.

"He sees how beautiful you are. And he is a young man. He is not impervious to your beauty, trust me." She shook her finger at Mazy. "That is why you must flirt with him next time. Smile. Lay your hand on his arm. Tell him how handsome he has grown. Or perhaps you did that when he took you to supper at the Sword and Shield."

"No, I did not. I am not depraved. I have no wish to tempt any man, especially a man as good as Sir Berenger."

Ro blew out a breath between her pursed lips, a scoffing sound.

"It is true. And if I thought there was any way Sir Berenger might be able to marry me, maybe I would flirt with him. But it isn't possible. Besides, I don't want him to think less of me. He is my friend, and I like it that way."

"Very well, very well. I will say no more. But I shall enjoy seeing him when he comes again."

"Please don't ogle him like you did last time."

"Ogle? I did not ogle. At least, not while he was looking."

Mazy shook her head. They had to stop talking of the handsome Sir Berenger when a woman came to buy some bread and cheese.

"Have you heard about the commotion?" the woman said.

"No, ma'am," Ro said. "What commotion?"

"Some men, riffraff from the docks, have been making trouble, talking of taking up Wat Tyler's Rebellion again. They were making their way through London. I'm hurrying to get what I need now before they come this way."

Ro's cheeks went pale and she grabbed Mazy's arm. "Wat Tyler and his men murdered people in the streets and burned houses. What if they attack us and try to burn down our booth?"

Mazy's mind went to how Wat Tyler's band of rioters had not only created chaos in the streets but stormed the Tower of London and executed the archbishop and other high officials. Would John and Sir Berenger be caught up in another mob of killers? Would they be hurt or killed defending King Richard?

"I'd advise you maids to get home and lock your doors." The woman paid for her goods and rushed away.

"Don't worry, Ro. It might not even be true." Mazy was trying to reassure herself as much as Ro. Surely they could not have another throng of people committing violence in London again so soon. After all, while King Richard had initially tried to reason with them, ultimately he made a harsh example of them, hunting them down and executing them in quick fashion, crushing the rebellion.

Ro was still pale, her freckles darker and more prominent on her whiter than normal skin.

Mazy asked the older man across the way if he had heard anything of another violent riot or rebellion.

"I heard tell of it from a man who had come from the east side of town. They was making their way through the streets, shouting about this and that, but they'll get themselves killed just like Wat Tyler, I imagine. Don't know why folks can't just stay at home 'stead of rioting in the streets."

Mazy thanked him and went to talk to one of the older women who sold vegetables a few stalls away.

"I heard about it too. You and Ro should go, just in case the mob comes this way."

Mazy looked around. No one else was leaving. But perhaps she was right. Ro might be loud and boisterous and always ready to try something new or go on an adventure, but she also became terrified when there was a possibility of danger.

After all, she didn't want to let anything happen to Ro.

"We might as well pack up our things for the day and go home," Mazy said as she came back to Ro, whose eyes grew wider. "There's probably nothing to worry about, but we'll be extra cautious, just in case."

"Oh, Mazy." Ro rushed around, throwing things into their packs, her hands visibly shaking. "What if they're coming here? They'll burn down our stall and kill us."

"Ro, it's all right. That's not going to happen. Besides, we will have time to get home, I am sure."

Mazy didn't want to alarm Ro, was trying to calm her down, but her own head was spinning with thoughts of what might happen if the rioters were on their way there. She and Ro might even encounter them on their way home. There was no telling what a crowd like that would do. After all, the violent throng that had attacked London and killed many people were just ordinary men and women, most of them very poor, but they had invaded the Tower of London in spite of its guards and gates and defenses. And it was a similar violent throng who had demanded Jesus be killed and who stoned the martyr Stephen.

The Wat Tyler rebels had killed numerous wealthy and powerful people, and they burned homes and belongings throughout the country for months before they were squashed. They'd wanted higher wages, which was a just cause in Mazy's estimation, but their violence confused her. Certainly Wat Tyler and his rioters hated the rich and powerful and blamed them for their meager existence, and revenge played a big part in their violent revolt. But killing people and burning buildings did not seem a wise way to gain favor with those in authority.

Mazy had to be calm for Ro's sake. She couldn't let her fear show, and it would do no good to panic.

Besides, she was the Knife Girl. She had to live up to her reputation of being brave.

The thought of herself as a model of bravery made her laugh inside. No one knew how frightened she was, how she did not consider herself brave at all. But at this moment she needed the reminder—she was good at throwing knives, and she would not shrink from defending herself and Ro.

She patted the knife in each hip pocket, hidden in her skirt. She just had to slip the knife out of its sheath as she pulled it out. She had not been practicing throwing the knives lately, but if the attackers came, she would be ready.

FOURTEEN

BERENGER NOTICED A MAN RUNNING ACROSS THE TOWER Green and went to meet him.

"I need to speak to the commander."

"I am the commander."

"Sir, a group of men calling themselves 'Wat Tyler's Sons' are beating and robbing people in the streets, and they're coming this way. They're coming to avenge Wat Tyler's death, saying his blood is on King Richard's hands."

Berenger hurried to sound the alarm and gather as many guards as could be spared from the Tower, but he put his best men at the Tower gates. He could not risk having a violent throng invading the Tower complex again, as had happened in the original Wat Tyler's Rebellion.

He urged his horse into a gallop, leading his men out of the Tower gates and into London.

Mazy. Was she safe? She and her friend were at their booth in the marketplace, no doubt. The little market where Mazy sold her goods was not far from the Tower of London, and the angry men who were beating and robbing people were on their way there.

The man could have been wrong. There were always rumors that another rebellion was coming. A few smaller revolts had begun, stirred up here and there, but had quickly been stopped, the leaders executed.

He was ahead of the other soldiers, but there were several who were close on his horse's heels. He headed straight for the market, and even before he got there, he heard screams.

Women were running and men were shouting and waving their arms at Berenger and his men. In the distance a man was running through the market with a thick club raised over his head. Behind him were more men with various weapons, beating anyone unfortunate enough to be in their way.

He urged his horse to go faster, searching the crowd for Mazy.

Heat rose inside him, but he set his mind on the battle ahead. He would not allow anyone to harm Mazy, nor any other innocent person. He prayed his battle prayer.

O God, send Your mighty angels with their flaming swords to help me.

Mazy and Ro rushed to pack up their things, tying the bags closed. But just as they were clearing off the last of the bread, getting ready to carry the bags to their horse and tie them on, shouts and screams sounded just beyond the street to the east.

"They're coming!" Ro froze in place, her face crumpling.

Mazy's blood went cold. "It's all right. Get on the horse and go get your father."

"I can't leave you!"

Mazy could see that Ro was about to become hysterical. Several women were fleeing the marketplace.

"Go now. Your father will bring men who can help us."

"No, I can't go without you." Tears were streaming down Ro's face as she shook her head from side to side and clasped her hands to her chest.

"You can and you must."

Ro just kept shaking her head. She wasn't going to leave without her. And the rioters were already upon them, chasing anyone who tried to flee. If she and Ro ran now, the men could come after them.

"Then we have to hide behind the counter." Mazy shoved Ro to her knees under the wooden plank that served as a place to display goods, then crouched beside her. The front of the stall would hopefully help hide them.

Mazy peeked over the table. Men with clubs, hoes, and long sticks were quickly pouring into the marketplace. They toppled stalls and booths with their makeshift weapons, swinging at everything in their path, including people. Mazy watched as one man came upon a woman squatting on the ground. The man used his foot to shove her onto her back as he swung his club at the stall next to her. Wood cracked. He hit it again and it collapsed, reduced to a pile of wood and tarp.

The man who was in the lead was shouting, "Death to tyrants! Death and mayhem until Wat Tyler is avenged!" He seemed to be the leader of the group, and he was coming toward her.

Mazy unsheathed her knives and prayed, *O God, protect me.*

She held a knife in each hand as the man was suddenly upon her. His gaze fixed on her and he sneered, showing broken and missing teeth. He looked just like the man who had accosted her after she visited St. Paul's Cathedral when she had first come to London.

Mazy glared back at him. Should she throw one of her knives? Was she truly prepared to kill him? His friends were right behind him, and a few of them were also fixing their eyes on her. She couldn't throw the knife if he came too close.

The man swung his club, connecting with one of the uprights on Mazy's booth and snapping it in two. Ro screamed as the side of the stall collapsed.

Mazy backed away a few steps and threw her knife. It stuck in the man's upper arm.

The man's eyes went wide. He roared with rage and ran at Mazy, raising his club to strike her.

Instead of throwing her other knife and losing her only weapon, she sidestepped and slashed at him, cutting his forearm.

He stopped midswing and grabbed his arm, his eyes still locked on Mazy.

If she ran, maybe he would follow her. She could lead him away from Ro.

Mazy started running, but another man grabbed her by the hair. She screamed and stabbed his arm. He howled and let her go, but the man with the broken teeth seized her wrist.

Over the evil man's shoulder she saw the king's guards rushing through the entrance on horseback. She tried to lash out at him with her knife, but his grip on her wrist kept the blade from connecting with his flesh.

More hands grabbed her arms from behind and she couldn't move.

"I'm going to kill you!" the man hissed as he forced her knife out of her hand. It clattered on the cobblestones. Her other knife's blade was still embedded in his arm, the handle the only thing visible.

Mazy screamed. He stuck his face so close to hers that she couldn't see the guards behind him. Were they coming? Did they see her?

She struggled to lean away from the putrid man, but his henchmen were preventing her. She could not get away, could not even put any space between herself and his stained and broken teeth.

"I'll cut off your ears with your own knife," he sneered. "And when we're done with you, I'll feed your tongue to the birds." His breath stank of rotting fish and ale, his nose nearly touching hers.

"Get off me." Mazy could feel hysteria rising from her gut to her throat.

"You wants a kiss from me," he taunted, laughing at her and leering in her face.

"Kiss her!" the men behind her said.

He puckered his lips, making kissing noises and coming so close she was afraid to turn her head, fearing his lips would touch her.

"Get off me," she said through clenched teeth, but he just seemed to get closer.

Her thoughts raced to come up with a way to get away from him. She could not bear it if he touched her lips. She could feel her own hysteria continuing to rise.

She did the only thing she could think of—she sprayed spit in his face from between clenched teeth and pursed lips.

The man backed away, wiping his face with his sleeve. "You little witch."

"Cut her!" one of the men behind her said, and someone handed the man her knife that had fallen to the ground.

He took the knife and pointed it in her face. Just then, a horse's hooves clattered up behind him.

Sir Berenger rose above them, his sword poised to strike her attacker.

The men holding her let go and ran, and the man with the broken teeth turned around just as Sir Berenger brought his sword hilt down on top of his head.

The man crumpled straight down onto his knees. Mazy snatched her knife out of his hand just before he fell on his face. He did not move.

Sir Berenger leapt from his horse. His hands were on

her shoulders, holding her at arm's length. "Are you hurt? Mazy . . ."

"No." Mazy could only stare at him as she tried to catch her breath.

"Thank God."

He pulled her into his chest, embracing her with one arm, his other hand still holding his sword. Weakly, Mazy placed her shaking arms around him, still clutching her knife.

How good it felt to have her face pressed against Sir Berenger's chest as he held her close. He came just in time. *Thanks be to God.*

"I have to find Ro." She suddenly pulled away. "I left her in our stall."

He let go of her and Mazy darted toward the broken stall, their bags scattered around it. Ro was just starting to stand up and look around.

Mazy ran to her friend. Tears still clinging to her cheeks, Ro stared hard at Mazy. "Are you well?"

"I'm well. Are you?"

Ro nodded, then noticed Sir Berenger.

"It was so frightening," Ro said, tears leaking from her eyes. "They were everywhere. It happened so fast."

"I must go and help capture them, but stay here." Sir Berenger stared intently into Mazy's eyes. "I'll return very soon."

Mazy nodded, her heart in her throat as he turned and hurried away.

Guards were tying the hands of the men who had laid waste to the marketplace, including the unconscious man who had grabbed her. And now she was certain that he was the man who had threatened her when she first came to London two years ago.

Sir Berenger rode out of the market after the men who had fled when the guards arrived.

"Oh, Mazy, I was so frightened." Ro was breathing hard while pressing her hand to her chest. "What happened?" She was staring at the bloody knife in Mazy's hand.

Mazy sat down on one of the stools they kept inside their stall. Her hands and knees were shaking like leaves in the wind. The danger was over, so why was she still shaking?

"I threw a knife at the man who broke our stall."

"Did you hit him?"

"In the upper arm. But he kept coming after me. I cut him across his forearm, then I had to run."

"Oh, Mazy." Ro covered her mouth.

"He caught up with me. His men were holding me and—" She pressed her fingers over her mouth. The terror of that moment returned to her so forcefully she couldn't speak.

"Oh, Mazy!"

Mazy forced herself to take a breath, then another, to calm herself enough to finish the story. "Sir Berenger saved me. I am well. They didn't hurt me. They didn't hurt me."

Was she trying to reassure herself as well as Ro?

"I thank God." Ro clasped her hands together in front of her chest. "Oh, that heaven-sent Sir Berenger. Did he take you in his arms and kiss you?"

"No, of course not." He had embraced her, but she'd share that with Ro another time. Besides, the thought of a kiss brought back the horrible man and his threat to kiss her. A sickening chill went through her stomach and she shuddered.

She had to think of something else. "Let us see if there is someone who needs our help."

They searched the area and found a man who was bleeding from his head. But he was able to walk and said he was well enough. People all over the market were trying to set their stalls and goods to rights.

"All my bread is spoiled," one woman said in a disgusted voice. She had run away at the first sight of the mob and was just now returning, as were several other vendors.

"He's one of the rebels!" a man shouted, pointing at a raggedly clad man who was skulking away.

Two guards gave chase, running him down and subduing him.

Mazy fetched their horse, rubbing his cheek to soothe him after the chaos. "Should we pack up and go home?" Mazy asked. Truly, she wanted nothing more than to curl up in her own bed and fall into a sleep of forgetfulness.

"I think we may as well. Father will have to fix our stall for us. We can go and fetch him. Do you think he will be cross about having to repair it?"

"I think he will be glad you were not harmed. Indeed, we are fortunate that we were able to save most of our goods by bagging them up before those evil men arrived."

Mazy's hands were still trembling. She crossed her arms and hid her hands under her armpits.

"But we can't go anywhere until Sir Berenger returns." Ro smiled as if she had not been crying just a few minutes before.

Mazy shook her head at Ro. She wouldn't admit it, but her heart pounded at the memory of him holding his sword over her attacker's head, of the way he looked as he pulled her into his arms.

"You can go and fetch your father if you wish."

"Oh no. I wouldn't miss seeing Sir Berenger when he comes back to you."

"At least you're no longer frightened."

"I'm so sorry, Mazy." Ro's face suddenly fell. "I was cowering behind the stall while you were fighting with those horrible men. But you should have hidden with me."

Perhaps she should have. She could still feel the way her knife had sliced into that man's arm. She suddenly felt sick, as if she might lose the food she had eaten earlier.

"Oh my. There is a bit of blood on your cheek." Ro rubbed at her face, using her sleeve.

"A lot?"

"No, just some little spatters." Ro shuddered.

"I'll clean up later."

Nervous energy flowed through her limbs. She paced around the market again, looking for anyone who was hurt and unattended. But no one seemed to be badly injured, and those who were bleeding had left. Some of the men were already trying to mend their broken stalls as people began filtering in, curious to see what had happened.

Mazy was finally rewarded with a glimpse of Sir Berenger coming back with two scruffy-looking men, their hands tied to the pommel of his saddle. He took the men to the huddle of others, who were surrounded by guards.

Sir Berenger spoke and the men listened. After a few more minutes and further discussion, they started toward the Tower of London, leading the prisoners in their wake.

Sir Berenger did not follow them. Instead, he turned and looked straight at her from the other side of the market, then started toward her.

FIFTEEN

"SIR BERENGER IS COMING THIS WAY!" RO SLAPPED MAZY'S shoulder with her hand.

"I see him."

"Should I leave you two alone?"

"No, that's not necessary." Mazy's heart thumped. And if she were honest, she did wish she could be alone with him, if only to keep others from seeing her embarrass herself, as she was not sure she wouldn't throw her arms around him and display more emotion than was appropriate.

"Oh, look! Father is here." Ro waved as her father appeared at the other side of the marketplace. He hurried toward them as fast as Mazy had ever seen him move.

Mazy greeted Sir Berenger, feeling strangely nervous, remembering how he had embraced her. "Did you capture all of them?"

"Hopefully. But are you sure you're not hurt?"

He reached his hand toward Mazy's cheek. Just before touching her, his hand dropped. "We'll take them to the Tower to be locked up until they can be tried and sentenced." He looked at the mess around them. "I'm sorry about your broken stall."

"Father can fix it." Ro smiled. "Thank you for saving us."

"Yes, thank you," Mazy said.

"And I am most grateful for you saving poor Mazy from those horrible men."

"You might not say 'poor Mazy' if you saw her knife sticking out of that man's arm." Sir Berenger raised his brows, letting his gaze linger on Mazy. "She is the bravest woman I know. But I am grateful to God that I arrived when I did."

Mazy swallowed hard to get past the lump in her throat. She wanted to say, "And I am grateful as well. You arrived just in time." But she didn't trust herself to speak.

"I wish we had gotten here sooner, before those men did all this damage. And before you had to defend yourself."

His gaze was intense as he focused on Mazy. But why did his nearness and his gaze send her heart racing? She took a deep breath to try to calm herself. Then she took another, determined to say something.

"I am very grateful. Thank you again for helping us and apprehending those men."

"Are you sure you're well?" He was so kind and gentle, while the gruff edge of his voice turned her chest inside out.

"I am not hurt. But now that it's all over, I just want to go home."

"Of course. I'll walk with you."

He paused to speak to Ro's father, who was moaning and grousing about the condition of their booth. He said he would stay and work on fixing it and let Berenger take Mazy home.

"I'll stay with Father," Ro said.

Sir Berenger checked the goods they had tied to their horse, making sure everything was secure. Then they started on their way.

She wanted to hold on to his arm, even imagined herself with her arms around him, crying on his shoulder, but she never could do that, never could let herself appear weak. Anyone from the market who saw her, especially those who called her Knife Girl, and Sir Berenger and Ro as well, would lose respect for her if they saw her crying. No, she had to be strong. But even more importantly, she didn't know if Sir Berenger would want her crying on his shoulder, or if he would think she was in love with him or that she wanted him to take care of her. And she could *not* make him think that. She would be mortified.

She could cry into her pillow when she was alone.

Berenger had watched Mazy being held at the mercy of those merciless men, but then, somehow, he had let the ice-cold calm flow through him, just as it did when he was fighting a battle. He'd done what he needed to do to capture the violent men. But now that it was all over, now that he'd talked calmly with Mazy and Ro and was walking Mazy home, the heat crept up his neck. He saw those men holding Mazy against her will while that other man leaned menacingly into her face, taunting her, then threatening her with the knife. He had wanted to rip those men apart. He even imagined running them through with his sword.

How dare they touch Mazy? She was sweet and strong and everything good. She was also soft and beautiful and deserved only good things and good people in her life.

Why couldn't this world be just? Why did it always seem that the best people suffered the most?

He took a deep breath and forced himself to expel the ugly thought with the air. She was safe. He could be thankful to God that he arrived in time, that she was unhurt. That was what he needed to focus on. She was not injured, and he had captured all the men who had threatened her.

After walking a few feet, Mazy stopped, as if to check her horse, but then turned to look at him, leaning toward him.

"Thank you." She said the words softly, her eyes shining with tears. She blinked them away. "It is good that you came when you did."

His heart warmed even as his head cooled. "God is faithful. He got me there in time."

"Yes. Thank You, God." She glanced up at the clouds, smiling. "All is well now. But why did those men do that? What made them start bashing everything and everyone in sight?"

"I don't know. I suppose that is for the king and his advisers and their appointed mediators to discover. Let us hope it was only what it seemed to be—a very small, short-lived rebellion."

His heart was strangely full as he gazed at Mazy. He didn't

want to leave her alone anymore to fend for herself. Perhaps someday the king would give him land and a title, a way to support a wife, and then . . . he could ask Mazy to marry him.

It was a rather startling thought. He'd always thought Mazy was beautiful, but when he first met her, she was Sir John's little sister. She was almost a woman, but with the innocence of someone unaware of the ways of men, even though she knew how to ride a horse like a man and could throw a knife and shoot a bow with amazing accuracy.

Was he tempting fate to think about marrying anyone? He was allowing himself to hope for something that, at this moment, was not even possible. But when he saw those men try to harm Mazy, he knew he could not bear to have her taken from him. He wanted to hold her and take care of her and never let anything evil get near her again.

But he didn't even have a home. Was it wrong to hope? Or did she only think of him as her brother's friend and Delia's brother? Hope thwarted led to disappointment, and sometimes even resentment and bitterness.

When they reached her home, he unloaded their goods from the horse. "I will return to look in on you soon," he said. "I must go and make sure the prisoners are all secured."

"Of course. Thank you, Sir Berenger." She gave him such a sweet smile, it made his chest ache.

He couldn't seem to tear his eyes from her face. He had an urge to touch her cheek, to feel how soft her skin was. Instead, he said, "Fare well."

He quickly mounted his horse and left.

A few days later, Berenger arrived at the palace. The king had specifically asked that Berenger be there today for the Feast of Saint Nicholas. He wasn't sure what to expect.

He looked around the Great Hall but didn't see any other knights in attendance.

"Sir Berenger? The king wants you to sit here." The chancellor came up behind him and indicated a place at a long trestle table set up on the dais that was quite near the king.

Berenger almost asked him, "Are you sure?" But he sat down where he was told.

A beautiful woman was already seated at the place beside him.

"Lady Bristow, may I introduce Sir Berenger of Dericott? Sir Berenger, this is Catherine Everdon, the Countess of Bristow."

"It is my pleasure to make your acquaintance, Lady Bristow."

The woman smiled quite warmly. Then she leaned over and said softly, near his ear, "The pleasure is all mine, Sir Berenger. And I am the widow of the Earl of Bristow." She emphasized the word *widow*.

"Please accept my condolences on the death of your husband."

She raised her brows, keeping her smile. "Thank you." The look she gave him, then the way she stared at his lips, put him on his guard.

It wasn't the first time a woman had looked at him the way she did, but she may have been the boldest, almost as if she was trying to get a reaction from him. He did not give her one.

"I have been very sad, but the king and queen have been

helping me with my grief. We are very fortunate to have such competent leaders, do you not agree? Though they are young, they are so wise."

Lady Bristow smiled in the direction of the king.

"Of course." Even if Sir Berenger did not agree—and in truth, he was not sure he did—he could not have said so. One uncomplimentary word against the king could easily be repeated and lead to many unwelcome consequences, including death.

"I am glad our majesties are able to help you in your time of mourning."

"Yes. But how long should a widow grieve?" She leaned toward him, a crease forming between her eyes.

"I don't know."

"There is nothing stipulated in either the Holy Writ or the laws of our land." She seemed to be waiting for an answer to her question.

"I never thought about it," he said.

"But what do you think, Sir Berenger?" She tapped her four fingers on his wrist where his hand lay on the table between them.

"I suppose it should be left up to the widow to decide when she is done grieving."

"Give me an amount of time. How long? Half a year? A year?"

"I cannot say."

She reached out for her goblet of wine with the long fingers that had been tapping his wrist.

Berenger slowly removed his hand and put it on his own leg, out of her sight.

She gazed at him over the rim of her goblet. She was a woman who knew she was beautiful, with black hair and brows, lips so red that she must have put something on them, and a long white neck. She wore earrings of pearl and precious stones, as well as a circlet and a necklace set with the same stones—a pearl and a green, a blue, and a red stone.

He guessed her age to be around thirty or thirty-five—a little old to be interested in him, as he was only twenty-three.

Berenger had a few good conversations with the person on the other side of him, a viscount from Northumberland, and a baron sitting across from him, but he ended up more often than not speaking with Lady Bristow. By the end of the evening she was confessing things he never expected.

"I was very young when I married my husband," she said, "but I truly loved him. He was the sun, moon, and stars to me, a young fifteen-year-old who had never traveled from home. But alas, he was cruel . . ." She sighed.

"I am very sorry he was cruel. No wife should be mistreated by the man whose duty it is to protect her."

Her eyes were soft as she blinked several times, her eyelashes fluttering. "Thank you. You seem like such a kind and chivalrous knight, someone who defends those who cannot defend themselves."

"I endeavor to be."

"Whoever marries you shall be a fortunate woman indeed. I only hope you find someone worthy of you."

He hated to admit it, but her words went straight to his heart like an arrow. That an older woman, and one as beautiful as

Lady Bristow, would think him so worthy felt very encouraging. Perhaps someday soon he would be able to marry well.

"I am tired and shall return to my room. But I hope I shall see you again soon." She stood and walked across the Great Hall in a swaying, fluid motion as her silk scarf and veil billowed out behind her.

"Sir Berenger."

He turned to see who was calling him. It was the king, who motioned with his hand for him to sit at the place his wife, the queen, had just vacated.

Sir Berenger obeyed. "Your Majesty."

The king, though not yet nineteen years old, already had an air of one who was used to being obeyed. He was no longer the boy who was afraid of his advisers. And yet, he was still probably more influenced by others than by his own experiences.

"Sir Berenger," the king said, leaning close, "how did you find Lady Bristow? Beautiful, yes? And an ease of manner that makes the conversation flow?"

"Yes, my king. She is both beautiful and easy to converse with."

"Forgive me for speaking so plainly, but she is as wealthy as she is beautiful. Her husband was the Earl of Bristow, and he left no heirs. I would like to marry her off to someone who will protect the castle in her possession, someone loyal to me. And since I desire to reward you for your service to me in Prussia, for your bravery and loyalty . . . I happen to know that the lady is most agreeable to the idea of marrying you."

"Sire, forgive me, but . . . the lady hardly knows me. We've never spoken before tonight."

"Marriages are often made between men and women who have never spoken, never even seen one another. My wife and I, for instance."

"Of course. Yes, of course." Berenger could feel the blood drain from his face. He could not insult his king. This marriage was King Richard's desire, and apparently the desire of Lady Bristow, though he could not think why. After having a husband who was cruel to her, why would she want to marry a man she hardly knew?

But if she had a castle and lands . . . was that not what he wanted?

Mazy.

He never should have let himself think of marrying her. He knew better than to let himself hope for something he had no control over. But he would have to forget he ever thought about her that way. Forget that she ever may have been a possibility for him. Because he could hardly refuse the king's gift.

Besides, how could he marry Mazy when he had nothing to offer her?

"I can see you are surprised. Think about it, and you can give me your answer when you are ready. And you can even ride out to Bristow and look around. See the castle. See the land. If you approve, and I am sure you will, then it is yours. I shall even confer the title on you. Berenger, Earl of Bristow. How does that sound to you?"

"It sounds very well." Berenger could feel his face burning, his emotions warring inside him.

"I must warn you, an offer like this may not come again."

He swallowed hard before answering. "I understand, my liege. And I am grateful to you. It is a very great reward for a humble knight."

"You may take your time to give me your answer, but the lady may prove to be more impatient than I am." He smiled. "You may go."

Berenger stood and bowed to the king. He left the Great Hall to go back to the knights' barracks, his stomach churning.

If he were to marry Lady Bristow, then she was the woman he would love and be true to. He would not be faithless, no matter whom he married.

But who would take care of Mazy? He could never hold her in his arms again, never be her rescuer, ever again.

Sixteen

Mazy and Ro went back to the market day after day, and everything went back to normal. Ro's father had repaired the booth, and he had even expressed his gratitude to God for keeping the two of them safe, choking on the words and making Ro and Mazy tear up at the gruff man's obvious emotion. And though all was well, Mazy was haunted by the face of the man who had threatened her, leaning in so close he was almost touching her with his lips.

But she would overcome this fear. She would stop dreaming about it at night, and she would stop trembling inside whenever she saw someone coming toward her stall who reminded her of him.

Why was she so haunted by what had happened? He had not managed to harm her in any way. And she had been through other attacks when she'd had to use her knives to defend herself.

Perhaps this time was different because he'd gotten so close to her and she'd felt so helpless to defend herself, with her hands held behind her back. Also, the other times she'd acted, the men had left her alone. This time she had thrown her knife, injuring the man, and yet he still kept coming at her. And then he'd puckered his foul lips so close to hers, she was sure at any moment he would press them against hers.

"Mazy? Are you all right?" Ro looked closer at her. She leaned toward her and Mazy jerked back.

Ro's eyes went wide.

Mazy pressed a hand to her chest, willing her heart to slow down. Why had fear suddenly gripped her when Ro leaned close to her? Why had she jerked away from her friend?

Mazy did her best to sound reassuring. "Forgive me. I was lost in my thoughts. I am well."

"Good, because I am thinking of going to that shop that sells Flemish dress material, and . . . Oh, look! It's Sir Berenger!"

Mazy's heart pounded, but not out of fear. Sir Berenger was dismounting from his horse. He left it with another guard, then came walking in their direction.

"I do love to watch him walk." Ro made a series of sounds in her throat.

"Behave in a seemly manner, please." But Mazy loved to watch him, too, as vendors in the market called out to him and he raised his hand and said something polite and kind. He was so mild and tranquil, except when he was clouting an evil man on the head.

"Mistress Mazy, Mistress Ro," he said, nodding to them. "Any trouble at the market in the last few days?"

"No, all has been calm." Mazy tried to smile without looking flirtatious.

"No trouble since you saved us," Ro said, arching her brows and smiling out of one side of her mouth. She just could not behave.

"I am glad to hear it. I wanted to let you know that I will be going on a trip to Suffolk and I shall probably be gone for some time."

Mazy felt her stomach drop.

"Will you be traveling on the king's business?"

He shifted his feet, glanced up at the sky, then said, "Yes. And no."

"Does this have to do with the king rewarding you for what you did in Prussia?"

"Yes." He spoke hesitantly, then finally looked Mazy in the eye and gave her a wan smile. "I have to decide if I want to accept what he is offering."

"Why would you not accept? Is it land? Property?"

"Yes, and a title, but I will have to marry the widow of the Earl of Bristow."

Mazy's heart stopped beating and the blood drained from her face. "Oh." She had to pretend she did not care. She could not act sad. Casting about in her mind for something to say, she said, "Have you met her?"

"Yes." He looked at his hands as he fidgeted with a knife handle that protruded from a belt around his waist.

Ro's mouth was hanging open. Mazy had never seen her speechless before.

"I wish you a safe journey," Mazy said. "I hope you find the information you need to make the best decision."

"Thank you." He gazed into her eyes, almost a questioning look, and then he glanced away. "Has Sir John been here to see you lately?"

"He was here two days ago. He asked me about the men who attacked the market."

"He was glad you were safe, I am sure."

"Yes, of course."

She could think of nothing else good to say about John's visit. He had seemed concerned at first, but then he became rather sullen after she assured him she had not been injured. He had little to say, did not stay long, and bought a flask of strong drink from Ro's father before leaving.

"I'm glad he came to see you. You know how to send word to him if you need him, do you not?"

"Yes." Mazy pulled her woolen cloak higher on her neck as the cold wind sent a chill through her.

Suddenly she wanted Sir Berenger to leave. Why was he here? Why come and tell her he was leaving, that he would not be there for her, any more than Warin or John was there for her?

Mazy saw Martin walking in her direction. She waved him over and began talking to him as if Sir Berenger was not even there. Let him talk to Ro. Mazy didn't want to talk to him anymore.

"It is always so good to see you looking so well," Martin said, placing his hand on his heart. "When I think of what might have happened, how you could have been hurt or even worse . . ."

Martin sighed dramatically. "You should marry me and let me watch over you."

Sir Berenger was looking at them, his expression going slack. He seemed to recover from his surprise and turned to face Martin.

"Sir Berenger, this is Martin Fisher. Martin, Sir Berenger is in charge of the king's guards."

"Thank you for your service to our king," Martin said, nodding to Sir Berenger, then eyeing him as if wondering why he was there.

Sir Berenger looked from Martin to Mazy and back again. She was fairly certain he had heard Martin say that she should marry him. He looked as if he might speak to Martin, but then he took a step back.

"I shall go," Sir Berenger said. "Fare well, Mazy and Ro. I shall see you when I return."

Why bother? You'll be married to someone wealthy by then, someone who can make you a landowner.

"Fare well, Sir Berenger." Mazy forced herself to smile and wave as if she were happy and his news had not affected her in the least.

As Sir Berenger turned his back and walked away, her chest ached.

"Are you well, Mazy?" Martin asked.

"Perfectly well. Did you want anything, Martin?" she asked a little brusquely.

"I only wanted to look in on you."

"We haven't a care in the world. How are you faring?"

Just then two customers came to buy bread. Martin, thankfully, took his leave. When the customers had gone, Ro turned to her with a woebegone look.

"Oh, Mazy." Ro sank down on a stool inside their stall and stared at her. "I thought Sir Berenger would marry you."

"I knew he could never marry me. I've told you that, Ro. You should not have been thinking that." But until this moment she had not realized how much she had been hoping . . . hoping against all reason that Sir Berenger would marry her.

O God, let her treat him well. Let her love him. I couldn't bear it if he were tied to a wife who was cruel to him. She knew he would never be cruel or faithless, no matter what his wife did to him. Sir Berenger was the best and noblest man Mazy had ever known.

Even now, though she felt hurt that he was marrying someone else, she had nothing to accuse him of or blame him for. Sir Berenger had behaved with nothing but kindness and chivalry. He couldn't know that she'd been hoping he would marry her.

And he would always be her ideal of what a man should be.

Berenger and a handful of soldiers, along with Lady Bristow and her servants, set out on their journey to Suffolk. The road was not bad, only a little muddy, as the first snow had fallen and then melted quickly, so they were able to travel at a steady rate.

Lady Bristow talked less than he had expected, which gave Berenger more time to be alone with his thoughts. He couldn't get out of his mind the man at the market who had been talking to Mazy. He'd sounded as if he had asked her to marry him before and she had refused. He tried to remember the look on Mazy's face. Had she been receptive to his proposals? Would she eventually say yes?

These thoughts made him sad and unsettled. He wished now he had stayed and questioned the man, found out what kind of man he was and if he could provide for her. But Mazy probably would have told him it was none of his business and that he had no right to ask such questions, which was true. But he was her friend, was he not?

He seemed to have two minds. One minute his thoughts were of a sober, apprehensive bent, as he wondered if he was making a mistake. The next minute he was of a hopeful mind, dreaming of having his own lands and castle and tenants, imagining passing his title of earl down to his son.

Mazy. Always Mazy was there in his thoughts as well. But why? She was Sir John's sister, and she was Delia's friend, but she was also his friend, and he cared what happened to her. It was foolish to feel as though he was letting her down by marrying a woman who was . . . Well, he had nothing to accuse her of, but there was something about her, something bold and a little less than circumspect. He couldn't help remembering how she had looked at him when they met, similar to the way lascivious men looked at a pretty woman in the street.

What did he truly know about Lady Bristow? She had singled him out when she knew nothing about him, but why? He should feel flattered, he supposed. Perhaps she knew more about him than he realized. Perhaps she was a good woman. Why should he think less of her just because she was flirtatious? She was nothing like Delia or Mazy, but did that mean she was not a good woman?

This was why he was going to Suffolk to Bristow Castle, to see Lady Bristow in her own home around her servants, to see how she treated people, to see if a marriage with her was possible. After all, she was beautiful. Anyone would think so.

His mind went to Mazy and how she had looked when he told her he was possibly going to be marrying a widow for her lands, property, and title.

She was disappointed in him. But she quickly changed her expression and told him she was happy for him. She smiled, but what was she really thinking? That he was greedy and grasping?

Berenger almost wished he could introduce the two women so he could get Mazy's opinion of her. But at the same time, something inside rebelled at that thought.

Two minds? He seemed to be of half a dozen minds at least.

The last day of their trip, the air grew significantly colder, the clouds darker and thicker, and snowflakes began to fall, small flakes at first, then big, heavy drops of snow.

The snow was so thick, Berenger could hardly see a hundred feet in front of him.

"Bristow Castle is at the top, just up there," Lady Bristow said, pointing.

Their horses had only started climbing the hill when a gray stone structure came into view. He stared up at Bristow Castle. The fortress was big and imposing, and yet it looked dark and not very appealing. But perhaps that was only because of the snow clouds.

"Bristow Castle. What do you think?" Lady Bristow smiled at him in that now-familiar way, out of one side of her mouth and with her brows raised.

"Very impressive."

She urged her horse into a trot and moved ahead of him. Her veil flowed out behind her in the way he was becoming accustomed to seeing.

No doubt she was anxious to be home. She quickly arrived, dismounted, and left her horse near the front door and went inside, while Berenger and the other guards took their horses to the stable and helped unsaddle them before going in.

Berenger heard shouting coming from down the corridor from the main entrance. The voice was sharp and high.

He broke into a run. A wide-eyed servant sidestepped out of the way.

At the end of the corridor he turned a corner. In front of him was the kitchen. Lady Bristow was standing before a handful of servants, their eyes cast down at the floor.

"Is everything all right?" he asked.

Lady Bristow turned her head, a look of annoyance on her face, which immediately faltered and was replaced with a smile.

"All is well," she said with a cheerful tone that sounded less than authentic.

"I thought I heard shouting."

"Oh, that was just me encouraging the servants to have everything perfect for you. They can be a little lazy when I'm not here with them." She turned to face the servants, whose eyes were wide as she addressed them. She clapped her hands. "Let us make everything ready, and be quick about it, shall we?" she said in a sweet but high-pitched voice.

She turned toward Berenger and smoothed her hands down her sides and hips. "And now I shall show you the castle."

She took his arm and hurried him away. "You don't want to see the kitchen. Come. I will show you around."

He let her pull him along to the staircase. Then she abruptly stopped. She sighed and reached out to him, placing her hand on his chest. "I am so glad you came. I so want to impress you while you are here." She made a pouty expression with her lips.

"You do not need to worry. I'm sure all will be well."

"I just wanted everything to be perfect."

"Were you scolding the servants earlier?"

"I was only instructing them. Sometimes I have to raise my voice because the cook is rather deaf." She leaned toward him, putting her weight against his chest with her hand.

Light footsteps sounded on the stone floor. They both turned to see a little girl walking toward them. She was wearing a ragged dress and her dark hair stood out against her pale face. She must have been about seven or eight. She froze when she saw them.

Lady Bristow said in a breathy, whispery voice, "This is my little ward." Then she turned to the child. "Darling, why are you wearing that? Be a good girl and go and change your clothes."

The little girl turned and ran away.

"She is your ward?"

"Yes, a distant relation. Her parents died, poor thing, and I took her in. I promise she will be no trouble to us. Only, I can't imagine why she was wearing that dirty old dress." She smiled as if amused.

"Does she have a name?"

"Of course. Her name is Juliana. I'm sorry she was not ready to greet you properly when you arrived."

"No matter. A girl her age should not be worried about impressing me, someone she's never met."

"Well, of course she should." Lady Bristow put both her hands on his chest now. "You will be a part of her life now that the king wishes us to marry." She suddenly pushed away from him and started up the stairs. "After that long journey, I need to refresh myself and change my clothing. But I shall see you in an hour in the Great Hall. Howard will take you to your room and get you anything you need."

She snapped her fingers at the young man who still stood in the hallway.

Howard stood up straight and bowed to Berenger. "This way, my lord."

When he was certain Lady Bristow was out of earshot, he said to the young man leading the way up the stairs, "I am Sir Berenger of Dericott. And you are Howard?"

"Yes, sir."

He still was not quite certain what had happened in the kitchen. But Lady Bristow's explanation that she had only raised her voice because the cook was hard of hearing did not ring true. Still, he didn't want to falsely accuse her either.

She was right when she said the king wanted them to marry. He had further elaborated his desires in a letter he sent just before Sir Berenger and Lady Bristow had departed on their journey, saying he wanted this castle in capable, loyal hands, especially since it was on the coast at a point that was easily accessible by ship.

Not only was this quite a handsome reward—a castle, lands, and a title—for the third son of an earl, a landless knight like Berenger, but it was a huge honor that the king had chosen him to control and defend this strategic castle.

He just had to marry Lady Bristow to get it, which would further endear him to the king as a loyal and dutiful ally. If the king were to come to rely on Berenger as one of his close advisers, he could only imagine the good he might be able to do—and the evil he might be able to prevent.

As he allowed the servant to fill a small tub with water so he could wash off the road dust and get clean, he thought about how Lady Bristow had greeted her young ward, Juliana. There was no warm embrace, and something in the child's expression and manner seemed a bit concerning, almost as if she was afraid of the woman who should have been something of a mother figure to her. It stuck in his mind like a cocklebur.

He was having misgivings about whether he should marry Lady Bristow, more of a gut feeling than anything else. But if he rejected the king's offer, he might never get another reward from him, and his refusal might even anger the king.

He needed to be really sure about this decision.

SEVENTEEN

BERENGER AND LADY BRISTOW HAD JUST SAT AT THE
table in the Great Hall when Lady Bristow exclaimed, "There
she is!"

The wide-eyed little girl he'd seen earlier came toward them
wearing a lovely pink dress, her hair hanging in curls by her
cheeks and over her shoulders.

"Come, come," Lady Bristow said, motioning to the child.
She picked her up and placed her in her lap. "Now, that is better,
is it not? A beautiful dress, clean face. Is she not a little beauty,
Sir Berenger, and nothing like the little beggar child we saw
before?"

"I am very pleased to make your acquaintance, Juliana. You
look very pretty." He smiled, but the child barely glanced at him.
Instead, she kept her head down.

"Look up, darling, so we can see you."

The child was sitting stiffly, with Lady Bristow's hands on

her shoulders. She lifted her head but looked on the verge of tears.

"She is learning languages with her tutor." She leaned back to look at Juliana. "Show off what you're learning to Sir Berenger. Say something in German or Italian."

Juliana's mouth turned down ever so slightly at the corners and tears welled up in her eyes. She sat very still.

"That is all right," Berenger said, trying to sound soothing. "When you are more accustomed to me, you can tell me something of what you are learning."

Lady Bristow frowned and shook her head.

"All is well," Berenger assured them both. "I wouldn't know what she was saying anyway, as I never learned German or Italian. But later I will teach Juliana some games I was taught as a boy. I think you will like them." Berenger leaned down to try to look into the child's eyes. She finally looked at him just as the first big tear slipped down her cheek.

Lady Bristow waved a young woman servant over and handed Juliana off to her. The servant hurried the little girl away.

"Is she not joining us for supper?" Berenger asked.

"She has her meals with her nurse. Children do not eat in the Great Hall." She sounded as if she were explaining something to him that he couldn't possibly know anything about.

But he happened to know that children did sometimes eat with their parents. He couldn't imagine Delia and Strachleigh turning their children over to a servant at mealtimes. But perhaps that was how Lady Bristow had been treated as a child and she did not know any other way. Perhaps Berenger could be a good influence on her, could help her learn to love and be loved, to take a more affectionate approach to her ward's upbringing.

He rather liked thinking he could be a help to her, could rescue her from a sad life. He'd always imagined he'd rescue a woman and fall in love with her. Was Lady Bristow that woman?

The servants began bringing in the food, and he ate heartily, as they had not had food this good since they left London four days ago.

"Everything is exceptional," he told Lady Bristow. She frowned, but before she could speak, he told the servant who brought in the next course, "Please tell the cook that the food is excellent and perfectly cooked and spiced."

Lady Bristow laughed. "You must be accustomed to eating at inns and alehouses. I was just thinking that the meat was over-salted and the sauces needed more spice."

Berenger caught a glimpse of the servant's face. He pursed his lips together and rolled his eyes toward the ceiling, but then quickly let his expression go blank.

"I don't think anything is wrong with this meal." Berenger raised his brows at Lady Bristow. "It is all very good."

Lady Bristow smiled and said, "The bread is very good, isn't it?"

Then she started talking about how lovely the castle would look in the morning, all covered in snow. "Did you know that this castle was built as a fortress to withstand any attack? The front door is reinforced with iron, and the stone walls are two feet thick."

"That is very impressive. How near is the ocean from here?"

"It is very close. In fact, you can see the ocean from the windows on the upper floors. Tomorrow we should ride through the estate so you can see just what it is the king is offering you." Lady Bristow laid her hand on his forearm and leaned toward him, smiling. "I think you will be pleased with how vast the estate is and approve of the condition of the land. It is very fertile for farming, and the fields are flat and free of rock. It is some of the finest land in England."

"I am looking forward to seeing it."

"I think we both need a good night's sleep after our journey." She said the words while gazing into his eyes quite intently. "But after tonight, we shall be spending a lot of time together. I hope you don't mind."

"Of course not." That was the most important reason for coming with her on this visit—to get to know her and decide if he wanted to marry her.

Most men would not concern themselves with a woman's character before marrying her, if they had much to gain from the alliance. Most men assumed they could subdue their wives, if necessary, and if a man was displeased with his wife, he would find another woman to love, while using his wife for heirs.

This was not at all what Berenger wanted. He wanted a love match like Delia and his brothers Edwin and Gerard had made. He'd always imagined having a wife who would love him and to whom he could give his love. Nothing less would ever make him happy.

At the end of the meal, Lady Bristow asked Berenger, "Will you accompany me to my room?"

He let her take his arm as they walked slowly to the stairs.

"I have put you in the bedchamber next to mine. I like feeling that I have a strong man nearby to protect me."

"Why? Do you feel yourself to be in danger here?"

She did not answer right away. Finally, she said, "No, but as I told you, my first husband was very cruel. He would often strike me when he was angry. I often wished there was someone to protect me and to rescue me from him." She said the last words in a soft whisper, clinging to Berenger's arm with both hands.

The thought of her husband hitting her made heat crawl up the back of his neck. He imagined defending her from the man.

"I am very sorry that happened to you. You did not deserve to be treated that way." The way she was clinging to him and gazing at him, as if she was entreating him to save her, made him think about kissing her. But it was not time for that. He wanted his mind to stay clear and alert. He needed to think of something that would steer his thoughts elsewhere.

"You have Juliana now, but did you never have children with your husband?"

"No, I never was able to conceive." She said the words quietly. "And he blamed me for that." She reached up and rubbed her eyes with her fingertips, as if brushing away tears.

"I am very sorry you weren't able to have children."

"Perhaps you will not wish to marry me, for fear that I will not be able to bear you a son, but I promise I shall try my best. I will consult the healer in the village. I have heard that she has an herbal concoction that can get barren women to conceive. I did not try it when I was married before. I did not want to have his child. But that was probably very wicked of me."

"I do not think that was wicked. You were probably afraid he would mistreat the child."

"Yes. You understand me so well, Sir Berenger." She stopped in front of a door and turned to him, pressing her forearms against his chest and gazing up at him. "I asked King Richard to allow me to marry you, of all the knights that he was considering, after he told me of your great bravery and honor on the battlefield. But we also have a mutual friend, Sir John of Wexcombe, who told me that you were a good man. Are you surprised?"

In fact, he was surprised that Sir John would speak so favorably about him. They were friends, but it was not Sir John's way to praise someone else. And how did she and Sir John even know each other? Before he could decide how to respond, she interrupted him.

"I believe you could be the one to save me from my loneliness and to protect me if anyone should ever try to mistreat me again."

Berenger's heart leapt inside him at the vulnerable look in her eyes. She needed a protector, and he suddenly wanted to be that protector, to save her from pain. How could he not? She was beautiful, with her large eyes, and she gazed at him as if she adored him already, even though he hadn't, as yet, done anything to deserve her affection. She stirred something inside him.

She closed her eyes, her face very close to his. He would only have to lean down a bit to press his lips to hers. But how could he do that when he had not pledged himself to her yet? He had to be certain first. He had no wish to behave dishonorably with her.

Besides, even as he thought about kissing her, his mind went to Mazy. And it would be dishonorable indeed to kiss one woman while thinking of another.

"Good night." He quickly kissed her hand and backed away. "Sleep well." He turned and went to his own room before he changed his mind.

Mazy sat with Ro's father while Ro tended the last of the alehouse customers for the night. He lay so motionless on his bed, Mazy leaned down beside him to watch his chest. There, it moved. He was still breathing.

He had become ill so suddenly, only two days before. It was frightening to see the illness progress so quickly.

"How is he doing?" Ro whispered, hurrying into the room.

"There's nothing wrong with me." Ro's father's voice was slurred as he opened his eyes and looked around. "Why do you make such a fuss? I'm just tired."

With great difficulty, he managed to roll over on his side. A coughing fit seized him, then gradually ceased.

"You can go now." Ro took Mazy's hand and squeezed it.

"Are you sure you don't need me?"

"You girls are like a couple of hens clucking and fussing . . . I'm well enough. Go on, Mazy."

Ro walked out with Mazy, then whispered, "I think his heart is paining him. At least he's trying to rest this time."

They'd been so worried when he'd had a similar bout earlier that year. He recovered, but he'd seemed a bit weakened afterward.

"I'll pray for him." Mazy patted Ro's shoulder. "Don't worry."

"Thank you."

Later that night Mazy awoke to someone beating on her door. She hurried to throw on a cloak before hearing, "Mazy, it's Ro! Please—" Her voice choked off, as if she was crying.

Mazy yanked open the door. "What is it? What happened?"

"It's Father. I think he's . . . Will you come down and see if you can wake him?" Ro sobbed into her hands.

Mazy ran down the stairs ahead of her. She entered their rooms and went to Ro's father's bedside.

He was still, his mouth open, his eyes closed. Mazy knelt beside him. "It's Mazy. Can you hear me?" But she suspected he could not, and never would again. She leaned over him, pulled her hair back, and placed her cheek against his mouth and nose. After a few moments she still felt nothing, no breath.

"I woke up and went to check on him, and I found him like this." Ro recommenced her sobbing.

"I'm so sorry, Ro."

"The worst part is that he died alone. I wasn't there to hear his last words, if he had any."

Mazy put her arms around her friend and let her cry on her shoulder.

Her own heart felt as if a boulder had settled on it. She knew the pain of losing a father, and she could easily imagine and empathize with what Ro was feeling. Besides that, she'd been quite fond of Ro's father, even though he was gruff and sometimes rude. At least he was a man of character who never harmed or cheated anyone and always was there to help. But what would she and Ro do without a man about the alehouse?

Perhaps it was selfish and unfeeling to think of that now, but they would need to think about it, and soon. They'd have to find someone to help them or they'd have to sell the place.

The next day they hung a sign on the door that the Swan was closed while they arranged for Ro's father's funeral and burial. They kept it closed for two days while Ro cried and talked about her father enjoying heaven and flitting around like an angel, and then a few moments later Ro would dissolve in tears again.

Mazy went up to her bed every night feeling more exhausted than she had when she worked all day at the market. And every night she wondered, *Is Sir Berenger married? Does he even think of me? Is he marrying someone worthy of him?* She didn't know. She only knew that she loved him and wanted the best for him.

EIGHTEEN

BERENGER AND LADY BRISTOW RODE THE PERIMETER OF the land that had been handed down to her first husband, the Earl of Bristow, by his father. Everything was covered with a dusting of snow as they surveyed all the farmland and pastures and meadows. The best part, however, was the seashore.

Berenger had always enjoyed the sound of the pounding waves against the shore, the sight of the ocean stretching as far as the eye could see, the majestic views both from high rocks above the shore and from the sand below. Just beyond the rise where Bristow Castle sat was a high, rocky place that overlooked a narrow shore beneath.

"A pity they did not build the castle here," Berenger said as he and Lady Bristow stood enjoying the vast ocean view. "It's not far, after all, barely five hundred feet away, I'd say."

"You do not approve of the castle, then? I suppose you will want to build another here."

"I did not say that."

"You will refuse to marry me because the castle does not have a better view of the ocean, won't you?" Lady Bristow's face crumpled, as if she was about to cry.

"Of course not. Not at all."

"I am accustomed to this sort of thing, of not pleasing . . . If only I could tear down the castle and rebuild it on this spot." She was wiping her eyes and sniffing.

Berenger patted her on the shoulder, not sure what to say. Was she sincerely worried or only trying to manipulate his emotions?

He stared out at the ocean. More snow clouds hovered overhead, making the sea look ominous and dark.

"The castle is built with a good view and prospect. You need not worry about such things. I am not so shallow or petty as that, and the walk from the castle to this spot is quite pleasant."

Lady Bristow sniffled some more and dabbed at her eyes with the back of her wrist.

"You must think I am silly. But I only want you to be happy with everything, to fall in love with the views of the sea, with the castle and the land and . . . to fall in love with me." She turned her head away as her voice cracked on the last word.

He wanted to fall in love with her as well. But truthfully, he wished Mazy was the one saying these words to him. If she said them, he would believe in her sincerity. But he simply didn't know Lady Bristow very well, and he was still wondering if he could trust her.

He almost felt as if he should apologize to her. It was unfair that he was thinking about Mazy.

"I don't think you're being silly," Berenger told Lady Bristow.

"Will you promise me one thing?" Lady Bristow wrapped her arms around his arm and leaned against him.

He gazed down into her eyes, feeling pity for her. Having had a cruel husband, she must be desperate for love. Was she the woman he'd always dreamed of loving, cherishing, and protecting?

"Promise me you will not take too long to make your decision. Every minute you make me wait is a pain in my heart." She pressed a fist to her chest.

"I will do my best to decide quickly." He smiled down at her, half-amused at her dramatic emotions and declarations, and half-spellbound by them. She was as intriguing as she was beautiful.

But something kept him from saying he would marry her. She was beautiful and she had the approval of the king, but he did not feel peace when he thought about marrying her.

"I would like to have Juliana take her meals with us. I need to get to know her as well."

Berenger watched for Lady Bristow's reaction to his request as they sat by the window watching the sun in the late afternoon sky.

She took a breath and let it out. "I haven't told you how difficult the girl is. She is very unpleasant and has a very bad habit of lying. I never know what she will say."

"That is all right. I wish to see more of her."

Lady Bristow raised her brows. "Very well. I cannot deny you anything." She smiled and placed her hand over his.

When the evening meal was served in the Great Hall, Juliana's nurse brought her in and seated her across from Berenger. Lady Bristow sat in her usual place at the head of the table.

The child was fair of face, but she kept her eyes cast down.

"How have you been occupying yourself today, Juliana?" Berenger asked. "It was a beautiful day. Did you take a walk along the seashore?"

The child looked up and stared at him but did not open her mouth.

"Answer Sir Berenger," Lady Bristow said. "He asked you a question."

"No, sir." The child cast her eyes down again.

"She is not allowed to go to the sea without my permission," Lady Bristow said. "I don't want anything to happen to her, and the sea is dangerous."

"Then we shall go together tomorrow, if the weather is fine." He couldn't help feeling pity for the child. He'd seen beggar children who looked happier than she did.

"An outing to the sea." Lady Bristow's lips smiled, but there was something about her tone that made him wonder if she was sincere.

"I hope that is agreeable to you, Lady Bristow."

"Of course. I always enjoy outings to the sea." She turned to Juliana. "Say thank you to Sir Berenger for inviting you on an outing."

The girl's head sank lower. "Thank you" was her whispered reply.

"She is very shy, but I am sure all will be well." Lady Bristow smiled cheerfully at Berenger.

Was something wrong with the child? He didn't want to think ill of Lady Bristow, but he needed to entertain the possibility that she was unkind to Juliana. The poor child seemed very sad. He must pay attention to how Lady Bristow treated her. He could not marry a woman who did not love children. What kind of mother would she be?

During the meal, Lady Bristow did not criticize the food or the servants, but chattered in a cheerful way. She asked Juliana a few questions to try to draw her out, but she replied in the fewest words possible. Berenger had a little more success.

"Do you like to draw or paint?" he asked her.

Juliana nodded. She glanced up at him much more often than she looked at Lady Bristow.

"What are your favorite things to draw?"

"Flowers and trees," the child said.

"You must have a favorite color."

She did not answer, just held his gaze.

"What is your favorite color?"

"Red and violet and blue."

"Oh, those are good colors."

"And yellow."

"I like yellow, too, especially the yellow sunlight in the sky."

She stared at him, not responding, but she had lost the half-defiant, half-frightened look.

"I rather like a good storm," Lady Bristow said. "A stormy sea, the fomenting waves. It's quite a sight to behold, especially when the sky is dark."

The child tucked her chin to her chest, looking down again. Lady Bristow frowned and shook her head.

After the nurse came to get the child and take her to bed, Lady Bristow said, "You see how she behaves toward me. She refuses to talk to me. I cannot imagine why. She spoils her best dresses because she knows it displeases me. You do not know how I have suffered with the child screaming at me, out of anger and frustration that her own mother and father are dead. I am the one who has taken her in to feed and clothe her, and yet for that very reason, I think she despises me." Lady Bristow sighed.

"That does sound very difficult. How did her parents die?"

She waved her hand and stared down at her food, picking off a bit of meat and putting it in her mouth. When she had swallowed, she said, "They caught a sickness and died within a week of each other. Very sad." That was indeed very sad. What if marrying Lady Bristow was God's plan to help this little girl?

He found himself looking forward to the next day's trip to the sea with Juliana and Lady Bristow.

The next day dense, wet snow blanketed the ground. It was cold but not overly, as they wore their warmest cloaks and walked the little trail that led from the castle to the sea. Berenger brought a cloth bag to carry seashells in if they should find some.

He paused as Juliana bent to draw in the snow with her finger.

"Are you writing your name?" he asked her.

She shook her head. "Drawing a flower," she whispered.

"Ah, very nice."

They continued on their way as Lady Bristow stood and stared out at the sea.

They came upon a large shell with a pale pattern of color on the outside, pearly white and smooth inside, large at one end, then tapering down to almost a point at the other end. He waited for Juliana to pick it up. She stared up at him. "Can I keep it?" she whispered.

"Of course. Hold it up to your ear and you can hear the hollow sound of the waves inside it."

She looked at it for a moment, then held it up to her ear. Her eyes went wide and her mouth opened into an O shape.

"All shells like this make that sound." He smiled at her, and she rewarded him with a wisp of a smile in return.

He held open the bag and she seemed reluctant to place it inside.

"I won't lose it, and I shall give it to you when we get back to the castle."

She dropped the shell into the bag and they kept walking, with Juliana staring at the ground as they went, occasionally finding another shell.

They came to a cove that jutted out into the sea. Juliana had been following him and focusing on the ground as she walked, but when he stopped, she looked up, gasped, and froze in place.

"What is it? Are you all right?" Berenger looked all around but could see no danger.

The little girl looked back as Lady Bristow was just rounding the bend and coming into sight.

"Is something wrong?" he asked Juliana again.

She looked at him with fear in her eyes, but then she whispered, "I'm not supposed to tell."

When Lady Bristow joined them, he asked, "Did something happen here that Juliana is afraid of?"

"She's probably remembering a ship that wrecked here during a storm a few months ago. Some men drowned. Poor thing. That is what's troubling you, isn't it, my dear?" Lady Bristow said. "No need to worry. There are no storms and nothing to worry about today," she ended cheerfully.

Juliana did not respond, just kept her eyes cast down, looking half-frightened, half-defiant.

He missed how happy she had seemed moments before when they were finding shells. That was all over now as she stood with her shoulders rounded.

"You are enjoying the sea and the treasures it yields, I see." Lady Bristow raised her brows at him.

"We found several shells, did we not, Juliana?"

The little girl glanced up at him, then dropped her gaze.

Lady Bristow looked heavenward, then whispered, though loud enough for Juliana to hear, "She is always so sullen. I don't know what to do with her."

Juliana seemed more sad than sullen, and she was only a little child, but Berenger said nothing to contradict Lady Bristow.

"Let us go back," Lady Bristow said, hugging her arms around herself as if she was cold.

Berenger let Lady Bristow walk ahead and stayed behind with Juliana. He held his hand out to her and was surprised when she took it and walked beside him. Her face lost the tense expression and she seemed to enjoy kicking the snow and once again looking for pretty seashells.

They made their way up the rocky trail from the seashore to the grassy path back to the castle.

"What do you think of our seaside walk? You can enjoy this walk every day when you are living here at Bristow Castle."

"I like it very much."

Juliana let go of his hand and started running. He saw her nurse waiting for her up ahead.

"It seems she likes her nurse," he said. "That is good. A child needs a friend."

"A nurse's job is not to be a friend. Surely you realize that children need discipline and structure and to be taught self-control."

"Of course, but a child also needs to have a friend they can play with and confide in."

Lady Bristow pressed her lips together, then quickly changed her expression and laughed. "I never realized you had such a soft heart. A knight with a soft heart." She reached out and tickled his arm with her fingernails.

"A knight should be compassionate, when the situation calls for it."

"And that is what I heard about you, why I told King Richard that you were the man I was looking for, the one I wanted to marry." She drew near and squeezed his arm.

Perhaps she was not so motherly to the child, but Berenger could show her how to be gentle and mild-tempered, could he not?

As they neared the castle, he suddenly remembered something he had been wondering about. "How do you know Sir John?"

"I met him years ago," she said, "when he was training at my uncle's castle."

"He must have been very young."

"Yes, I believe he was sixteen or seventeen. And then I saw him again when I was visiting King Richard. I had heard about your exploits and asked him if he knew you." She spun around suddenly and pointed back at the ocean. "What do you think? Is it not a magnificent view?"

He had to admit it was.

He wouldn't ask her again, but he was also pondering what she'd said about Juliana and the shipwreck.

Later that evening Howard came into his bedchamber to stoke up the fire against the chill of the winter night.

"Howard, what happened when the ship wrecked near here and some sailors drowned?"

"When, sir?"

"A few months ago, I heard."

"No, sir." Howard shook his head. "There haven't been any shipwrecks near here in many a year."

"Not for many years? Are you sure?"

"Yes, sir."

Why had Lady Bristow lied to him? Very strange. What was she concealing? He tried to remember how the child had reacted when Lady Bristow mentioned the shipwreck, but Juliana had said nothing.

"How long have you served Lady Bristow, Howard?"

The man suddenly cut his eyes away from Berenger and even shuffled so that his back was to him as he stoked the fire.

"I served under the master, Lord Bristow, since before Lady Bristow came here as a bride."

He wanted to ask him what he thought of her, but that would be unfair. A servant could not speak ill of his master or mistress.

The man lit an extra candle, then said, "Will there be anything else you need, sir?"

"Thank you, Howard, no. You may go."

"Sleep well, sir."

In truth, Berenger had not slept well since he had come to Bristow Castle. The night before, he'd had a dream that a wolf was chasing him. When he turned to face the wolf with his drawn sword, he found not a wolf at all but a woman, although he couldn't see her face, as it was hidden in a thick mist. He could still hear her wolfish snarling.

He'd had other dreams for the rest of the night—that is, when he was able to sleep between waking up and wondering how long the night would last. But he did not remember the other dreams.

Berenger had a feeling he would not sleep any better tonight than he had the night before.

NINETEEN

MAZY AND RO HIRED TWO MEN, WIMARC AND SILVESTER, to help run the alehouse, but they had to confront them after two weeks. They caught them lying about how much ale and food they were buying and selling, which enabled them to steal the profits. With Mazy's experience at keeping her father's books, she only had to examine the records and inventory to deduce their theft. Thankfully, she'd thought to examine their accounting before more time had passed.

Silvester had seemed like an honest person, and he was a relative of Ro's, though not a close one. Ro had not known Wimarc and had trusted her relation's word about the man. Clearly that was a mistake.

"Miss Roesia knows I'm not a bad man, Miss Mazy. You're accusing me of stealing, but I would not do that to two such maids as yourselves. Besides that, Roesia's my kinfolk."

But Ro stared back at him with her arms crossed, unmoved and unmoving.

"We are sorry it has to end this way, but you and Wimarc will have to leave the alehouse at once."

Wimarc, whose greasy black hair had a prominent white streak in front on one side, leaned toward her with an angry stare. "The Swan be our alehouse now, as we be the ones running it. We'll not be leaving on the say-so of two women still wet behind the ears."

"This alehouse belongs to Ro. It belonged to her father, and everyone knows that. My brother is Sir John, a knight in the king's service at the Tower of London. I will send word and he will bring his fellow knights to remove you if you will not leave on your own. So I suggest you get out now." Mazy crossed her arms over her chest, doing her best to glare at the two men and hide the fact that her heart was pounding against her chest.

"We'll not be leaving." Wimarc also crossed his arms.

"That's right." Silvester followed suit.

Ro looked at Mazy, fear making her eyes wide and her cheeks pale.

Mazy's mind went to the knives in her pockets. How could she threaten them and get them to leave? If she drew her knives or threw them, the men might retaliate. She could not risk them harming Ro.

Mazy glared back at the two men while Ro stood close to her side. What should they do now? Just wait for the men to leave? Could they stay awake all night until some patrons came the next morning and hope for assistance from them?

She moved farther back into the alehouse, bringing Ro with her. "This is Ro's home and business," she told the men. "We are not leaving. But you will be leaving, either tonight or tomorrow, it matters not to us." Mazy propped her back against the wall as if she was very comfortable.

"It's ours now. We're not going anywhere." Silvester sneered at her.

How could she and Ro have been so wrong about these two men? They had seemed so trustworthy. Was she such a poor judge of character?

But she couldn't think about that now.

Would the men attack them during the night if they fell asleep? Ro was looking more and more frightened.

Mazy whispered to her, "Look mean, and don't you dare cry."

"Getting scared, are you?" Wimarc sneered.

"We're not afraid. Are you?" Mazy did her best to sneer back at them.

"You'd better get afraid." Silvester took two steps toward them.

"Come any closer and I'll throw my knife straight into your heart." Mazy grasped hold of her knife handle inside her pocket. She would do it. To defend herself and Ro, she would.

He stopped and eyed her, as if trying to decide if she meant it. But she had given him fair warning. He would not get another.

Wimarc made a guttural sound.

"I've heard about you," Silvester said. "They call you the Knife Girl."

She waited to see if he would take another step toward her. She was ready.

She could see Ro's hand was trembling, but she said nothing and did not move.

They stood staring at one another for what seemed a very long time. Finally, the two men sat down on the floor and started talking in low whispers. Mazy hoped they were speculating whether Mazy would slit their throats should they fall asleep. She wouldn't, but she hoped they thought she would. She continued to stare at them while keeping her hand in her pocket on her knife handle.

"You can go now and I will not tell my brother, Sir John of Wexcombe, to take his vengeance out on you for how you have behaved toward Roesia and myself."

Silvester looked at Wimarc first. He was weakening. She could see it in his face.

Honestly, she wondered if John would even notice if something happened to her. But right now she had to convince these two miscreants that she had a loving, attentive brother, a knight with connections to the king.

"My brother belongs to the king's own personal guard. He has the king's ear, and if the king finds out you harmed his guard's sister, he will have you drawn and quartered."

Silvester cut his eyes at Wimarc again, and Wimarc suddenly stood to his feet.

Mazy gripped her knife.

Wimarc went around the heavy plank counter, grabbed a flask of ale, then tapped Silvester's arm.

"We won't forget how you wronged us. You'll regret this."

Wimarc's expression was spiteful as he and Silvester stalked out the door.

Mazy ran to the door, closing and then barring it with the heavy crossbar. "Is the back door locked?"

Ro met her gaze. "I think so."

They both ran through the alehouse to the back door and locked it, then found the crossbar and threw it down over the door. Then Ro burst into tears.

Mazy held her friend, a dull, lifeless feeling falling over her.

First the riot in the market, then Ro's father dying, and now this. What was next? And how were they going to run the alehouse and continue to sell goods at the market? She didn't want to abandon the women whose goods they sold in the market. They were mostly widows, and this was their only income.

God, I'm tired. I'm just so tired.

Mazy did not go to the market the next day. Instead, she helped Ro in the alehouse and tried to find someone they could trust to help them run the Swan. So far they had found no one.

"Perhaps I should sell the Swan." Ro's expression was as sad as when she was mourning her father's death.

They stood looking at each other over the counter, finally experiencing a lull in customers and their orders.

"I don't want you to sell it if you don't want to." Mazy couldn't bear to think of Ro losing something else she loved so soon after losing her father. "Besides, where would you live?"

"I could live with you on the top and the new owner could live on the middle floor." She frowned and shrugged her shoulders. "The only other option is to get married."

"You can't just go and get married." Mazy stared hard at Ro. "Has anyone asked you?"

Ro fidgeted with the towel she had tucked into her belt, looking down. "I think Anselm would marry me, if he thought I was interested."

"Anselm?" Mazy tried to remember who she was talking about. "The young man who sits in the corner and stares at you?" Her stomach felt a little sick at the thought of Ro marrying him. His hair always looked greasy and he was not very good-looking, with a paunchy belly and otherwise skinny frame.

"He's quiet but very clever. I've never seen him spending time in bad company, nor ever heard him say anything debauched or unkind."

"Do you love him? Or think you could love him?" Again, Mazy's stomach churned at the thought.

"I don't know." Ro stared down at her towel again.

"You don't have to get married, Ro. We'll think of something."

"I don't know what else to do."

"But, Ro, you would only be marrying him for protection. We can find someone to help us, I'm sure. I don't want you to feel as if you must marry. There are surely some trustworthy people in London. I—"

"All right, Mazy. But we have to find someone who won't try to cheat us this time. I'm not brave like you. The next men who threaten us just may carry it out."

"I know. I understand."

Marriage. A few men had proposed marriage to them when they were selling at their booth in the market, but Mazy never took them seriously, except Martin Fisher, and she didn't want to marry him. And she hadn't thought Ro wanted to marry anyone either. But now that she thought about it, Anselm was often at the Swan in the evening when she and Ro came back from the market, and he also visited them in the market at least once a week.

On the day of Ro's father's funeral, Anselm had hovered around Ro, offering to fetch whatever she needed, staying the entire day while other people came and went. Even if Ro was not in love with him, he seemed to be in love with her.

"You don't have to marry Anselm if you don't want to," Mazy said, touching Ro's arm.

"I know. You know I only do what I want." Ro grinned and lightly slapped Mazy's shoulder with the end of her towel.

She wanted to point out that Anselm might be clever, but he always looked like a lost dog who hadn't eaten in days. But then, that wasn't very kind.

Ro smiled. "If I get married, I hope you know what my next goal will be."

The look on Ro's face was too diabolical for Mazy's comfort. "What?"

"Getting you married."

"Oh no. Ro, no. Don't you get any such notion in your head." She didn't want to get married for the purpose of protection or help.

The truth was, she could not imagine marrying, now that Sir Berenger was getting married to an earl's widow. She didn't think anyone would inspire feelings of love in her, anyone besides Sir Berenger.

Berenger had passed a couple of weeks at Bristow Castle, including Christmas, with winter turning quite cold. He was having trouble falling asleep at night, so it happened that he was still awake when he heard a knocking sound.

He opened his eyes. All was completely dark except for the glow of the embers in his fireplace.

The loud knocking came again, from just the other side of the wall of his bedchamber, and this time it didn't stop. Someone was pounding on the wall in Lady Bristow's room.

Berenger leapt from his bed and quickly pulled on some hose and a shirt. He yanked open his door, strode to Lady Bristow's door, and yelled, "I'm coming in!"

He threw open the door and all was pitch black, but he could hear something like bare feet shuffling along the floor.

"Help me!" came the raspy cry.

"Lady Bristow?"

Soft crying was coming from several feet away.

"Lady Bristow, can you hear me?"

More crying.

"Come toward me," he said, still unable to see anything. "You should be able to see me in the doorway. Come."

Shuffling sounds came nearer and he went to meet them. "Lady Bristow, it's Sir Berenger."

"Oh, Sir Berenger." She grabbed his shirt and started crying again, pressing her face to his chest.

"Let me light a lamp."

"No, please, just hold me." She clung to him.

"All's well. You're safe." He patted the back of her shoulder. "Did you have a bad dream?"

"It was so real." Her voice sounded strangled. "Lord Bristow was choking me, hitting me in my face. It was so real, just like he used to . . ." The rest of her sentence was too garbled to understand.

"All's well. Nothing can harm you now."

His heart constricted painfully at the thought of her former husband striking her. How could any man do such a thing to the woman he had vowed to love and cherish for as long as they both should live?

"Will these dreams never stop?" Her voice sounded anguished.

He held her close, rubbing her back as soothingly as he could. Her hands rested on his chest.

"You are so kind, Sir Berenger, so strong and brave. I have been so much better with you sleeping so close to me, in the next room." She sniffed and seemed to be breathing more calmly.

"I am glad you have felt safe with me nearby."

"Forgive me. I should get a lantern and light it." She pushed out of his arms and stepped away from him.

She moved to the fireplace and stirred up the embers, setting them to glowing. Then she lit a lantern and came back to him.

"Better now?" he asked her, taking a step back.

"Are you leaving me so soon?" She narrowed her eyes at him.

"I think I should go."

"You can stay another moment or two." She set the lantern down, and before he knew what she was doing, she had slipped her arms around him and pressed her cheek to his chest.

"You're so warm," she said in a low, throaty voice. "You have no idea how good it feels to be in your arms."

Her soft, rather frail body pressed against him, along with her low voice telling him how safe he made her feel . . . It was intoxicating. He couldn't help wrapping his arms around her, and then he noticed how thin and silky her clothing was.

His heart beat hard against his chest, heat rising up the back of his neck. Was this the woman he would marry?

Lady Bristow raised her head. He could feel her breath, soft and feathery, against his jaw. "I can only imagine how good it would feel to have you kiss me . . ."

She was tempting him. He should go. But the desire in her voice seemed to turn him to stone. He couldn't move.

Her lips were on his chin. He was so much taller, she was probably standing on her toes to reach him.

He leaned his head down and her lips touched his. The gentle pressure quickly turned insistent and passionate, and he pulled away.

"Forgive me, Lady Bristow." He tried to step out of her embrace and had to pull her arms loose.

"Stay with me." Her words were commanding.

"I must go. It would not be right." He stepped quickly to the door. "Good night." He closed it in her face.

Back in his own room, he locked the door and broke out in a sweat across his forehead and down his back.

The new year had begun, and the castle had become a fortress covered in snow. It would be difficult to leave now because of the ice and snow, but he found himself feeling more and more conflicted and confused by Lady Bristow's behavior. Was she truly having nightmares? Or was she only trying to manipulate him into her bed?

God, show me what to do. He wasn't sure how much longer he could resist the persistent Lady Bristow.

TWENTY

"MAZY, A LETTER CAME FOR YOU TODAY FROM LADY Delia."

Ro handed her the rolled-up missive while Anselm sat recording expenses in the Swan's ledger.

"Thank you." Mazy clutched the letter in her hands, looking forward to sitting down in her room and reading it.

"How are we doing?" Mazy asked, looking over Anselm's shoulder.

Christmas and the New Year celebration had just passed, and winter had set in with a hard freeze and a thick layer of snow on the ground.

They had hired Anselm to help them with running the Swan, and so far he was proving to be competent and things were going smoothly. And he seemed as trustworthy as they had hoped.

Ro, however, had ceased to think about marrying him. She seemed happy to pay him to do a job rather than to marry him.

"We are doing better this month than last," Anselm said, looking at the record book. "But this colder weather may keep people at home."

"I found a woman to help me with the selling in the market."

"Oh? Who is it?" Ro exclaimed.

Mazy explained that one of their suppliers, the one who provided them with woven baskets and embroidered table linens, had moved to London since her ailing husband had died. "She has a daughter who is old enough to stay home with the younger children while she helps me in the market."

"That is wonderful!" Anselm said.

"I'm so glad to hear that, Mazy." Ro indeed looked happy. Now she wouldn't have to run back and forth, helping Anselm in the Swan during the busiest hours, then hurrying back to the market to help Mazy.

Mazy went up to her room and read Lady Delia's missive alone as she rested on her bed.

My dear Mazy,

I still worry so much about you being in London without a protector, since your brother hardly ever visits you. I suspect that there are more dangers than you are telling me of, and I hope you are staying safe. Please try to be careful.

I worry now about my brother Berenger. He has gone to Bristow to decide whether or not to do as the king wishes and marry Lady Bristow, but my dear husband has heard some rumor that is causing me alarm on his behalf. I cannot bear to think of him married to someone who not only is not worthy of him but who may actually harm him. I know I should not worry you, but I only say all this to ask you to pray for him. Pray that God will give him wisdom to act as he should. If this Lady Bristow is truly as bad as the rumors say, then he will need God's wisdom to extricate himself. Forgive me for troubling you, but I know you will pray for him. You have been such a good friend to us both.

Please tell me if you need any help. I would gladly have my husband send you one of his guards, if you needed him, to protect you from the evils of London. There are far too many people there for my taste. I much prefer the quiet and calm of Strachleigh, but I was never as brave as you are, dear Mazy.

After a few more small matters, she closed the letter with, "Your faithful friend, Delia."

Mazy's heart was beating so fast it seemed to trip over itself as she reread the letter. Was Sir Berenger in trouble?

If Lady Bristow had done something bad, surely the king would not have asked Sir Berenger to marry her. But perhaps the king didn't know.

It had been a long time since Mazy had visited John at the Tower of London, and it was only a short walk, hardly a quarter of an hour. So she left Lady Delia's letter in her room, donned her warmest clothes, and went to see him.

Her brother was standing near the gate talking with some other guards when she walked in.

"Sister," John said, turning his back on his fellow guards. He never introduced her as his sister to the other guards. Did he not want them to know her? Or her to know them? Perhaps it was his way of protecting her. The other men cut their eyes at her and dispersed.

"How's everything at the Swan?"

"The man we hired to help us is doing a good job, and Ro and I are well." She knew that if she gave him much more detail than that, he would interrupt her and change the subject.

"How's everything at the Tower of London?" she asked.

"Good." His gaze wandered slowly past her and over his shoulder, as if he was already bored with the conversation.

"I was wondering if you knew anything about Lady Bristow."

"Lady Bristow? Why would you ask about Lady Bristow?" John's eyes snapped back to her, his brows lowering.

"As you know, the king wants Sir Berenger to marry her. Do you know anything about her? Lady Delia mentioned some rumor to me—"

"What rumor? What did Lady Delia say?"

Mazy's stomach churned at how sharply John was looking at her, as well as the edge in his voice.

"She didn't say, just that there was a rumor about Lady Bristow, something bad, but she didn't know if it was true. She was concerned for Sir Berenger."

John was slow to speak, kicking the dirt at his feet, staring down, then out across the Tower Green. "I'm sure Sir Berenger can fend for himself," he drawled, "make his own decision about marrying."

John could be so maddening in his responses.

"But have you heard anything about her? Is there any gossip around the Tower, with the other men?"

"I don't know anything." John did not even glance her way, and she got the sick feeling that he was lying to her. But why would he?

"Did you see her a few weeks ago when she visited the king?" He must have, since he was part of the king's personal guard.

"I saw her."

"Is she a handsome woman?" Her heart sank. Why did she ask that? She didn't want to know.

Again, John was very slow to answer. Finally he said, "She is known for her beauty. Tall, dark hair." He still wasn't looking at her.

"Can you ask around, see if anyone here knows her character?"

"I'm not some old woman who has nothing better to do than gather gossip."

"I know that. I just thought maybe you might hear something about her, if she is a good person or bad, what she is known for, for our friend Sir Berenger's sake."

John said nothing, just shuffled his feet. "Well, I could stand here talking all day, little sister, but I have duties."

"Of course. I don't want to keep you from them."

"From what?"

"Your duties."

He grunted and nodded, then turned and walked away.

His behavior was not so different from the way he usually

acted. But she couldn't help feeling that he knew a lot more than he was saying.

Now she was even more curious to find out about Lady Bristow. If only there was someone she could ask, but her brother was the only person she knew at the king's palace and the Tower of London.

God, please protect Sir Berenger.

Mazy had once heard one of the Swan's regular customers tell Ro that his wife worked as Queen Anne's favorite lady's maid and therefore heard a lot of the gossip about other nobles. And now that she had someone working for her in the market, she could go back to the Swan early to watch for him.

Mazy looked up from the letter she was writing to Lady Delia and saw the very man enter and sit on a stool near the door. Ro started toward him, but Mazy stopped her.

"I'll wait on this one." Mazy approached the man. "What can I get for you?"

"Ale and stew," he said.

"I'll get it forthwith."

Ro was already dishing up the stew, then she fetched the ale. "He always gets the same thing," Ro said. "I'll go with you and tell him who you are, and maybe he will be more inclined to trust you."

"Good idea."

They delivered the man's meal and Ro said, "Mazy, this is Reginald Worsley. Reginald, this is Mazy, the daughter of the

Baron Wexcombe. She and I have been working together for years."

The man leaned back, studying Mazy.

"She's a trustworthy soul, just looking for some information to help a friend. You may not be able to help her, but . . ." Ro shrugged her shoulder.

"What is it you want to know?" Reginald Worsley looked out of heavy-lidded eyes, and Ro went back to her duties.

"I have a friend," Mazy began, "a knight named Sir Berenger, who has been asked by the king to marry a widow. There have been some rumors about this widow, and . . . I'd just like to help him know the truth before he marries her. He is a good man, you see. A very good man." Tears sprang up out of nowhere. Mazy coughed and cleared her throat to get rid of them.

"The widow of the Earl of Bristow."

"Yes." Mazy's heart leapt. Perhaps he did know something.

The man eyed Mazy a moment before speaking. "I have heard of this knight and the likelihood of marriage to Lady Bristow. I shall—only because I trust Ro—I shall see what I can find out."

"Thank you. I would be very grateful. Thank you."

The man nodded, grabbed his spoon, and began to eat his stew.

God, thank You. It was nothing yet, but at least it was the first step toward possibly discovering something that would help Sir Berenger.

The next day Mazy was helping serve customers when Reginald Worsley came in and sat down at the same table as the day before. He locked eyes with Mazy.

She hurried toward him.

"Sit." He nodded at the stool beside him.

She sat and waited.

"What I'm about to tell you can never be tied to me or to my wife. You are never to say that we told you anything."

"Of course. You have my word. I will not tell."

"I don't have facts, only hearsay, you understand."

"Yes, I understand."

"Though the king refuses to believe it, many say that the lady in question poisoned her husband with death cap mushrooms. The king apparently questioned her over the matter, but she persuaded him after much weeping and protesting that the rumors were lies. She also has misled the king about the little girl who lives with her, saying she is her cousin, but she's actually the dead earl's brother's child. The child is the true heir to Bristow Castle, which is why she keeps her parentage a secret."

Mazy's heart pounded sickeningly. "That is so evil."

"But I never told you any of this." Reginald stared intently into her eyes.

"No, but I am so grateful to you. Very grateful. If you ever need anything . . ."

"Ale and stew are all I need today." His expression lightened a bit. "And I'm glad if it helps save the young knight's life."

Mazy fetched the man his ale and stew and whispered to Ro, "Don't charge Reginald Worsley anything."

Ro's eyes brightened. "He helped?"

"Yes."

Mazy had to warn Sir Berenger, but she could not trust this information to a letter. She would have to tell him in person.

Berenger kept thinking about Lady Bristow's behavior the night before. He remembered the way she had practically begged him to kiss her, the feel of her lips on his.

She could be crafty and sly. He still wondered why she had likely lied about the shipwreck. He also still felt quite unsettled about the way she treated Juliana, though he'd never seen her mistreat the child, and she often spoke kindly to her. Juliana had warmed up to Berenger but was stiff and untalkative when Lady Bristow was nearby. But he did feel much compassion toward Lady Bristow regarding the way she'd been so wronged by her first husband.

He was not ready to make a decision about marrying her. He knew he would have everything he always wanted if he married her, as she did seem to love him and have great affection for him. But he still had doubts that nibbled at the edges of his mind like a mouse nibbling a sheet of parchment. And he couldn't help but feel that little Juliana was the key to understanding and to either putting his doubts to rest or confirming them.

He didn't want to upset Juliana, but perhaps he might be able to talk to her about it, since she seemed to trust him now. So he went in search of her in the tiny room where he had been told not to disturb her, as she was being tutored by her nurse.

He kept his footsteps quiet and eased up to the doorway and peeked inside.

Juliana was bent over a white cloth in her lap. The needle in her hand went in and out of the cloth as the child gave it all of her attention.

She suddenly sneezed.

"Juliana!" the nurse exclaimed and hurried over to her. "Did you sneeze on the cloth? If Lady Bristow sees that you soiled your work, she will have both our heads on a platter."

"I am sorry. I don't think it's soiled. It will dry and—"

Her nurse gasped.

"What?"

The nurse tried to snatch the cloth from Juliana just as a drop of blood dripped from the child's nose onto the cloth.

"No!" The nurse's anguished whisper seemed to echo through the room as they both stared at the bright red stain.

Juliana burst into tears, holding her hand to her nose to try to stop the bleeding.

The nurse put down the embroidery and found a cloth and gave it to Juliana. "Here, take this and try to stop crying. It will only make it worse. Stuff it up your nose and hold your head up." She gently tilted the child's head up, even as she continued to cry.

Juliana held the cloth to her nose, tears streaming down her cheeks as the nurse tried to comfort her.

"It's not your fault," she said. The young servant looked ready to cry herself.

Was Lady Bristow so cruel and exacting? Juliana looked hardly old enough to be learning to embroider, especially not anything important, and it was not her fault if the cloth became soiled from a nosebleed.

Berenger's chest ached as he wanted so badly to stride into the room and reassure the child and her nurse that Lady Bristow would not be angry and that all would be well. But something held him back.

He needed to see Lady Bristow's reaction when she did not know he was watching. He didn't want to be foolhardy, after all, assuming he knew her, when he had only known her a few weeks and several incidents had raised concerns.

He shrank back out of the doorway and went in search of Lady Bristow. He found her in the kitchen, instructing the cook about what to prepare for the evening meal.

"Sir Berenger. I was just about to go and find you," she said with a radiant smile.

Such a smile should have made his heart leap in his chest, but somehow all he could see was the panic and horror on little Juliana's face and her nurse's when they contemplated this lady discovering the stain on the child's embroidery. Suddenly Lady Bristow did not seem so beautiful and appealing.

But he couldn't judge her. Not until he saw her reaction for himself.

"Shall we take Juliana for another walk on the seashore?" he asked Lady Bristow.

She continued to smile at him, but her eyes changed, darkening. She moved away from the cook and took his arm.

"I would be pleased—delighted—to take another walk with you," she said in the same low voice she had used the previous night, leaning very close to his ear. "But we can go without Juliana. She is still engaged in her lessons."

"Can she not take a rest from her lessons and walk with us?"

Lady Bristow laughed, a short, throaty chuckle. "I am sure you think girls have nothing very important to learn, but if we take her away from her lessons every day, she will grow up to be a know-nothing simpleton."

"Well, we cannot have that. But it can do no harm for one day. Only for an hour or two. As a favor to me?" He looked her straight in the eye, stopping in the middle of the hallway outside the kitchen.

"How can I deny you anything?" She stared at his lips. "Anything you want."

"Good. Will you go and fetch her while I change my shirt?"

Lady Bristow seemed to bristle. "Fetch her?"

"Forgive me. I do not mean to offend you."

"Very well, go on and I shall fetch the child." She waved him away with her hand.

"I shall be back down shortly." He hurried to the staircase and took the stairs two at a time while Lady Bristow watched him from below.

As soon as he was out of her sight, he waited but a moment before peeking back down the stairs. The lady was moving away toward the room where Juliana and her nurse were probably still trying to repair the stained embroidery.

Berenger did his best to sneak silently down the stairs. At

the bottom, he peeked around the corner to see Lady Bristow entering Juliana's room.

Berenger hurried the rest of the way down the hall, stopping just outside the door and standing very still.

Lady Bristow's voice was harsh and strident. "What is this? A stain? On the pillowcase you were told to make?"

There was silence, and then soft sobs.

"I shall teach you to be careless," she said in the same cold rasp. "You shall not go on the walk with Sir Berenger. You shall not be allowed outside the castle until you learn to be more careful." The accusation in her voice made it sound as if she were blaming the child for some heinous crime or outright rebellion.

Berenger could stand it no longer. He stepped into the room and said, "Is Juliana ready to go for a walk?" Then he feigned surprise at seeing her crying. "What is the matter, little one?" He went to her, sank to one knee beside her, and gathered her in his arms, though her body was stiff, as if she was terrified.

"It is nothing," Lady Bristow said quickly. "She has been naughty and says she does not wish to go for a walk with us." She changed her voice as she addressed the child. "No matter. We shall go on our walk without you, Juliana, but I hope you shall have thought better of your little temperamental fit by the time we return."

Berenger's heart broke in two at the obvious pain of the child while he grew warm at hearing Lady Bristow lie so blatantly.

"I think I'd like to stay here with Juliana," Berenger said. "You may go on a walk without me." He smiled gently at the child, whose wide eyes fastened on him.

"Well." Lady Bristow huffed out a breath. "May I remind you that taking a walk was your idea, Sir Berenger?"

"You are right. But I was only using that as an excuse to spend some time with Juliana. What are we doing?" he went on quickly, speaking to Juliana. "Surely we are not knitting a blanket or sewing a dress or some other dull thing like that?" He winked at Juliana and smiled at her poor nurse, who looked nearly as wide-eyed as Juliana.

"We should play a game." He glanced around the room. "Are there no games here? No nine-men's morris or backgammon?"

"Not in here," the nurse replied.

Lady Bristow's arms were crossed over her chest and she was staring with a blank expression at Berenger.

"I have important matters to attend to." Lady Bristow turned on her heel and left the room.

Berenger looked at Juliana. "What would you like to play? What is your favorite game?"

The child gazed at him, still frozen in place.

"She likes it when I tell her a story," the nurse said, "but she doesn't know any games."

"I shall teach you one, then."

Berenger taught them what he called the small-child version of blindman's buff, in which no one can hit, only tap with one finger. After a few minutes of playing, he finally saw a smile on Juliana's face.

"You caught me! You win!" He leaned down until his face was level with hers.

Juliana let out a giggle, then gasped, putting a hand over her mouth as if she was afraid of the sound coming from her own throat.

"I am so glad to see you smiling and happy, Juliana. It's good to laugh and play. Did you know that?"

But she kept her hand over her mouth.

His decision was made. But what would happen when he told Lady Bristow that he could not marry her? And how could he leave this child here to be treated so coldly, devoid of all joy in life?

His stomach sank at the thought that Lady Bristow was not all that he hoped she might be. He would have to inform the king as well. Would the king be angry? Would he even believe Berenger?

He certainly had many things to ask God for, not least of which was His protection over himself and Juliana, for Berenger now knew that he could not leave the child to Lady Bristow's guardianship.

TWENTY-ONE

WINTER HAD WRAPPED ITS ICY FINGERS AROUND ENGLAND, but in spite of foul weather, Mazy would carry the information she had learned to Sir Berenger.

She packed a saddlebag the very night she heard what Reginald had to say about Lady Bristow, and the next morning she went to the Tower of London to ask her brother if he would go with her.

"How long will this trip take?"

"Three or four days there and three or four days back."

"Can you not ask Ro's father to go with you?"

"He died." She had told him that.

Sir John grunted, a squinting look on his face. "Where are you going?"

"To Bristow Castle to see Sir Berenger."

He flinched when she said Bristow Castle. "I know something of this Lady Bristow. You had better not be thinking of crossing her. She is not a sweet, innocent maiden like you, Mazy, so stay away from her."

"What do you mean?" Ah, so he hadn't been forthcoming with her before. Would he reveal what he knew of Lady Bristow? Her heart was in her throat. She was more convinced than ever that she needed to warn Sir Berenger.

After so long a pause she thought he wasn't going to speak, he said, "Do not go to Bristow Castle."

"I'm going, with or without you."

Again, he was silent for several moments, then finally said, "You can't go by yourself."

"Then go with me."

"I can't."

Mazy tried not to let herself feel disappointed. After all, she hadn't really expected him to leave his duties to help her. "Can you recommend someone, a knight or a trustworthy guard who would go for a small amount of money?"

He said nothing for a long time, then, "I know of one guard who might go with you. But I'm telling you, you shouldn't go. If you go, your fate is in your own hands. I am not responsible for you."

"I understand. Can we ask him now? I would like to leave today."

"Today? You're not asking for much, are you?" He raised his brows and frowned. "I can't promise I can find him. Wait here."

She waited as her brother set out across the Tower Green at a rather slow pace. He couldn't be bothered with hurrying, not for her.

John's behavior had many times made her realize how little he must care about her, but if he found a trustworthy guard to go with her to warn Sir Berenger, it would be more than he had done for her since her father died.

Once she'd been a baron's daughter, protected and loved by her father. Now she was alone. She'd learned to trust Ro and her father, and to trust in her own abilities, but her place in the world was precarious at best.

At least she still believed in Sir Berenger's character. He was a good man, with a good heart, who loved his brothers and sister very much, and he'd always been attentive to her, she who was no actual relation to him. She had to try to protect him.

She saw John coming toward her with a man by his side, a man with gray hair and a gray beard.

"Mazy, this is Giles. Giles, this is my only sister, Mazy."

Giles bowed to her. "You need my assistance, my lady?"

"If you are willing to accompany me to Suffolk, I need protection for eight days of traveling, possibly nine." She told him how much she was willing to pay him. "Is it sufficient?"

"Yes, my lady."

She should probably stop him from calling her a lady, but it hardly mattered, she supposed. But since John had not called him "Sir Giles," she assumed he was not a knight but only a guard.

"Can you set out with me today?" she asked him.

"I shall be ready in less than an hour."

"Good. Meet me at the Swan when you are ready."

He nodded to her and hurried back the way he had come.

"Mazy, I hope you are not going to get into some kind of conflict with Lady Bristow," John said, turning his head to spit on the ground.

"I was not planning to."

"Good, because she may look like a kitten, but she has the teeth of a lioness and would not hesitate to tear you apart."

Mazy wanted to assert that she was capable of taking care of herself, but since she wanted him to elaborate, she tried to look confused. "What do you mean? You make it sound as if you know her and have had dealings with her."

John stared into the distance with a blank look on his face. "Just stay away from her. That's my advice to you, little sister. Sir Berenger is a man. He can take care of himself."

"I am no one. I am not even a baron's daughter anymore. I will be invisible to Lady Bristow, so don't worry about me."

"Just don't become her enemy." And without another word, he turned and walked away.

"Thank you for your help," Mazy said. But John did not acknowledge her thanks, if he heard her.

An hour later, true to his word, Giles arrived at the Swan, leading his horse by the bridle. Mazy had already bid Ro fare well, and moments later, they set out on horseback on the north road out of London.

After her brother had warned her about Lady Bristow, she had prayed and asked God if perhaps she should go to Strachleigh to tell Lady Delia what she had learned. After all, Lady Delia could send her husband, the Duke of Strachleigh, and some of his men with her to tell Sir Berenger what she had learned about Lady Bristow, in case there was trouble.

But going straight to Bristow Castle in Suffolk would save a couple of days. And if Sir Berenger was in danger, a few days could make all the difference.

As she rode, she closed her eyes, quieted her mind, and prayed, *God, where should I go? To speak to Lady Delia? Or to Sir Berenger?*

In her mind the words instantly appeared: *Go to Sir Berenger at Bristow Castle.*

God, are You sure? She waited, wondering at herself for asking God such a question, but she heard nothing else.

God was sending her, so He would surely protect her and Sir Berenger.

God was also with the martyrs, but they still died.

She shook her head at the morbid thought.

God, Sir Berenger is a good man, and he is my friend. Use me to keep him safe. Help him, God. And help me.

They would have to cover long distances every day to reach Bristow Castle quickly, so they only stopped when the horses needed water and a rest and kept going until the sun was setting, sleeping under the trees most nights.

Giles said very little. Before they left, she did find out that he was a guard at the Tower and had been from a young age, that his wife had had a child a few months before who was sickly, and that they had spent a lot of money on physicians and healers trying to make him well. She was glad she had paid him so well.

Berenger had been dreading seeing Lady Bristow, knowing what he had to do. He still hadn't quite decided how to tell her or how he would take Juliana with him when he left. And as they sat together at the evening meal, Lady Bristow touched his arm, and he had to force himself not to recoil.

"This castle was rebuilt fifty years ago after it was destroyed by fire." She had told him this before.

"Yes, I know." He continued to eat, trying to behave as if nothing was amiss.

"It is very solid, and King Richard called it essential and strategic in defending England."

"It is a very impressive castle. I am sure King Richard values it, and so should he."

"So you like the castle?"

"Of course."

"It is only me you do not like."

"I never said I did not like you."

"But you are judging me for not being more motherly to Juliana. You think I am too . . . I can't imagine what. And now my heart is broken from your rejection." Lady Bristow covered her face with her hands.

"I have not rejected you." *Not yet.*

What could he say? He did not want to lie, and he had made

up his mind not to marry her. He just was not sure how to tell her, and it seemed she had noticed that he was not believing her deceptions anymore.

"You do not know what I have suffered, the cruelties at the hands of the earl, my husband." She dabbed at her eyes with a cloth.

"I do not know. You are right." He was reluctant to think she was lying about her husband. Perhaps he had been cruel to her and that much was true.

"And the child has hated me since she came to live here. Besides that, I don't know how to be a mother. But if you help me . . . with your help, I can change. Will that make you happy?"

"I am sure I would never ask you to change for me. You must do what you know to be right."

Her jaw hardened as she pursed her lips.

"You speak in riddles, and still you refuse to tell me if I will be your wife, if you will do as the king wishes and marry me."

Perhaps it was wrong of him not to tell her the truth now. But something made him wait.

"I shall give you my answer very soon." After he had notified his men and packed up his things.

Again, her jaw clenched. "Very well, but you should not let Juliana convince you that she is always calm and good and behaves well. She has given the servants so many bruises with her tantrums, kicking and screaming, biting and hitting. It has taken me a year to get her under control, and I fear you will undo all the good I've done for her."

Lady Bristow stared down at her food, pushing it around with her knife.

"I am sorry you have had so much trouble with Juliana. We played together quite pleasantly with her nurse."

Lady Bristow continued to stare down at her food.

"You understand nothing about children." She looked up, gazing at him with round, wide eyes.

He bristled at her condescending remark. "As you know, I have no children and have not been responsible for any, but I was a child once. Children do have feelings and thoughts, just as adults do."

"Why are you punishing me for the child's sake?"

"I am not punishing you. That is not something I would do."

She huffed out a breath. "Then perhaps you should trust my judgment instead of trying to take control. I have had charge over the child for a year now and I know what is best for her."

"Very well." Berenger was determined to say nothing more. He just had to bide his time and be ready to leave in the next couple of days.

He would pretend to acquiesce to her, but he was not willing to leave Juliana to this woman's care, even if he had to take her away by force.

"Men never understand the care of a child the way women do." Lady Bristow shook her head and smiled, as though trying to lighten the mood.

He could point out that she admitted she did not know how to care for a child, giving the excuse of her husband's bad treatment. Although now that excuse seemed like manipulation.

She may truly have suffered at the hands of her first husband. He may have abused her, as Berenger knew for certain that many women were treated abominably by their husbands. But at this point he couldn't help but question the truth of anything she might say.

The plight of women was so often ignored by those who should rescue and support them. Berenger would always consider it his privilege and duty to rescue any woman who needed his help. But in this case it was Juliana who needed his help.

The servants had brought out the last course of food and Lady Bristow had eaten very little.

"Are you well?" he asked.

Lady Bristow rubbed her temple. "I have a headache. I think I will go to bed early tonight." She rose from the table. "Will you walk with me to my room?"

He didn't want to, but he also couldn't deny her request, in case she was truly ill.

She clung to his arm all the way up the stairs.

"Should I send for a servant to take care of you? Do you need something—a glass of wine, perhaps—to help you sleep?"

"No, no, I will be well."

He feared she would try to kiss him again, as she had the night before, but instead, she gave him a wan smile and went into her room, slowly closing the door behind her.

Berenger went into his own room to get his cloak. He wanted to speak to his men about being prepared to leave at a moment's notice. While most of the guards were Lady Bristow's, he had brought two of his own guards.

But as he glanced out the window toward the sea, he saw a ship on the water. It seemed to be heading straight toward the cove where he and Juliana had explored when they were searching for shells.

He strained his eyes to see what sort of flag the ship was flying, but there was none.

A soft knock sounded outside in the hallway, seemingly from Lady Bristow's door.

He hurried to open his own door just a crack so he could listen.

He heard Lady Bristow harshly whisper, "Do you not think I saw it? Go away."

The door shut with a soft *click*.

Berenger stuck his head out and saw a male servant hurrying away from her door.

He ducked back inside his room. The ship was getting closer and soon appeared to be anchored inside the cove.

He remembered how Juliana reacted when she realized they were in that very cove.

He put on his cloak and left his room as quietly as he could, then made his way outside. Thankfully it was a bit warmer tonight, and he set out toward the shore where the ship was anchored.

Behind him, he heard a noise. He stepped off the path and hid behind a tree, hoping whoever had made the noise had not seen him.

As he watched, a figure came down the secluded, dark path carrying a lantern. The figure looked to be the height of Lady

Bristow, but the person wore a hood over her head that concealed her face. Was it one of the servants?

The woman passed by his hiding place and continued down the path. Berenger waited a few moments, then, carefully picking his way to avoid making noise, he followed.

The moon was pale and not very high in the sky, so he could clearly see the light from the lantern, except when a bend in the path caused trees to block his view. He stayed what he hoped was a safe distance behind.

On the sandy shore he continued in the dark behind the figure. The wind lapping the waves against the shore masked any sound his footsteps might have made on the crunchy layer of snow.

The figure made its way to the cove where the ship was anchored. As the woman rounded the bend, he hurried to catch up so he could see what happened next.

He rounded the same bend just as the hood blew off and revealed Lady Bristow, her skirt blowing against her legs, striding toward a man dressed in the clothing of a sailor.

Berenger tried to stay in the shadows, but he drew nearer, hoping to hear their exchange. Thankfully the cove was partially sheltered from the noise of the wind.

"Milady," the man said with a French accent, bowing. Then, speaking in French, he said something Berenger did not understand.

Berenger could see Lady Bristow's smirk in the lantern light. The man was leaning close to her now, his face less than the span of his hand from hers.

Lady Bristow held out a small, rolled-up parchment, and the man took it from her. Then he placed in her hand a leather pouch, like the ones used for carrying coins. Lady Bristow put it in her skirt pocket, just before her arms came up to wrap around the sailor's neck.

He put an arm around her and they kissed rather violently—quite unlike the kiss Lady Bristow had planted on his lips. Berenger's stomach twisted.

The two parted. The man seemed to be trying to coax her to go with him back to the ship, but Lady Bristow shook her head and pulled back.

There was nowhere on the sandy shore for him to hide, so Berenger turned and hurried away. Would Lady Bristow's light catch him? If she sounded the alarm, no doubt the French sailors or pirates or whoever they were would have crossbows and would give chase.

But he rounded the bend without being detected. The only light now was from the pale moon, and he could barely see anything, even his feet beneath him. But that was good. Lady Bristow would not be able to see him either.

He must have missed the path that led back to the castle. Instead, he plunged into the trees that came up to meet the sand of the shore. He waited there, watching for Lady Bristow to come into view.

He did not have to wait long. She must have refused the man's invitation and continued on her way back, alone, with her lantern. She found the path and set out up the hill to the castle, her stride purposeful.

This was serious indeed. Mistreating the child was enough to make up Berenger's mind against marrying her, but was Lady Bristow consorting with the French, England's enemy? She was handing over missives and receiving money. Could she be anything other than a spy for them? A traitor to King Richard and to England?

Though he had no real evidence, certainly it was enough to speak to the king about. In fact, he had a duty to tell the king, who would then no doubt question Lady Bristow about it. But how much better would it be if Berenger could get to the bottom of the lady's treachery?

Could anything this lady had said be true? The worst part was how she may have duped the king. Could she have discovered important information through her friendship and visit with the king and divulged it to the enemy?

He wished he could find some kind of evidence he could show the king.

He waited a few more moments, then found the path the lady had just taken and walked back toward the castle. He took a turn around the other side of the castle, coming in from the opposite side, away from the ocean shore.

A few candles were lit near the castle's front entrance, so he took one to light his way back to his room. All was quiet as he mounted the stairs, but as he was passing Lady Bristow's door, it opened.

"Sir Berenger." She looked surprised.

"My lady." He bowed to her.

Be calm. Don't look nervous or she'll be suspicious.

Twenty-Two

"Where have you been?" Lady Bristow asked him.

"I took a walk to the village." *God, forgive me for the lie.*

"To the village? Why?"

"I was restless. I thought I would get some air and stretch my legs."

She stared hard at his face, holding up her lantern. "You look a bit flushed. Did you encounter anyone on your way there and back?"

"No one. Everyone must be abed. And you, my lady? Are you feeling better? Did you get some rest?"

"My headache is gone and I feel much better. Thank you for asking."

"You do look remarkably well," he said.

"As do you. Would you like to come into my room and have a cup of wine?"

He did need to see the inside of her room.

"Yes. I will come in, for a moment."

She gave him a smile as she stepped aside to let him into her room, but her eyes remained cold.

Berenger quickly glanced around. There was a screen to one side, a large trunk against the wall near it, and on the other side of the room was her bed; beside it a tall mullioned window looked out toward the sea. Would the ship be visible from that window? He was almost certain it would be, any lights on the ship serving as a beacon or signal.

Lady Bristow started walking toward the bed, letting her fingertips lightly tap his arm.

"Come and sit here beside me." She sat in a cushioned chair, and Berenger sat in the one next to it. Lady Bristow poured wine into two cups.

She smiled that beguiling smile—the one he had thought so warm and inviting just a few days ago—as she handed him the cup.

They each took a sip, then he set down his cup on a small table.

"Do you not care for this wine?" Her voice took on a deeper tone. "I'm sure it would take much more than this to make a man like you drunk."

"I rarely drink wine."

"The French have their wine and the English their ale." Lady Bristow laughed, a guttural sound. "Honest to a fault, are you not, Sir Berenger?"

"I try to be honest, Lady Bristow."

"Call me Catherine. I should dearly love to hear you say my Christian name." She leaned quite close, her eyes heavy-lidded. She was staring at his lips.

The image of her kissing the stranger on the beach flashed like lightning through his mind.

"Catherine, tell me about your father and mother. I don't think you've ever told me about them."

Her expression changed, going hard. She straightened.

"Whyever would you want to talk of something so dull as that?"

"Is that dull?"

"My father was a baron, my mother the daughter of a baron. What else is there to tell?"

He'd hoped she might reveal a connection to France. To ask outright about any French relations might cast him in too suspicious a light.

"My mother was the daughter of Lord Fairchild," Berenger said. "He was a landowner in Bedfordshire. Tell me something about your mother."

"My mother? She had my two brothers and me. My older brother inherited my father's barony when my father died a few years ago. My mother died when I was fifteen. Is there anything else you wish to know?"

"I am very sorry you lost your mother at such a young age. I lost my mother when I was almost nine years old."

"That must have broken your heart." She made a sympathetic moue with her lips.

"Yes, but my brothers and sister and I are very close. We have always taken care of each other."

"My brothers were not very good to me, I'm afraid. I grew to especially hate my older brother."

"Was he cruel to you?"

"Are you always so inquisitive? Drink some more wine." She tapped the cup with her fingernail, a playful smile on her lips, but her eyes seemed cold, staring back at him.

He took another sip but watched her carefully.

"There. Isn't that a pleasant taste? I must say, I can't imagine how you men can drink so much ale. Wine is much better, do you not think?"

"Indeed. I have heard the best wine is grown in France. Where is this wine from?"

"France, I would wager." She gave him a narrowed look from over the rim of the cup as she took a healthy gulp.

He stared at her, wondering how he might ask her more about her connection to France, and also wondering if the ship was still just off the shore.

Perhaps it was not so wise to come into her room. He was playing a rather dangerous game.

"It is late, and I won't keep you awake any longer, especially since you were not feeling well earlier."

"I am quite well now, as you see, so do not use my health as an excuse for leaving." She leaned closer to him.

"Very well. Then I think I should leave for the reason that it is not seemly and does not set a good example for the servants for me to be alone with you in your room so late at night."

"Ah. It is for the servants, and for my reputation, that you wish to go. But if we intend to marry, you will not have to worry about my reputation."

"That, of course, is the reason I am here at Bristow Castle—to decide if we are to marry. And if we do not marry, you will marry someone else. Therefore, I must go."

He rose quickly and headed to the door.

Lady Bristow caught up with him just as he opened the door, her long fingers closing around his arm. "Stay with me," she whispered. "I shall make you glad you did."

She pulled his head down and kissed him. He did not kiss her back this time.

"I'm sorry, my lady, but I must go." He tried to be as gentle as possible, even tried to look as if he was tempted to stay. "You are so very beautiful," he whispered, then leaned down, as if he was about to kiss her. Then he turned, pulling out of her grasp, and hastily stepped out the door.

Once in his room, he closed the door and slid the crossbar into place.

He rushed to his own window and looked out. The ship was now so far away he could just make it out on the dark sea.

He rubbed a hand down his cheek. What sort of predicament had he almost married into? Lady Bristow consorting with the French, possibly selling information to them, and mistreating her child ward? He took a deep breath and let it out slowly.

He had to find the answers to his questions, protect the innocent, bring the guilty to justice, and then make his escape from this fortress of snow and ice.

TWENTY-THREE

BERENGER HAD KNOWN SINCE THE DAY BEFORE THAT HE had to tell Lady Bristow he couldn't marry her. He'd even quietly packed his things into his saddlebags. As for the lady, she seemed to be avoiding him.

When he had finally found himself alone with her earlier at the evening meal, he told her.

"I know this is not what we both had hoped, but I have come to the decision that I cannot marry you. Please forgive me, but I am sure you will have no trouble finding someone else to marry you and—"

"You would reject me like this? Am I to have no explanation for why you would give up everything you could ever want?"

He knew this wouldn't be easy. "I am sorry. I will leave in the morning."

"No explanation." She stared at him, her expression tense, her eyes wild.

"I have made observations that convinced me that we are not suited for one another."

She just stared. "After all that I said to you, how I was willing to give you everything."

"Forgive me for causing you pain."

"I do not forgive you." Her face crumpled, but he no longer trusted the sincerity of her tears.

"I cannot believe this."

She made a face of one who was crying, but he failed to see any tears.

"You will leave me, after I've fallen in love with you? I never thought you were so cruel."

She leaned toward him, and he actually had to force himself not to take her in his arms. Was he so easily manipulated? He reminded himself of how insincere she could be, and the memory of her treatment of Juliana soon helped him to steel himself against her machinations.

"I am also taking Juliana with me," he told her. "She needs a change, I think, and my sister, the Duchess of Strachleigh, is very fond of children."

"Who do you think you are? You will do no such thing."

"I think it best for both you and the child."

"I shall write to the king and tell him how you are trying to steal the child for your own purposes."

"Do as you please, but I will be leaving with Juliana."

She glared at him. Finally, she stood up slowly, then regally walked toward the stairs. He heard her footsteps as she went up to her room.

Berenger quickly left the table as well, going to talk to his men about being ready to leave the next day and warning them that there might be trouble.

"We are leaving in the morning," Berenger said, making sure to speak to them outside the guards' barracks. "The lady has been treating the child cruelly, so we will take her to Strachleigh until I figure out what to do."

"Yes, sir. We will be ready." They both looked resolved, and he left them.

Finally, just after dark on the fourth day, Mazy and Giles rode up the hill toward Bristow Castle.

Soon, perhaps within minutes, she would see Sir Berenger.

Her heart beat fast. What would she say to him? He would think she had lost her mind, but she would tell him what she had heard from Reginald Worsley.

Would he be offended? Would he believe her? Would he be embarrassed at her coming all this way to warn him? Or would he be grateful for the information? If he tried to embrace her, would she jerk back in fear? She would soon find out.

The road was dark, lit by only a small bit of moonlight. Giles led the way.

When they reached the top of the hill, she could see the massive castle, with its multiple levels and towers. This was what Sir Berenger could expect to be master of, could pass down to his children, if he were to marry Lady Bristow.

Perhaps he had already married her.

The thought sent a cold chill through her.

Mazy and Giles dismounted near the entrance to the castle, as no one had been guarding the gatehouse. Giles took their horses to the stable and Mazy approached the front door.

As she reached out to grasp the brass knocker, the door opened. Sir Berenger stood holding a candle.

"Good evening." Mazy gave him her best smile and waited.

"Mazy?" His mouth fell open, then he quickly put his arms around her, pulling her into his chest.

She didn't shrink back. Instead, she embraced him. All too soon, though, he pulled away.

"How did you get here? Did you come all this way alone?" He looked behind her, then motioned for her to come inside.

"I was accompanied by a guard. His name is Giles. He's taking the horses to the stable now, as we have ridden hard for four days." She said abruptly, "I have something important to tell you."

This was not how she had intended to greet him, her words tumbling out in this way.

She wanted to say, "You look so handsome." The breath went out of her and her hands started to shake. Why had she come here? Was it truly for his safety? Or was she so in love with him that she could not bear for him to marry another woman? *God, tell me what to say.*

When Berenger got back to the castle, coming in from the back, he heard someone at the front door and opened it.

Mazy. How could it be that she was here in Suffolk? Had his thoughts conjured her up? He'd been thinking about her all day, how glad he would be to go back to London and see her.

He stared at her beautiful face, her earnest expression, and his heart seemed to beat out of his chest. He brought his attention back to what she was saying when he heard, "I have something important to tell you."

Steps on the stairs. Was Lady Bristow coming down?

"Come with me," he said, hurrying her out. "It is so good to see you."

As soon as he'd closed the door and was sure no one could see them, he embraced her again. Oh, how he had missed her, and how good it was to have her in his arms. But not wishing to make her uncomfortable, he soon let her go, much sooner than he would have liked.

"It is good to see you too." Mazy looked relieved and happy, and his heart did a strange flip inside his chest.

"I must be frightful to look at after riding for four long days." She looked down at herself.

"On the contrary, you look beautiful." He said it with a smile, hoping his words did not make her uncomfortable, his breath a white fog in the cold evening air.

They were standing in the bailey between the castle and the gatehouse, but a small stand of trees would block them from view of the castle if anyone was looking out.

"I know you must be exhausted. Forgive me, but it's safer to talk out here." Perhaps he shouldn't have said "safer." He didn't want to alarm Mazy.

"That is good. I shall tell you quickly why I came and pray you don't get angry with me."

What could Mazy ever say that would make him angry with her? "You may always speak freely with me."

"Very well." She lowered her voice, forcing him to lean down to hear her. "I have heard from a reliable source that Lady Bristow's child ward is not her cousin but the deceased Lord Bristow's brother's child, a child who would inherit this estate if her parentage were known."

This was an important revelation indeed. If it was true, Juliana could be free from Lady Bristow!

"It is good of you to come here and tell me this." Truly, it was more than good. His heart ached at the self-sacrifice of her actions, traveling in the dead of winter.

"I wanted to warn you about her character," she whispered. "There is more. There are also rumors that she poisoned her husband, that he died at her hands. There is no proof and it is only a rumor, but I wanted to tell you to be cautious. Even John said she was dangerous."

Had she really killed her husband? Rumors weren't always true, of course, but they usually had at least an element of truth.

"Thank you, Mazy. I am grateful. Where is your guard, so that I may thank him too?"

"He will probably stay the night in the stable with the horses or the grooms."

"I will pay him for his service."

"There is no need, as I am paying him."

Berenger took her hand between both of his. "You are so brave and capable."

Again, his heart was beating out of his chest. He'd saved Mazy once, and now she was here to save him. Truly, she scrambled his thoughts until he could think of nothing but taking her in his arms and kissing her.

But that thought brought him back to where they were and who was nearby.

"We must take great care. Lady Bristow is inside the castle."

"Should I stay in the village tonight? Lady Bristow will find my presence suspicious."

"We will tell her that you are on your way to Strachleigh to visit my sister. Besides, I want to keep you close so I can be sure you're safe. Come." He started to lead her toward the castle and stopped. "Mazy? Thank you."

"Of course." The way she gazed up at him . . . those innocent but courageous eyes . . .

He had to think clearly, to keep her safe and to get Juliana out of the castle, and soon.

They proceeded toward the castle, still not encountering anyone until they were inside.

"Sir Berenger? Is that you?" Lady Bristow was coming down the stairs. Her face was red and her eyes were wet. "The guards say that a strange man asked to put up two horses in the stable and—oh. Who is this?"

The way she approached them put him in mind of a wild cat he had once seen stalking a rabbit.

"Lady Bristow, this is Mazy, the daughter of Baron Wexcombe. She is on her way to visit my sister in Strachleigh and stopped here with her guard to rest their horses."

"Oh." Lady Bristow tilted her head to one side. "And how does she know you?"

"I stayed with Lady Strachleigh for a short time when I was younger, after my father died," Mazy answered.

"I see."

A short silence ensued, then Berenger said, "Perhaps she could have something to eat and the servants could get a room ready for her?"

"She is to be our guest, then." Lady Bristow's expression was quite cold. She turned and walked away without another word.

Mazy's heart was still in her throat after meeting Lady Bristow. She was as cold and frightening as Mazy had imagined. She was also quite beautiful. Was Sir Berenger still hoping to marry her? He hadn't said he wouldn't, and this castle was most desirable for any knight, as valuable as Lady Bristow was beautiful.

Sir Berenger walked with Mazy toward the kitchen.

Mazy whispered, "I shall leave first thing in the morning."

"The child and I will be leaving with you," Sir Berenger whispered back.

As they entered the kitchen, two servants were still inside, working. They smiled when they saw Sir Berenger.

"Good evening," he said pleasantly. "Is there anything you can gather together for a late supper for this young lady?"

"Yes, of course," they said, quickly scurrying about. "Shall we take it to her room?"

"I can eat it here," Mazy said, "and I'm sure Giles would appreciate some food as well."

"He already came and we supplied him," a servant said.

"Oh, thank you very much." Mazy sat down and realized just how tired and sore she was, almost too tired to be hungry. One of the servants put down a plate of food in front of her. She took a bite of a fruit pasty, the flavor of plums and fried dough spreading over her tongue, making her close her eyes and exhale in bliss.

Perhaps she wasn't too tired to eat after all.

Sir Berenger talked to her while she ate, though she could tell he was only talking about unimportant things, not what was truly on his mind. He couldn't speak freely, of course, with the servants in the room. Mazy paused between bites to tell him a little bit about what she had been doing and the things happening in London, at the Swan, and at the marketplace.

When her stomach was full, she thanked the kitchen servants. Giles had brought in her bag of clothing, so Sir Berenger picked it up to carry it to her room.

Just outside in the corridor, an older woman servant was waiting, frowning. She said, "I'll take you to your room."

They followed the woman to a room on the ground level of the castle.

"Is there not a room on the same level as my bedchamber that our guest could stay in?" Sir Berenger asked the servant.

Was he afraid for her safety?

"Lady Bristow instructed me to put the lady here." The servant did not turn around or look at him.

Sir Berenger met Mazy's eye but said nothing.

They followed the servant to the room. "Will there be anything else?"

"Thank you, that will be all," Sir Berenger said. When the servant had left the room, he whispered, "Come, I will show you to a room near mine. I don't trust Lady Bristow."

Her heart actually expanded and she let out a pent-up breath. He didn't trust Lady Bristow. Surely that meant he would not marry her. *Thank You, God.*

He looked both ways in the corridor before motioning her forward. When they reached the stairs, he again looked all around. When he had stood still for several moments, he started up.

He seemed to walk extra carefully when they reached the next level. He passed two doors before opening the third one and letting her inside.

He inspected the room, checked the bed, and locked the door that led into a smaller servant's room.

"Will you be able to manage without a servant?" he asked.

"Of course. I am not accustomed to having a servant." She smiled, stifling a chuckle.

"I will leave you, then. I know you are tired." He pointed to the wall. "My room is there. Just come and get me, or pound on the wall if you need me. But be careful. Lady Bristow's room is on my other side." He took her hand in his. "Thank you for coming to warn me. You are very kind and good, Mazy of Wexcombe, and I am grateful for you."

She stared up at him, her heart in her throat. How good he looked—not good as in handsome, although he was certainly that, but good as in a person whose heart was without guile, blameless and full of compassion. Oh, how she wanted to be close to this man, both in proximity and in spirit.

"I . . ." She probably looked like a fish just plucked from the water. She closed her mouth, swallowed, and managed to say, "I'm glad I could help. You are very kind and good too."

She sounded like a child, her words simple and stilted. Why could she not think of something more eloquent?

He squeezed her hand and left, slipping out the door and closing it noiselessly.

She lifted her hand to her lips, the hand he had just been holding, and imagined she was kissing him. *God, forgive me for my foolishness, and let me not be too brokenhearted when I have to part from him again.*

He might not marry Lady Bristow, but someday he would marry someone, a lady, no doubt.

Berenger was awake before dawn. Indeed, he had not slept much all night, as he listened for any sign of distress or danger from Mazy's room. When the sun was up, he went to knock on her door, but softly.

She answered immediately, fully dressed, and was even carrying her bag.

"You are coming with me, yes?" Mazy said.

"Yes, but I have to tell Juliana's nurse to gather her things."

"Be careful." Mazy's brows rose into her hair. She looked so sweet and innocent, not like Lady Bristow, who had obviously been feigning those same qualities.

"But first I want to walk you down to the stable and meet your guard."

They passed through the hallway and down the stairs without spotting anyone. But as they were walking through the ground level, an anguished cry rang out from Juliana's room.

Berenger broke into a run, dropping Mazy's bag.

He rushed into her room as the head housekeeper was trying to pry Juliana's hands away from her mouth.

"What is happening here?"

"The child refuses to eat," the woman said, hesitating, a guilty look on her face. "Lady Bristow said she was to have this."

Berenger strode forward and got between the servant and the child. "She will eat when she wishes to eat."

"What is that you're feeding her?" Mazy stepped forward, staring at the bowl and spoon in the servant's hands.

The servant pulled the bowl away, hiding it under her arm. "That is not your concern."

"Give it to me." Berenger held out his hand.

The servant started to run from the room, clutching the bowl to her chest, but Berenger grabbed her by the arm, taking the bowl from her.

Juliana said, her voice sounding as if she was choking back tears, "I hate mushrooms."

Mazy gasped, and her eyes met his. "The rumor was that she gave her husband death cap mushrooms."

Berenger examined the contents of the small wooden bowl. Scrambled eggs with tiny bits of what looked like mushrooms mixed in. Heat crept into his forehead.

He squatted in front of Juliana. "Did you eat any of this?"

"No." Juliana shook her head.

"Thank God." He rubbed his forehead. "Juliana, this is my friend Mazy. Would you take a journey with us?"

She looked at Mazy and then stared at him with large eyes.

"We will take you away from here, to a safe place. You won't ever have to come back here. Would you like that?"

"Yes."

"Let's pack up your things."

Mazy helped him stuff the child's clothing into a bag that they could tie onto a saddle.

"What is the meaning of this?"

Lady Bristow stood in the doorway. Her eyes were as black and cold as the bottom of a well in January.

"I told you, we are taking Juliana on a trip to visit my sister." Berenger went back to gathering the child's things, but since she had very little, they finished quickly.

"The king will have your head for this. She is my ward."

"She will be safe with us." Berenger bent down as Juliana reached up to him. He picked her up and carried her with one arm while he carried Mazy's saddlebag and the child's bag in the other hand.

"How dare you?" Lady Bristow reached for Juliana, but she cried out and wrapped both her arms and legs around Berenger.

He and Mazy walked past Lady Bristow.

"I will send my guards after you," the lady said. "You will not get away. The king will not let you take her from me."

"She is coming with us."

He could hear Lady Bristow's footsteps behind them, Juliana clinging to him.

Mazy walked close to his side and said quietly, "I have my knives."

Mazy did not even look frightened as she put her hand in her pocket.

"I shall tell the king what you have done," Lady Bristow threatened as she followed them out to the stables. Her soldiers were standing to the side, watching them.

"Guards," she said in a sharp voice. "Stop this man and this woman from taking my child."

Berenger's men stared hard at Lady Bristow's guards, who looked uncomfortable, shifting and whispering among themselves.

"Hear me!" she screamed. "Detain them. Now."

"This child is now in my protection." Sir Berenger addressed the guards as he kept moving. "I am not doing anything wrong, and you know me well enough by now to know that the child will be safe with me."

The guards looked from Berenger to Lady Bristow and back and did not move.

"I will have you all flogged," she screamed. Running into the stable, she came out with a riding crop. She tried to hit the nearest guard, but he yanked the crop out of her hand.

Meanwhile, Mazy's guard, Giles, appeared, having already saddled his and Mazy's horses. He started helping Berenger saddle his own horse.

"Get out of here, if you are not here to help me!" Lady Bristow was screaming at her guards. "Go on! Leave me!"

Juliana kept hold of Berenger's leg with one hand while he worked to saddle his horse, and she kept her other hand in her mouth, sucking on a knuckle.

By the time they were ready to mount their horses, Lady Bristow was nowhere to be seen.

Sir Berenger placed Juliana in front of him on the saddle. When everyone was ready, they all set out toward Bedfordshire and Strachleigh.

TWENTY-FOUR

MAZY'S HEART WAS FULL AS SHE SAT WITH LADY DELIA, her husband, the Duke of Strachleigh, their child Alfred, whom she had not seen in more than two years, and a new baby.

Sir Berenger and Strachleigh were talking about Lady Bristow.

"She will certainly have people at the king's court who are loyal to her," Sir Berenger told his brother-in-law.

"No need to worry. She cannot hurt the child now." Strachleigh exuded confidence. "I will send a number of my knights and soldiers with you for protection."

"I sent a letter by courier to the king the day after we left," Sir Berenger said, "but we will make our way to London to speak to King Richard in person. Although Lady Bristow will have reached him before us, no doubt."

After a good night's sleep, they set out the next morning accompanied by Strachleigh's men. Juliana seemed content as long as she was with Sir Berenger, but she was warming up to Mazy as well, letting her do little things for her. Mazy already loved Juliana and felt fiercely protective of her.

They rode all day and stopped at an inn in a small walled town to sleep.

"Welcome," the innkeeper said as they walked inside. "May I offer you our best room?"

Of course the innkeeper thought they were a family—husband, wife, and child.

"Thank you, yes." Sir Berenger turned to glance at Mazy.

Mazy suddenly wished with all her heart that they were just what the innkeeper thought them to be.

She thrust the thought from her mind as they sat and let the innkeeper serve them stew, warm bread, and ale. While they ate, Juliana sitting on Sir Berenger's knee, he looked Mazy in the eye and spoke in a low voice.

"Are you comfortable with us staying in the same room tonight? You have my word that the child will sleep between us and nothing unseemly will occur."

"Of course. I trust you. And the best way to stay safe and to avoid suspicion—and to keep Juliana feeling safe and taken care of—is for the three of us to remain together."

Later, after they had gone up to the room, Mazy washed Juliana's face, then laid her down on the larger of the two straw mattresses. The child's eyes were closed before her head even touched the bed.

"Poor little thing," Mazy said as she washed her own face in the washbasin. "She was so tired."

"I don't think I shall have any trouble sleeping either." Sir Berenger groaned as he stretched out on the smaller mattress, leaving the bigger one for Mazy and Juliana.

"Did you not sleep well at Lady Bristow's castle?" She hid her smile. But she felt a slight pang at realizing she was gloating over his not being able to marry Lady Bristow. After all, it was quite a misfortune when she remembered that he also would not be able to inherit the castle and all the wealth of Bristow.

"It was not a restful experience."

"I'm sorry." Mazy covered her mouth in an attempt to hide her amused smile.

"Oh, you think that's funny?" He shook his head.

"I was laughing at the situation—a knight afraid of a woman."

"I wasn't afraid of her, only afraid of being married to someone without integrity. But I suppose there have been a few men who were afraid of you. How many men have you cut since you've been in London?"

She wasn't sure why, but his comment and question made her stomach feel sick. How could he jest about that? She had been absolutely terrified every time she had been forced to use her knives against someone.

"Do you think I enjoy harming people?" She inwardly flinched at how defensive she sounded, but she couldn't tamp down this anger, even as she had no idea where it was coming from.

Sir Berenger sat up and stared at her. "Forgive me. I have offended you." His voice was low and soft.

"I had to defend myself. Do you think I had anyone else to

defend me? If I had not hurt them, I would have been harmed, and I am not sorry I did it."

Her hands were shaking. She wanted to yell but kept her voice low, almost a whisper, to keep from disturbing Juliana.

"I am glad you hurt them, as you have every right to defend yourself. And I'm sorry." He leaned toward her, a pained look on his face. "I wish I had been there to defend you. I am beyond sorrowful that you had no one to depend on to watch over you."

"I don't need anyone to watch over me. I am doing very well for myself." But was she? She hated every time she felt threatened enough to put her hand in her pocket, to contemplate another man attacking her and having to defend herself with her knife.

"I can't rely on anyone but myself, and that's all well and good." She was overreacting to what Sir Berenger was saying. She knew she was, but she didn't know how to stop herself or even what had provoked this overwhelming emotion. She only knew she was very angry with Sir Berenger for . . . what? For not marrying her? He could marry whomever he wished.

Mazy quickly blew out the candle and lay down on the bed beside Juliana. "I don't know why I said all that," she whispered. And yet she could feel similar words bubbling up, angry words that still threatened to leap out of her mouth.

"Did something else terrible happen to you? Something you haven't told me? I will make them pay for what they did—"

"No, nothing beyond what you already know. Although two men did try to take the Swan from Ro and me. I had to threaten them. There was a tense couple of hours where they wouldn't leave. But Ro and I were not hurt."

"You must tell me their names so I can apprehend them and make them answer for their actions."

"I'm tired. I don't want to talk about it." She was glad it was too dark for him to see her face.

Sir Berenger was a good man. But he was only a friend. He didn't want to marry her, and he had no real responsibility for her. If anyone should be asking her forgiveness or saying they were sorry, it was her brothers. One was a baron and the other a knight, but neither of them cared enough to protect her.

She'd even had to come to Ro's aid, as Ro became fearful in dangerous situations and did not carry a weapon to defend herself, much less Mazy.

Help me, God, to overcome this selfishness inside me. She should not be resentful of Ro. Ro was good to her, was a good friend and partner, and Mazy was happy to protect Ro whenever necessary.

But it was further proof that Mazy could not rely on anyone but herself. Depending on someone else only caused disappointment and pain. And yet none of this was Sir Berenger's fault.

"Forgive me for what I said." Sir Berenger's voice sounded regretful. "And when we get back to London, I will see if I can hire Giles, or someone equally reliable, to be your personal guard, to protect you."

His words—kind and thoughtful, yet hurtful at the same time—made tears sting her eyes. Part of her wanted to retort, "If I need a guard, I will hire one myself." But she bit her tongue and said, "No, I thank you. I would prefer you did not hire a guard for me. Good night, Sir Berenger."

"Good night." His voice was sad.

As she lay in the dark, she had to keep wiping the tears, praying, *Please, God, just let me fall asleep and forget this pain.*

Berenger could not stop thinking about Mazy's words from the night before as they traveled the next day. Why was she so angry?

Juliana had decided to ride with Mazy, and the two of them kept up a cheerful banter, playing games, telling stories, and singing children's songs and rhymes. Their interaction was so beguiling. Did Mazy understand how appealing she was?

He kept trying to sort out what Mazy had said and why. He'd never seen her angry before. She said she could take care of herself. Was she angry with her brothers and lashing out at him, since they were never around? But that seemed like something only a very immature person would do, not Mazy.

He'd taken great pleasure in being the one to reach her before anyone else when the crowd of ruffians attacked the marketplace. He'd saved her, but what if he had not been there? What if he had not reached her in time? The thought made him physically sick. And what was to stop something like that from happening again?

He'd learned that the way to keep the people he loved safe was to stay in good favor with the king and to stay far away from people like his stepmother, who were selfish enough to destroy lives to get what they wanted. And already he had broken the second rule by nearly agreeing to marry Lady Bristow, and he might very well break the first rule by telling the king he would not marry Lady Bristow.

So far nothing was going according to his own plans and desires. Would he also cause bad things to happen to the people he loved?

But as he listened to Mazy and Juliana, shoving his gloomy thoughts away, he couldn't help but smile at the adorable picture they made, as well as the happy sounds of singing and laughing with each other.

Was this not what he'd always wanted? He saw how happy Edwin and Gerard were with their wives, and Delia's contented life with her husband and children. But if he lost favor with the king by not marrying Lady Bristow . . .

There was no knowing what trouble he could bring down on his family by refusing to marry the woman the king had chosen for him. But he could not marry Lady Bristow. He recalled what happened when his father married an evil woman. His father had been murdered, and his entire family, all seven sons and one daughter, were nearly beheaded.

Berenger rode close to Mazy. Every time he looked at her, his thoughts whirled in different directions almost simultaneously.

He wanted to wrap his arms around her and tell her how much he admired and cared for her. And he now knew for certain: he wanted to marry Mazy.

His heart was full just thinking of marrying the maiden he admired above all others, the woman he trusted and respected. He had no doubt that she would be a good wife, although he had no idea what their marriage would look like, now that he would be displeasing the king, besides the fact that it would be full of love and affection.

He also wondered if marrying her would endanger her, himself, and even his family.

He should not allow himself to even think of marrying Mazy, as sweet and beautiful as she was, until he spoke to the king and received his permission. But first he had to tell King Richard that Lady Bristow was not what she appeared to be and turn down the king's idea of a reward.

He couldn't bear the thought of Mazy being threatened or attacked again, of her having to defend herself from bodily harm. If she would not allow him to hire someone to protect her, to follow her to and from the marketplace and see that she made it safely home each night, he would have to do it secretly. He couldn't leave her unprotected again.

"Giles thinks it might rain tonight."

Mazy was helping Juliana fill up their water flasks at a spring of fresh water where they had stopped to rest the horses. Mazy turned to gaze up at Sir Berenger. "Should we look for an inn to stay the night?" she asked.

"I don't think there are any towns near here. We might find a barn or stable to take shelter in for the night."

"In a stable? With animals?" Juliana looked frightened.

Mazy and Sir Berenger exchanged glances. Mazy said, "All will be well. Sir Berenger and I shall take care of you."

"It will be nice and cozy and warm," Sir Berenger said, rubbing his hands together and smiling at the child.

Juliana was already less quiet and timid than when Mazy had first met her, but she did not look comforted by Sir Berenger's words.

When darkness was closing in and the clouds had completely obscured both the waning sunlight and the moon, they found a farmhouse and Sir Berenger asked the owner if they could sleep in his barn. "I am a knight in the king's service, and these men are our guards," he said.

"You are welcome to the barn and stable," the farmer said.

Thankfully, the weather had grown warm enough for most of the snow to melt, so as they lay down in the fresh straw on their blankets, making sure no animals were near Juliana, the child fell asleep immediately. The guards bedded down on the other side of the stable.

From a couple of feet away, Sir Berenger said softly, "I'm sorry I upset you last night."

"It's nothing. I shouldn't have been so angry." *Please let him understand that I don't want to talk about it.*

"I still would like to hire Giles to protect you, to be your personal guard, if you will let me."

Why was he speaking of this again?

"I don't want you to go to that trouble and expense for me. It's not necessary anyway, and I am not accustomed to someone following me around."

Sir Berenger was quiet.

She went on. "I can take care of myself. And I have enough

money to hire a guard myself if I need someone. Already I have two women who work for me, which allows me to travel to the countryside to get more goods."

Truthfully, she did not know how things had gone in her absence.

After a few moments of silence, Sir Berenger said, "I'm glad things are going so well. You deserve your success."

"Thank you."

Truthfully, it would take most of her extra earnings to hire a guard who would accompany her, a large man who would scare away anyone who might wish her harm. And someday, if she was very fortunate and God so willed it, she would have a husband who loved and cared for her, and during what little time she was away taking care of business in the marketplace, her children would be safe at home with a kind and gentle woman servant to care for them. Her husband would love her too much to restrict her to the home, and he would love her too much to leave her without a guard to protect her.

In her mind—and only in her mind—she told Sir Berenger, *You aren't responsible for me, Sir Berenger, so stop trying to be so good. It is not your place. You are not my husband.*

No matter how much she might wish he was.

TWENTY-FIVE

BACK HOME IN LONDON, BERENGER STRODE ACROSS THE lawn toward the door of the Palace of Westminster for his meeting with King Richard.

He'd dressed carefully for the occasion, and he had to take several deep breaths to try to calm his breathing and his heart, which was beating twice as fast as normal.

Once inside, he was led to a private apartment where the king was alone with only one guard standing in the corner and another at the door.

Berenger tried to read his expression. Was that disappointment on his face?

"Come, Sir Berenger." The king motioned him forward with his hand, and without the usual greetings, the young ruler said, "Tell me why you have decided to reject Lady Bristow."

Berenger had to swallow past the dry spot in his throat.

"My liege, did you receive the missive I sent explaining everything?"

"I did, but I could hardly believe your words. And Lady Bristow has been here, quite distraught at the way you have treated her. I hope you have a better explanation than you gave in your letter."

Berenger felt the blood drain from his face. Lady Bristow had beaten him to London and to the king. Of course she had, and of course she would have told the king some sad story in which she was the victim and Berenger was the villain who had wronged her.

In the letter, Berenger had told the king about his suspicions of Lady Bristow mistreating her ward, about the rumor that the child was the heir to Bristow Castle, and about finding the child being forced to eat poisonous mushrooms. He had even told him of her late-night meeting with the French sailor on the beach. How were all those things not a good explanation for his refusal to marry the woman?

"You have kidnapped her ward. What do you have to say for yourself?" the king demanded in his eighteen-year-old voice.

"Your Majesty, I have good reason for taking the child. As I told you in the letter, Lady Bristow's servant was trying to feed the child deadly death cap mushrooms. And it is rumored that Lady Bristow poisoned her husband as well."

The king's expression hardened.

O God, help me. It was four years ago all over again—falsely accused, being tried before the king, the king being influenced by corrupt advisers, and Berenger and his brothers being found

279

guilty and sentenced to death. Had he stumbled into the same situation again? Would his brothers and sister all share in the consequences of his running afoul of the king?

"Your Majesty, in good faith I went to Bristow Castle with the Lady Bristow, intending to marry her if she proved of good character. But one thing after another after another . . . Surely Your Majesty knows of my loyalty and willingness to serve you, to even die for you, my king. But Lady Bristow, I believe, is selling whatever secrets she knows to the king's enemy, France. She is selling something, for I saw the exchange with my own eyes and heard the French language with my own ears. I saw her kissing the French sailor, or ship's captain, whatever he was."

The king chewed the inside of his lip, his brows lowered.

"The child was afraid of Lady Bristow, and my sister's friend helped care for the child on the journey here. The child's welfare was of utmost concern in taking her from Bristow Castle."

"I am hearing two distinctly different accounts from you and Lady Bristow. And now I must consider who to believe. I am sure you understand, Sir Berenger."

"Of course, Your Majesty. I understand that you must weigh what is truth and what is falsehood."

"Yes." The king said nothing for a moment, then waved his hand. "You may go. I will send for you when I have determined who is telling the truth."

"Thank you, Your Majesty." Sir Berenger bowed to the king and made his way out in a daze of racing thoughts.

After all he had done to be the most dutiful knight, without fault in the king's service, would his life once again be in jeopardy, this time because of Lady Bristow?

Mazy took Juliana with her to the marketplace the next morning, showing her all the sights, buying a sweet confection made of almond paste, and introducing her to all the friendly vendors in the market. The child smiled at everyone, her eyes sparkling, and Mazy's heart grew full at the thought that Juliana would never have to be at Lady Bristow's mercy ever again.

Now all would be well. Juliana could receive her inheritance, once Sir Berenger told the king the truth about the child's parentage, and Lady Bristow would be exiled, at the very least. No one would be hurt by that lady's treachery.

And Sir Berenger would move on to the next wealthy widow whom the king chose for him to marry. After all, wealthy widows of England's nobility—as well as their lands and castles—needed the protection of a strong knight like Sir Berenger. Knights were too valuable to be allowed to choose their own spouse, and women were too unimportant to choose theirs.

Mazy would have to check her bitterness. What an ugly root it was, twisting around her heart, making her think angry, sarcastic thoughts. This was not who she was or who she wanted to be. She was Mazy, Knife Girl, defender of innocent women and children, helper of the poor widows who needed to feed their children. She was strong and brave, and she did not think bitter thoughts about a man she knew to be good at heart.

But when would she be loved and defended by a good man?

It was a legitimate question, but she didn't need to be thinking it. She needed to think about her business plan, how to proceed next. Life was like a chess game, after all, always dependent on the next move.

"I've raised six children," said the woman who had taken care of Mazy's booth while she was gone, pulling Juliana onto her lap, "and I will show you how I used to make them all laugh." The woman started making her knees jump up and down while holding Juliana's hands out to the sides. She chanted a singsong rhyme as she jostled Juliana.

"Ride a little horsey, ride to town. Ride a little horsey, and don't fall down!"

At the word *down*, the woman dropped her knees, letting her skirt catch Juliana while she held her hands. Juliana laughed and said, "Do it again!"

While Juliana and the woman played the game several more times, Mazy caught the eye of Martin Fisher, who was talking with the old man who sold walking sticks that he had whittled and sanded to an incredible smoothness. They were staring at Mazy, smiling, then waved.

Mazy waved back as Martin broke away from the man and made his way toward her.

"Beautiful Mazy, how glad I am that you're back at your booth again."

"Thank you, Martin. I haven't seen you for a while."

"Yes, it has been a while, but I have been coming every day for the last week and you were not here. I feared some harm had come to you, and I could not bear it." He leaned down close to her, then sank to one knee. "It made me realize that I still want, more than anything, for you to marry me. Beautiful Mazy." He grabbed her hand between his. "I beg of you, say you will marry me. Marry me today, and I shall dedicate my life to making you the happiest woman in London."

"I heard a rumor a few weeks ago that you were marrying Harriet of Cheddar."

"Oh no. Harriet was just a passing fancy."

"A passing fancy? That sounds like quite an insulting and cruel thing to say about a young woman who agreed to marry you."

"We had a bit of a falling out . . . That is, we are not to be wed."

"I see."

"Dear, sweet Mazy, in your heart you must feel some love for me." He passionately kissed the back of her hand. "Marry me, please, and put me out of my misery."

Part of her wanted to chuckle, and another part wanted to jerk her hand away in disgust.

"I am sure you will find someone else just as quickly as you found Harriet."

"Do not tease me so cruelly. You had told me you would not marry me. Are you saying I should have waited for you? Well, perhaps you are right. But I have realized my error, and my heart wants none but you."

She almost asked him, "Did you hire a troubadour to teach you these overly sentimental declarations?" But instead she said, "Forgive me, Martin, but my heart belongs to my business partners. I must think of them. If I were to marry, I would leave them without a way to care for their families. You would have me betray them. Alas, I cannot be so cruel."

"I would allow you to keep working in the market if you wished. In fact, I would help you expand to help more women sell their goods in the market. I am considered somewhat wealthy, as I am my father's heir, and you know that I am starting my own merchant business, importing goods from the East."

In truth, it was a good offer. A girl like Mazy could hardly hope for more than a man like Martin, who was not poor, could give her a good home, and would no doubt be able to provide the protection her brothers had refused to give her.

As she looked at Martin—he was not bad to look at, he had all his teeth and hair, and he did not seem to have a lot of vices—she tried to imagine herself married to him. Yes, she could probably love him. If he was her husband, she would love him. But she simply could not reconcile herself to marrying him. She could protect herself with her knives. Her business was doing well. And she wanted love, an exceptional love from an exceptional man.

But then she heard herself saying, "Let me think about it, Martin." Though she still thought about Sir Berenger every time she pondered the idea of marriage.

He narrowed his eyes at her. "I will see this as an opportunity."

"An opportunity?"

"Yes, an opportunity to convince you that I will make a good husband and you will not be sorry to say yes."

"I'm afraid I must work now, Martin."

Juliana was eating a fruit pasty, cherry juice dripping from her chin, while a customer chose some of the fruit that had come in from the countryside that morning from one of Mazy's suppliers.

The woman who manned the booth next to Mazy's cackled. She must have been listening to their conversation. "Don't be an inconsistent lover!"

Martin's cheeks were tinged red as he stared down at Mazy. "I won't be inconsistent this time, Miss Mazy. You shall see. I shall be as constant as the sun and moon and stars."

He kissed her hand again and slowly walked away.

While Mazy helped the customer, weighing her cherries on the scale, her heart smote her. Was she leading poor Martin on a fool's path, only to ultimately say no to his proposal? Wouldn't it be kinder to tell him he had no chance now rather than later?

But no one she had ever met could compare to Sir Berenger's good humor, good character, and ability to make her want to tell him everything that was in her heart. He was kind and compassionate, not just to her but to everyone, whether humble or noble. And he felt . . . safe.

A pain went through her chest. Sir Berenger didn't want her. He wanted to treat her like a friend, to hire someone to watch over her, not *be* the one to watch over her.

Well, she didn't need him. She had friends already, and she had her knives.

Berenger gave Giles enough money for six months' worth of wages.

"Look after her, but don't let her know you are doing so."

"Yes, sir." Giles went toward the market to find Mazy, staring down at the heavy bag of coins in his hand.

Giles was a good man. Even if Berenger had to flee the country or, God forbid, the king arrested him and had him beheaded for whatever lies Lady Bristow was telling him, Giles would do as he had asked. He would protect Mazy.

But what would happen to her after six months?

His heart sank. He had been forced into considering marriage to Lady Bristow, and because he would not follow the king's wishes, he had possibly let his family down . . . again. Hadn't he let Edwin down when he failed to prevent him from losing his arm and nearly being killed? Falling out of favor with the king had been the cause of nearly losing his brothers and his own life. He'd been determined not to let that happen again. But all his efforts had led to just that—losing favor with the king.

His heart weighed him down as he left his barracks. He could not tell any of his men or his fellow guard captains what was befalling him or anything about the king's words to him. He set out to wander London Town until most of his men would be asleep.

He walked without knowing where he was headed. He passed inns and bakeries, chandlers and cobbler shops, but he had no wish to enter any of them. Finally he saw the Swan up ahead, its sign like a beacon, with its big white bird on a bright blue background.

His heart stuttered like a horse stamping in place, then

quickened to a fast trot. He suddenly wanted to see Mazy more than anything.

He walked inside and, when he didn't see her, he sat down.

Ro and her new helper, Anselm, were bustling about, with several customers and a lively little crowd at their biggest table singing a pirate song. The crowd of four men and three women were loud and looked happy, without a care. They were not particularly poor, it seemed, but perhaps somewhere below merchant status. They were not encumbered with worries about the king bestowing his favor on them—or having their heads for displeasing him.

Ro suddenly called out to him from across the room. "Stay there! I'm coming!"

She topped off two big cups of ale from the barrel behind the counter, set them down in front of two men, then hurried over to Berenger.

"Mazy said you were seeing the king today. She should be here very soon." She glanced at the door as if looking for her.

He wished Mazy would appear, especially before Ro asked him how things went with the king. Mazy was the only person he wanted to talk to about that.

"Ale and stew?" Ro asked.

"Yes, thank you."

She hurried off. And then Mazy came through the door with Juliana, holding on to her little hand.

His heart stuttered again, as it had when he'd seen the sign of the Swan. The sight of her evoked such a yearning inside him. Why did his heart long for her? Was it because she was so lovely and fair? No. He'd seen other lovely and fair women who did not make his heart yearn. It was more because she was so kind and compassionate, and she always held his attention, always made him want to tell her more than he ever wanted to share with anyone else. She was good and honest, and she was brave enough to defend herself, to be strong and resilient and even help other women survive.

He loved her.

He'd wanted to marry her before, but now he realized that he was in love with her. A fine time to realize such a thing, when his life could be forfeit. But somehow nothing seemed to matter except this love. Could she ever love him in return?

He would not trouble her with a revelation of his feelings. It could have no good outcome at this point, when he could be exiled, becoming a mercenary, possibly even forced to fight for one of England's enemies just to survive.

But he was getting far ahead of himself.

Juliana spotted him the same time Mazy did. The child immediately held out her arms toward him.

He got up and picked up the child, and she wrapped her skinny arms around his neck. "Did you have a good day with Miss Mazy at the marketplace?"

"I ate cherry pasties and played 'Ride a Little Horsey' with a woman."

"Oh? And did Miss Mazy have a good day?" He looked at Mazy, his heart thumping.

"Of course."

"A man named Martin asked Mazy to marry him. He said he would make her happy."

Mazy's eyes grew big. "How did you . . . Juliana, I don't think that's exactly . . ."

"Martin said that you were waiting to see if he would be consistent."

"Juliana." Mazy shook her head and tickled the child under her arm, making her laugh.

Berenger's stomach was sinking, his thoughts churning. "What did you say to him?" he asked Mazy, trying to keep his voice bland.

"I told him to let me think about it."

"What? Think about what?" Ro had arrived with cups, Anselm right behind her with bowls of stew.

"Oh, just Martin." Mazy wouldn't meet anyone's eye.

"Martin Fisher? Oh yes, he's been after Mazy to marry him for at least a year now. He has money too." Ro raised her brows and nudged Mazy's arm. "He is handsome enough, and he seems kind."

"You could do worse," Anselm chimed in. "Me, for instance."

Ro said to Anselm, "I saw Muriel Finch eyeing you yesterday like you were a side of beef."

Anselm shook his head at her. The two walked back to the counter with Anselm muttering, "You're just jealous."

Surely Mazy didn't love this Martin Fisher.

Berenger wanted her to be protected and loved, but the

thought of her marrying anyone besides him made him feel empty and numb.

Dear God, help me be able to give her more than Martin Fisher ever could.

TWENTY-SIX

BERENGER SET JULIANA ON THE BENCH BETWEEN HIM AND Mazy, then handed her the cup of water Ro had brought for her.

"How did your meeting with the king go today?" Mazy stared straight into his eyes. "Well, I hope."

"Not so well." Berenger briefly explained what the king had said, trying to speak softly and not too explicitly, lest Juliana understand and repeat his words.

"This is not good." Mazy's cheeks turned pale, her eyes widening. "Let me speak to the king. I can explain everything, as I was there with you."

"No offense intended toward you, Mazy, but the king probably would not grant you an audience with him. You've never been introduced—"

"We can tell him I am the daughter of Baron Wexcombe and the sister of one of his knights. He doesn't have to know that

Warin cast me off. He listens to nobles, does he not? I know I am a woman, but—"

"I cannot let you endanger yourself for me." The very thought of her in danger made him sorry he had told her any of this.

"I can at least try. I will not be endangering myself just by talking to him and telling him what I saw and what I know."

Berenger knew how capricious the young king could be, but he didn't argue with her.

"All may yet end well," Berenger said. "After he thinks it over, and perhaps discovers more information about a certain child's parentage, the king may realize I am telling the truth and Lady Bristow is lying."

"I know you are accustomed to helping other people, not accepting help, but I do wish you would let me try to help."

He didn't speak as he thought about what she said.

"Please. Let me try."

"The truth is, I can't abide the thought of you coming to harm, but especially if you are hurt because you were trying to help me."

She sighed. "It is not a sin to let someone help you, someone who wants good things for you."

"I could give you the same advice. Did I not have only your welfare at heart when I offered to hire a guard for you? You should accept my help—if you trust me."

"A woman shouldn't accept assistance from a man who is not her relative nor her husband."

"I am someone who cares for you. It is the same as—"

"Very well, very well. I suppose you are right." She gave him a wry grin. "I won't argue with you. I don't want to make you angry."

"I am not angry, just tired. I should probably try to sleep."

"You should eat first." Mazy nodded at the bowl in front of him.

He didn't feel hungry, but he ate a few bites of the stew so as not to upset her.

When Juliana had eaten a little bit, she fell asleep in Mazy's lap.

"Let me take her to bed."

Ro hurried to her side before she could get up. "I'll take her so you and Sir Berenger can talk a bit longer. I'll put her in my bed until you come and get her."

Mazy started to object, then relented.

They talked until Ro returned. "She's sleeping soundly. You can leave her all night if you wish, or you can go and take her when you're ready."

"Thank you, Ro." Mazy gave her friend's arm a brief squeeze.

"You've had a long day," Berenger said. "I will accompany you to your room."

He and Mazy made their way to the small storage room at the back of the Swan. They were alone now. He wanted to tell her how he felt, but he wasn't sure if that was wise. Had he done something that might be keeping her from returning his feelings? He remembered how upset she'd been on their way back to London.

"Forgive me for upsetting you when I offered to hire someone to watch over you."

"There is nothing to forgive. I don't know why I was so angry."

"I have a confession to make." Berenger knew he might make

her angry again, but he didn't want to be deceptive. She would no doubt discover it on her own eventually. "I hired Giles to watch over you. He is paid up for the next six months."

As they stood facing each other, Mazy gazed at him but said nothing. Finally, after several moments, she said, "I know you did it because you want to be helpful."

"I just want you to be safe."

"You are very kind. Thank you." But her eyes had clouded over. She was thanking him, but she was not altogether pleased. Something was bothering her, and he needed to discover what it was.

"I don't know what will happen if King Richard decides Lady Bristow is telling the truth. I wanted to make sure you were safe as long as possible."

"Do you truly think the king will believe Lady Bristow over you?" She wrapped her arms around herself.

Her brown hair fell down around her shoulders, a lovely, wavy curtain that only enhanced her beauty. One strand was lying against her cheek, drawing his attention to the smoothness of her skin. His heart clenched as he suddenly wanted to touch her, to feel how soft her hair was and how silky her cheek.

"I don't know what will happen, but we must trust that all will be well." His mind was numb. He felt as if he was only saying what he should say, what he should feel and believe, when in actuality he was grieved at what the king had said, afraid he might never be able to have the one thing he now realized he wanted.

"If the worst happens," she said, gazing intently at him, "I want you to go into hiding, to save yourself. Promise me you will." Mazy leaned close and put out her hand, placing her palm against his chest as if to steady herself.

"Hiding is not befitting of a knight."

"Is it better to let an evil woman cause your death? Please. Tell me you will not let the king arrest you."

The anguish in her expression and in her strained voice made him lose his breath for a moment. Did she care so much for him? Was this why she had never accepted a marriage proposal? For he was sure she had had many, as beautiful and confident as she was.

"Do not worry about me. The king undoubtedly will have realized who is in the right by tomorrow morning and will send for me."

"I can see that you do not believe that." Mazy's eyes filled with tears and she lowered her head, resting her forehead against his chest.

Berenger encircled her shoulders with his arms, pulling her close. She slipped her arms around his back and stood very still. After a few moments, she lifted a hand to wipe her eyes, but still she did not look up at him.

"Don't cry, Mazy." His heart was breaking, a pain shooting through his chest. "There is no reason to think the worst. All may turn out well."

"You are the best man I know," she said softly against his shirt.

"And you are the best and most beautiful woman I know."

She laughed, a short, gentle expulsion of air. "I know that cannot be true."

"Do you not know how beautiful you are? Look at me."

Slowly she raised her head and her eyes met his.

"You are as beautiful as a sunrise, as pretty as any meadow full of flowers. To me you are the most beautiful woman in the world." And he meant every word. He was so in love with her.

Her eyes were glowing in the dim light. Her lips looked so soft, so close.

His heart beat fast as he leaned toward her. Never had he wanted a kiss so much. Never had anything seemed so good and pure and precious.

She did not move, did not turn away. Indeed, she stared at his lips, then closed her eyes.

He closed the gap between them and pressed his lips to hers.

His heart stopped, then beat heavy and fast. Her lips were perfect—soft but firm as she kissed him back, though awkwardly, which was more endearing than he could have imagined. His must be her first kiss, and the way she leaned into him caused him to groan.

One kiss quickly became two and then three. Soon they were holding each other tighter, kissing more urgently, as if afraid it would end as suddenly as it had begun.

He'd never felt this way before. If only it never had to end. And why should it?

"Mazy, will you marry me?"

They were both breathing as if they'd been running uphill. She stared at him with a dazed look.

"I'm in love with you. You're good and brave and you're always so kind." He sounded like a man with only half a brain.

She kissed him again, pulling his head down to hers, before breaking away and whispering, "Are you sure? Why?"

"Why?" What kind of answer was that? "I love you. I want to spend the rest of my life with you. I want to protect you and love you and treat you as you deserve to be treated."

She smiled. "Very well. I will marry you."

Her smile was as beguiling as her answer. He pulled her up onto her toes and kissed her thoroughly, deeply.

When the kiss ended, she was slow to open her eyes. She sighed and said, "I love you too. I've never loved or wanted anyone but you."

She rested her head against his chest. Then, after a blissful moment of silence, she cried out, "And now you will be killed and I'll be alone again."

She tried to pull away but he held on to her. Then he felt her body tremble, as if she was sobbing.

She did love him. This wonderful, clever, courageous, emotional woman loved him.

Mazy was going to lose him.

Now that he had said he loved her and wanted to marry her, he would be ruined and possibly even killed because of that evil Lady Bristow, and Mazy would be completely alone.

Sobs overtook her before she could stop them.

Foolish, unrestrained girl, she berated herself. She tried to breathe in deeply, to force back the sobs. She concentrated on breathing in and out, her forehead pressed against Sir Berenger's chest.

Oh, the dear, dear man. How she loved him. She never let herself admit that she was in love with him, but she had loved him since she was sixteen years old and living at Strachleigh, basking in every bit of attention he paid to her, marveling at how kind and modest he was. He was never boastful, never rude, never treated anyone—from the least to the greatest—with anything less than respect and kindness. He was so good. Could it be possible that he loved her?

But the very next moment a knife pierced her heart. He was in danger, through no fault of his own, and now the terrible event from his younger years was coming back to haunt him, as he was put in danger once again because of false accusations against him.

"Don't worry." He was rubbing the back of her shoulder, touching her hair with his other hand.

Even now he was only thinking of her.

"All may turn out well. I will make sure you are taken care of."

"Please stop saying that." She buried her face in his chest.

"Saying what? All may turn out well? Or I will make sure you're taken care of?"

Mazy let out a burst of laughter amid her tears. "That you'll make sure I'm taken care of. How can I bear it if you die?"

"Oh, heavens above!" Ro cried out behind her. "Is Sir Berenger in danger?"

Sir Berenger let Mazy pull away. She quickly rubbed the moisture from her eyes and faced Ro.

"Possibly," Sir Berenger said. "But probably not."

"Lady Bristow is spreading falsehoods about him," Mazy

said, keeping her voice low, taking deep breaths as she tried to control herself. "But we shall hope for the best."

She gazed up at him as he surreptitiously put his hand on her back.

"Will you tell her, or shall I?" He was smiling.

Mazy felt her cheeks start to burn. "Sir Berenger and I . . ."

"You're getting married!" Ro squealed and clapped her hands together.

"We can't tell anyone yet," Mazy said in a loud whisper.

"It might be best," Sir Berenger drawled, "if the king doesn't know I asked someone else to marry me."

At Ro's look of consternation, he added, "But I would tell the whole world this moment if I could, because I am never"—he pulled Mazy close to his side—"never going to let this beautiful woman out of my sight again."

Mazy wasn't sure if she should scoff at his dramatic—and impossible—declaration, or just smile indulgently. But since the former might hurt his feelings, she chose the latter.

"I am so very happy for both of you," Ro said, her smile as wide as Mazy had ever seen it.

She squeezed Mazy's arm. "I'll leave the two of you alone. In fact, you can spend the night in our extra bedroom tonight if you wish." She gave Sir Berenger a sidelong grin.

When Ro had left, Mazy let herself sink into his embrace again. With her cheek resting comfortably against his shoulder, she said, "Although I won't do what Ro may be suggesting, I do think you should stay here tonight. If you go back to the knights' barracks, the king may have you arrested. Or Lady Bristow may do something terrible, may have hired someone to murder you. I cannot bear to let you go back."

"Perhaps you have a good argument. But I need to go back. My things are there and—"

"But you don't want me to worry."

"Oh, I see how it will be." He gave her a half smile, half frown. "Now that you know how much I love you, you plan to use that control over me."

"No! No such thing." She shook her head, smiling as she saw the way he was looking at her. "I just don't want anything to happen to you. And I don't want to worry about you. There. Is that honest enough for you? Not controlling, is it? To say that I'm worried and I want you to stay here?"

"Then I shall stay."

He bent and kissed her lips, making her stomach turn inside out. How wonderful to be kissed by this man. Each kiss was better and more breathtaking than the last.

Kissing Sir Berenger was like soaring to the heavens and drifting dreamily back to earth. And she couldn't bear the thought that his life might be destroyed by the evil Lady Bristow. Surely God would not allow such a terrible thing.

As promised, Sir Berenger stayed the night in the extra room at the Swan. The next morning Mazy left little Juliana in Ro's care.

"She shall be my helper today as we make sweetmeats and pastries." Ro smiled at Juliana.

"I can knead the dough for Aunt Ro." Juliana giggled as she pounded a small amount of dough the size of a man's hand with her fist.

Already Juliana seemed much happier, almost as if she had forgotten Lady Bristow and Bristow Castle. Mazy's heart felt warm at seeing the child secure and happy.

As Sir Berenger and Mazy walked to the marketplace, she turned and motioned to Giles, who followed several horse-lengths behind them.

"Come and join us!" she called to him.

When he caught up with them, she said, "You don't have to keep it a secret anymore that you are my guard, that Sir Berenger is paying you to protect me."

Giles looked uncomfortable as he glanced at Sir Berenger, as if wondering if he had done something wrong.

"It's all right. I told her."

"Good," Giles said, his shoulders relaxing. "I don't like keeping secrets."

After they arrived at the market, Sir Berenger gave her a brief kiss before going back to the knights' barracks, leaving Mazy with Giles and the women who worked in her booths.

"I'll try to see if I can find out any news of my situation."

"Promise me you'll be careful."

"I promise."

Her heart rose at the look of love in his eyes. She watched him leave, leading his horse down the London street, and she felt as if her heart was going with him.

But now she had to tell Giles another secret.

"I did not tell Sir Berenger, since I didn't want him to try to stop me, but I am also going to the palace to try to see the king."

"Sir Berenger will not like that." Giles, ever calm and serious, did not blink as he stared back at her.

"I know, but I must try to help him. He deserves to have someone on his side."

She had to do something.

She left the two women in charge of the market booths and she and Giles made their way to the Palace of Westminster. Mazy was wearing her best dress. Though she was sure it was not as fine as the king was accustomed to seeing, at least she did not look terribly poor.

Giles was able to get her past the gatehouse, and then past the second set of guards, as he was well-known to them.

When they came to the entrance of the king's private chambers, Giles whispered something to the two guards at the door.

"He's in there," one of the guards said, nodding to a door across the hallway.

Giles turned to Mazy. "You'll have to make your appeal to the king's chancellor first."

Mazy's heart leapt. "Will you go with me?"

Giles nodded. They started toward the door, which flew open before they could reach it.

A well-dressed man glanced at Mazy and Giles before striding toward the king's apartments.

Mazy glanced at Giles, who nodded, indicating that the man was the chancellor.

"Sir, please forgive me," Mazy said, hurrying after him, "but I need to speak to the king."

The chancellor finally stopped and looked down his thin nose at her. He was quite tall and wore a shiny silk tunic of deep red.

"Who are you and what is your business with the king?" His voice was quiet and polite, but his eyes were sharp and intent on Mazy's face.

"I am Mazelina, daughter of the Baron Wexcombe. I need to speak to the king, to tell him what I know of Sir Berenger of Dericott and Lady Bristow."

"What do you know of them?"

"That is what I need to tell the king."

"The king is not accustomed to speaking with daughters of barons whom he has not summoned."

"I am sure that is true, but I think he will want to hear what I know of the knight and lady in question."

Truly, she did not know anything that Sir Berenger had not already told the king. But if she could corroborate Sir Berenger's story, he might listen. At least, she hoped he would.

After staring at her for a few moments, the chancellor sniffed and said, "If His Majesty is in good humor, I will ask him if he would wish to speak with you. Wait here."

"Thank you, sir." Mazy bowed as the guards opened the door for the man. He quickly disappeared behind the closing doors.

She turned and saw her brother John coming toward her.

John had a cold but concerned look as he broke away from a

group of guards and approached her. Without any sort of greeting upon reaching her, he said in a low voice, "You need to distance yourself from Sir Berenger. Lady Bristow plans to take the child away from him. She's sent men to get her, bad men."

Mazy immediately grabbed Giles and whispered in his ear, "Go to the Swan and protect Juliana. Hurry."

He nodded and left.

She turned back to John. "How do you know Lady Bristow? What do you know?"

"I knew her when I was training with her uncle's men. Even then she was someone who got whatever she wanted. You need to stay away from her, Mazy." He turned and went past the group of guards, disappearing down a long corridor.

TWENTY-SEVEN

MAZY STOOD WAITING OUTSIDE THE KING'S APARTMENT doors. At least the chancellor had not outright rejected her request to see the king.

Mazy tried to pray silently that she would remember everything she had hoped to say, and for Juliana's safety, but it was useless. Her mind was a jumble. She would simply be honest and tell the king in a straightforward manner what she knew of Sir Berenger and what she had seen of Lady Bristow.

No one spoke, and time seemed to drag on and on. Mazy began to think of all the terrible things that might happen if the king refused to speak to her, or worse, refused to believe her. Might she make things worse for Sir Berenger?

Just when her heart was in her throat at the imagined consequences of talking with the king, a servant opened the doors from inside the king's apartments.

"The king will see Mazelina of Wexcombe now."

Mazy stepped forward, a burst of energy flowing through her limbs. She followed the servant, hiding her hands in the fabric of her skirt by her sides to keep them from shaking.

They walked down a long corridor, the floor made of pale marble, but Mazy couldn't take note of her surroundings because her thoughts were racing around in her head even as she tried to calm them and bring them into order. *I just have to be honest. I will tell him the truth.* But even if she said the wrong things and the king hated her, rejecting her as Warin had done, God was in control. If God wanted her to have favor with the king, then she would.

All too soon, the servant stopped in front of a door, then opened it, letting her pass through ahead of him.

A young man sat on a high throne at the other end of the room. She did not look at anything else but fixed her eyes on the king.

"Mazelina of Wexcombe," the servant boomed from behind her.

Mazy sank into a deep bow.

"Come forward," the king said. Was he annoyed that she was taking too long? She hurried toward him, her breathing fast and shallow.

"Your Majesty, forgive me for imposing on you, but I wished to tell you what I am sure Your Majesty would want to know about the Lady Bristow and Sir Berenger, who is your loyal knight and captain of your guard, as you know. You see—" She had to pause to swallow, pressing her hand to her chest. Why was it so hard to breathe? Try as she might, she could not seem to squeeze a deep breath into her chest.

"You may speak."

But the king's words made her even more nervous. She paused to try to calm her breathing. It didn't help. Finally she continued, speaking haltingly.

"Sir Berenger and I have known each other for years. His sister, the Duchess of Strachleigh, is my friend, and we correspond with each other. Sir Berenger became my friend when I was just a girl and living at Strachleigh temporarily after my father died. He is the kindest and best man I know. He is honest and loyal—very loyal to you, our king—and he would never harm a child.

"But I shall come to the purpose of my . . . Forgive me." She pressed a hand to her chest, feeling the sweat under her arms. "I went to Bristow to warn Sir Berenger that the lady, Lady Bristow, had poisoned her first husband, the Earl of Bristow, and that the orphan child, her ward, whom she claimed was her cousin, was actually the earl's brother's daughter and therefore the heir. So when—"

"Who told you this?" The king looked as though this was the first time he was hearing this. Had Berenger not told him?

"I promised I would not tell, but it came from a reliable source."

"Go on."

"I came to tell Sir Berenger this information, but he had already witnessed the lady treating the child very ill. And while I was there, we found the lady's head house servant trying to force the child to eat some cooked mushrooms, which turned out to be death cap mushrooms. As I am sure Your Majesty knows, they are very poisonous."

"You saw this with your own eyes?"

"Yes, Your Majesty. The child was keeping her lips closed, refusing to eat the mushrooms. Sir Berenger stopped the servant from forcing her to eat them. And that is why we took the child with us when we left Bristow." Mazy's words were finally sounding less breathless. But she sounded so stilted.

"I see. And what else do you know of Lady Bristow?"

"Nothing, Your Majesty. I do not know her at all, but I know Sir Berenger would have married her because his king wished it if he hadn't discovered such treachery, and that he would never lie about anyone, especially not a woman. He takes his vows as a knight very seriously. He is a very honorable knight." Did she sound as if she was in love with Sir Berenger? Would the king tell her that her testimony meant nothing, as she was giving him opinions rather than facts?

"And his fellow knights and guards must know what a good man he is. That he is a knight of good character and good courage."

"And you, Mazelina of Wexcombe. Why are you in London and not in Wexcombe?"

Her heart stopped beating for a moment. "Shortly after my father died, I came to London with my brother, Sir John, who is a knight in your service."

"Who is your husband?"

"I am not married, Your Majesty. I sell goods in the marketplace. I buy the goods from women in the countryside, mostly widows who have children to feed, and I sell them. I have two booths in the market and two workers."

"More widows?"

"'More widows,' Your Majesty?"

"Are your two workers also widows?"

"Yes, Your Majesty."

The king smiled. "Is there anything else you wish to tell me?"

Was there? She tried to think of something important to share. "I thank you for allowing me to speak to you. I just wanted to plead with you to believe Sir Berenger. He is truthful and is truly the best man I know—good and compassionate and loyal to God and to his king and to England. He would never mistreat anyone. He only wants to do what is right." *And he loves me.*

She had to blow out a breath through her mouth to stave off the tears that pricked her eyelids.

The king stared at her with a mild expression. Finally he said, "I am glad you came to speak to me, Mazelina of Wexcombe. You may go now."

Was that all? Did he have no questions for her? But all she could do was to bow and leave.

As she was escorted from the king's chamber, she began to breathe freely again. Had she said the right things? Her cheeks were hot and her sides and hairline were damp and sweaty as the guards opened the door, then closed it behind her.

Giles was not waiting for her, as she had sent him to protect Juliana. Had he arrived in time and was Juliana safe? Why had she not mentioned that Lady Bristow was trying to take Juliana back? But perhaps it was best that she had not said anything about that. It might seem as if the lady cared more about the child than she actually did.

She hurried as fast as she could toward the Swan and prayed,

Thank You, God, for letting me meet with the king. I cannot know what the outcome will be, but I pray You will show Sir Berenger—and me—mercy and favor. God, please give us favor. And please don't let those bad men take Juliana away.

When she arrived at the Swan, Ro was sitting on a stool, hugging Juliana, and Giles was standing over them. All the customers were standing around talking, their eyes wide. Everyone turned toward her, nervous looks on their faces.

"Mazy!" Juliana called out.

She went to her and asked Ro, "What happened?"

"Wimarc and Silvester were here. Giles chased them away." Ro let out a long breath.

"I don't think they'll be back," Giles said, sheathing his sword.

"They wanted to take Juliana," Ro said.

Juliana reached for Mazy and clung tightly to her, squeezing her neck and pressing her cheek against hers.

"Don't worry," Mazy told her. "No one is taking you from us."

For once, John had served her well.

Berenger had not been summoned by the king. He still had not been given any duties at either the Tower of London or the king's palace since his return, so Berenger went back to the Swan that evening to see Mazy.

"Did you hear anything from the king?" she asked, a bright, hopeful look in her eyes.

"No, not yet."

"Don't worry." She patted his chest. "I'm sure you will hear good news, and soon."

Why did she seem so sure? "What have you done?"

Mazy's mouth fell open and she looked slightly guilty.

"Very well, I will tell you, since I don't want to keep secrets from you."

He waited, his heart in his throat.

"I went to the palace today and spoke with the king. He listened to all I had to say about what I knew about Juliana and you and Lady Bristow, and he seemed to believe me. He even said he was glad I came to talk to him, and he was actually quite pleasant."

"Mazy, you shouldn't have gone to the king." His stomach sank. "If he decides to believe Lady Bristow, you could be in danger."

"I don't think so. Besides, I think he believed me and will decide in your favor. After all, we have the truth on our side."

"But you don't know how treacherous Lady Bristow is. We have no idea who she might have on her side. She may come after you. I'm so sorry for putting you in danger." He covered his face with his hand. What had he been thinking? He'd never forgive himself if something bad happened to her.

"She did send two men to the Swan to try to take Juliana, but Giles protected her."

"Juliana is safe?"

"Yes, she is well and safe."

"How do you know it was Lady Bristow who sent them?"

"John warned me. Somehow he knew. It was the same two men we hired to run the Swan."

"I'll have them arrested and thrown in the Tower."

Juliana came hurrying up to him, and he picked her up, lifting her high, then hugging her. "There's my Juliana."

"Two scary men tried to take me, but Giles took out his sword." She held up her hand as if she were brandishing a sword. "Then they ran away."

Berenger took a deep breath and let it out, giving Juliana an extra squeeze. "I am glad. We won't let them take our Juliana."

"Come and take your bath," Ro said, walking up behind Berenger and taking the child from his arms. She smiled at him before walking with Juliana to the back of the alehouse.

"I'm so sorry I put you and Juliana in danger." He rubbed a hand down his face.

"You're not putting us in danger." She placed her palm on his cheek. "All will be well. Lady Bristow is not so powerful if she had to resort to hiring Wimarc and Silvester to do her evil bidding. I wonder how Lady Bristow found those two? Evil attracts evil, I suppose. But Giles, thanks be to God, was here to protect Juliana."

"I should be the one protecting you. Instead, once again I left you to be harassed and threatened by evil men. Truly, I am no better than your brothers, who left you to fend for yourself." He'd become the thing he hated—a person who did not take care of the people he loved, but instead focused only on getting what he wanted. *O God, I am a wretched man.*

"You have done nothing wrong, and you are the opposite

of my brothers. They refused to take any responsibility for my well-being, while you try to take on responsibilities that are not your own." She pulled his hand from his eyes, bringing her face close to his. "And you did take care of me by hiring Giles."

Indeed, there was a heaviness in his heart, a rebellion of his spirit, at the thought of her going out of her way to help him.

"It was for the best that I had to fend for myself. God has watched over me and protected me. It could have been a lot worse. You are here now. That is enough for me."

She put her arms around him and buried her face in his chest.

This woman was so good, everything a man could desire in a wife. His mind was racing with thoughts of the terrible things that might happen and the things he could do to make sure she stayed safe if he was executed or sent away. Was she right about him taking on responsibilities that were not his own?

But he would marry Mazy, Lord willing, and then he could rightfully take on the responsibility for her welfare and provision. But he also knew there was a limit to what he could control. He would do what he was able to do and pray and trust God for the rest.

Mazy was in the market the next day when two of the king's guards found her.

"Mazelina of Wexcombe, the king has summoned you to the palace."

Giles said in a booming voice, "What is this about? Why does the king wish to see her?"

"We were not told that," one of the guards said, "but she must come with us."

Mazy left her booths with the women in her employ and went with the guards. Giles accompanied her, always making sure to walk between her and the king's guards.

When they reached the palace, Sir Berenger was waiting outside the king's chamber. Their eyes met and he winked at her.

When the chancellor saw Mazy, he said, "You may go in now."

Sir Berenger took a deep breath and let it out, but then he gave her a brave look, pressing his lips together.

Mazy smiled at him. She wanted to hug him, kiss him, or at least squeeze his hand, but she refrained, as the doors to the king's chamber swung open.

"Come forth!" the king commanded. "Sir Berenger and Mazelina. How fares the child, Juliana?"

Sir Berenger looked at Mazy, indicating that she should answer.

"She is well in body and spirit, Your Majesty."

"I am glad to hear that. I made some inquiries and discovered that the child is, in all likelihood, exactly who you said she was." King Richard stared at Mazy.

There was silence as no one spoke. Finally, the king continued.

"I also discovered that you were both right about Lady Bristow. She has close connections to the king of France. In fact, after I told her what Sir Berenger had said about her, she left in the middle of the night. I sent my men after her. They arrested her as she was trying to board a ship bound for France in the company of two ruffians named Wimarc and Silvester and intercepted an incriminating letter she had written to King Charles of France."

Sir Berenger met Mazy's gaze before looking back at the king.

"She is a traitor, and she will be dealt with as such. I do not think she had enough information to do much damage to England, but if she could have, she would have. But I asked you both here because I might never have known either of these schemes of Lady Bristow's if it had not been for the two of you."

"It is our privilege, honor, and duty to help our king and our country," Sir Berenger said with a bow. "We are relieved that she has been captured and can no longer harm Juliana."

"I am now even more eager to reward you, Sir Berenger, and you, Mazelina of Wexcombe. But how shall I do it? Do you have any suggestions for me?"

Mazy could not tell if the king was serious or in jest. Again, Sir Berenger spoke first.

"Your Majesty, if I may be so bold, and if you will allow it, I have two requests. The first is that you would allow Mazelina and me to be the guardians of Juliana, the rightful heir of Bristow Castle and its holdings."

The king stared, his expression unchanging, before finally saying, "That request is granted, as I believe the two of you will take care of the child and her assets. What is your other request?"

"That you would allow me to marry Mazelina of Wexcombe, as I am in love with her."

"And what are the lady's wishes? Does Mazelina wish to marry Sir Berenger?"

"Yes, Your Majesty, I do." Mazy's heart leapt.

"Then your wish is my command. The two of you shall be married forthwith."

"I thank you." Sir Berenger reached out and put his arm around Mazelina.

Her heart was so full, tears welled up in her eyes.

"But as these are merely small requests, there is still the matter of a reward. And since your ward, Juliana of Bristow, is the heir of Bristow Castle, and since I wish to bestow a reward on you for yourselves and your heirs, I have decided to create a new title. From henceforth you shall be Berenger Raynsford, first Earl of Saynborne, and your holdings will be Saynborne Castle and all its demesne. It is not far from Bristow, so I believe you shall be able to watch over both until the child is of age."

"That is very generous of you. I thank you, on behalf of myself and any heirs God shall bless me with. We are very grateful, Your Majesty."

"Very grateful," Mazy echoed, unsure what else to say. She knew nothing of Saynborne Castle or its holdings, but Sir Berenger seemed sincerely pleased.

The king sent them on their way, and as soon as they were outside the doors of the king's chambers, Sir Berenger embraced her, holding her tight and burying his face in her hair.

He murmured something that sounded like, "Back from the dead."

"I can hardly believe it. All is well." Mazy squeezed him as hard as he was squeezing her.

Sir Berenger held her for a long time, right there in the hall with the king's guards and Giles looking on. When he finally loosened his grip, he was blinking fast and his eyes were watery.

She wished he could kiss her privately. But when they left the palace, their arms around each other, Sir Berenger stopped her on the green for a long kiss.

Sir Berenger gave her a quick peck on the nose, then asked, "Where would you like to get married?"

"Dericott."

"Not Wexcombe?"

"No. Your sister is more my family than anyone in Wexcombe."

"We shall do whatever you wish, for I want you to be ecstatically happy."

Her wonderful Sir Berenger. Her future husband. How she loved him! She even loved how dramatic he could be. Her brothers were both so unemotional, undemonstrative, uncaring; she was filled with joy to be with someone who was just their opposite.

Twenty-Eight

IN THE FEW DAYS BEFORE LEAVING LONDON TO TRAVEL TO Dericott for the wedding, Mazy and Ro hired a man to help Anselm at the Swan, and Mazy hired another widow to help in the market. Mazy and Sir Berenger asked Giles to help Ro with gathering the goods from the various suppliers, who were mostly widows. And Mazy turned the entire market business over to Ro, as Mazy would be too far away to travel back to London often enough to keep the business going.

When Mazy, Sir Berenger, and Juliana departed, Ro wished them well and saw them off, intending to travel with Giles a few days later after she had made sure everything was running smoothly with their market booths and the Swan. Ro was also tasked with informing Martin Fisher that Mazy would not be able to marry him, though she thanked him for his offer and wished him well.

Lady Delia was there when they arrived at Dericott Castle. She helped Mazy design her dress and had her own seamstress sew it. The dress turned out quite beautiful, with an embroidered and fitted cote-hardie, an embroidered belt at the hips, a bright-blue silk bliaud over it, which was open on the sides, and a light silk cape attached at the shoulders that went all the way down her back to her ankles.

Ro arrived the day before the ceremony, and she and Lady Delia helped Mazy dress the morning of her wedding, which dawned bright and clear, with only a few fluffy white clouds in the late winter sky.

Mazy made her way down the steps in her flowy, brightly colored dress, and Sir Berenger was waiting for her in the front entryway of the castle. If it had not been for the way he looked at her, with his deep blue eyes staring at her as if he could not believe his good fortune, she might have been impressed by his six handsome brothers standing around him. But she locked eyes with his, and no one else seemed to exist.

"You are so beautiful," he said, reaching out with one hand, his voice starting to choke up on the last word, his eye shimmering with tears. He cleared his throat, as if to dispel the tears.

"You are so handsome."

And he was. His face was clean-shaven, and his blue eyes seemed even more distinct and bright. His brown hair was perfect in its slight unruliness. He wore a blue sleeveless tunic, embroidered with silver thread, that perfectly offset her blue dress. And his white shirt set off his tanned skin, his perfect neck and throat, his masculine chin, and his hair, which was nearly touching his shoulders.

But the best part of her new husband-to-be was the sweet look of love and tenderness on his face.

She'd thought she wanted to travel with her father, that that was her dream and dearest wish. Then she'd thought she wanted only to take care of herself. And finally, she realized she wanted someone who would love her and whom she could love. But with Sir Berenger, she had all of that and so much more. She had someone whose gentle, kind heart was all hers, and yet he was his own person, and he respected and admired her for being her own person as well.

They belonged together, and they loved and respected each other enough to let them be themselves, a whole person whether they were together or separate.

But they much preferred being together.

All of these things went through her head as they walked, arm in arm, toward the church in the village below the castle.

Roger was with Martha and a small group of servants from Strachleigh Castle. Sir Berenger saw the boy first, and he and Mazy waved and called to him. He waved back with a huge smile that made tears spring to Mazy's eyes. Roger and Martha walked along with Mazy and Sir Berenger, shouting well wishes and streaming ribbons on the ends of sticks, laughing and smiling.

Sir Berenger's family also walked with them, all six of his brothers, including his oldest two and their wives, and Lady Delia and the Duke of Strachleigh. Sir Berenger waved at them, but most of the time he kept his eyes on her face.

When they were nearly to the church, he leaned down and whispered, "You have made me the happiest man in the world."

"And I am the happiest woman." She couldn't help smiling. In fact, she couldn't seem to stop smiling.

Mazy wanted to remember every detail of this day—the way the sun looked on Sir Berenger's hair, his family looking so happy, the way the village church seemed to wink at them as the sun reflected off the colored glass of the windows, and the happy tears in Lady Delia's eyes. Most of all, she hoped she never forgot how Sir Berenger was looking at her, the way he held on to her arm that was looped through his. The way she felt today should sustain her through whatever trials might come their way.

The priest was waiting for them at the top of the steps. They said their vows before the crowd, then went inside for the rest of the wedding ceremony. And when they made the trek back up the castle mount, they seemed even giddier and more celebratory than they had earlier.

Lord Dericott, who was Berenger's brother Edwin, along with his lovely wife, Lady Audrey, had set up trestle tables on the grassy area in front of the castle, spread with food and drink to share with the villagers and guests.

The guests all bestowed on them a wedding blessing and wishes for their health, an abundance of children, prosperity, and every happiness. But no matter who came to wish them joy, Berenger kept his hand in Mazy's.

By the end of the day, after they had feasted and danced for hours, Mazy was ready to give all her attention to her husband, and he was looking at her like she was the only person in the castle.

After spending a few nights in a small guesthouse about a hundred yards from Dericott Castle, they set out on their journey with Juliana to visit Bristow Castle, which they would place in the hands of a steward until Juliana was of age. Then they'd be traveling thirty miles north of Bristow to Saynborne Castle, where they would all live together.

When they were still half a day's ride from Bristow Castle, they saw a man on horseback galloping toward them, a small cloud of dust behind him.

"It's Lady Bristow's steward," Berenger said. They had sent word to him that they were coming, so it was not so strange that the man was coming to meet them, but there was something about the expression on his face that told Berenger something was wrong.

The steward rode straight up to Berenger. "Sir, Bristow Castle has burned. The walls are still standing, but the roof and all inside it are gone."

Mazy was glad Juliana was asleep in her new nurse's lap so that she wouldn't hear anything that might upset her. But just imagining that great and mighty fortress burned to the ground gave her a sick feeling in her stomach.

Berenger sent a few men ahead of them to survey the damage and to see if there was anything that could be salvaged.

He and Mazy exchanged a look. Could Lady Bristow have been responsible for burning down the castle? Mazy would not be surprised if the woman had ordered one of the servants to set fire to the castle in retaliation. She couldn't have it, and she wouldn't want anyone else to have it either.

When they were nearing the castle in the late afternoon, Mazy could smell the smoke. Juliana was waking up, and she whimpered and reached out for Mazy. She took the child and placed her on her horse in front of her. Juliana hid her face in Mazy's chest.

"Please don't let Lady Bristow take me away," Juliana said.

"No, no, we will not let her take you. She's nowhere near here. The king has arrested her and locked her away. You are safe with us."

But when they came into sight of the blackened ruins of the castle, Juliana began to sob.

"All is well." Mazy tried to comfort the child, but her eyes were wild, and she would not stop clinging to Mazy and crying.

"What are you afraid of?" Mazy said.

"Lady Bristow is coming to get me."

"No, she won't. She will never hurt you again. She's gone forever, and you are safe with us."

"There was a ship and some men. I heard her talking in French, and she slapped me. She said if I ever told anyone, she would strangle me in my sleep."

"What ship, Juliana?" Mazy was staring, horrified.

"She must mean the French ship that landed in the cove. Probably the same one I saw. But don't worry, Juliana. Lady Bristow will never hurt you again. You can tell us anything you wish and she cannot harm you."

Mazy smoothed Juliana's hair back. Her eyes had a haunted look, and she was obviously still not sure she believed she was safe.

"Why don't you take Juliana and get back on the road to Saynborne?" Berenger said. "I'll send most of the guards with you."

"Will you catch up with us?" Mazy clung to his hand much the same way Juliana had been clinging to her.

"We will. I will be back with you before night falls."

"If you don't, we will stop and wait for you."

Berenger nodded, then gave her a kiss on the lips before addressing the guards and telling them the plan.

Mazy did her best to smile and keep Juliana calm and happy, trying not to worry about Berenger. They rode the rest of the day at a slower pace, putting distance between them and the burned-out castle.

Later that day, when she saw Berenger coming toward her looking healthy and strong and peaceful, the air rushed out of her and she whispered, "Thank You, God. Thank You."

Berenger rode his horse straight to her. "Did you encounter any problems?" he asked.

"No. Did you?"

"No." He obviously didn't want to speak of the fire in front of Juliana.

That night as they bedded down in a small stand of trees between the road and a stream, Mazy lay facing Berenger. "Did you discover who burned Bristow Castle?"

"Not for certain. But I spoke to Juliana's former nurse. She heard that a letter had arrived for the head house servant, who was very loyal to Lady Bristow. The rumor is that Lady Bristow ordered the head house servant to set the castle aflame."

"You don't seem upset about it burning," she whispered.

Berenger didn't reply right away. After a few moments he said, "I am sorry for the people who no longer have a position and are worried about their future. But the king will most likely order that the castle be rebuilt, since it was in an important location for the country's defense. But even if the king does not provide, Juliana is our daughter now, and if her holdings in Bristow are not enough to rebuild the castle, she will be well, as we will always take care of her. I know you feel the same way."

"Of course. But it still seems like a sad loss."

"It is, but think about it like this. Now Juliana will never have to see the place where she was bullied and abused. Perhaps if there is nothing to remind her, she will forget completely the unkind things that were done to her."

Mazy placed her hand against Berenger's cheek. "You are so wonderful and kind. God was so good to give me you."

"I feel the same." Berenger brushed her cheek with his fingertips. "There is no other woman I could ever want. Just my Mazy Mazelina, the Knife Girl of London, the sweetest and bravest woman in England."

Mazy smiled at his compliments and kissed his hand. She fell asleep holding his hand against her cheek.

Today was the day they would see their own Saynborne Castle and its lands.

Already Mazy had seen so much of the country that her father had once promised to show her. And soon she would see the vast waters of the sea that she had heard described but had never beheld.

"Slow down," Berenger said, smiling as if about to laugh at her.

Mazy hadn't realized she'd been going any faster than usual. "I'm just so eager to see it. Aren't you?"

"I don't want you to be disappointed."

"How could I be disappointed?"

But then she started thinking, if it turned out to be a ruin, with the roof leaking and no functional shutters on the windows, or if there were no trees or flowers . . .

"I won't be disappointed." She smiled to reassure him and herself.

Juliana was riding with her nurse and was bouncing up and down. "I hear the sea!" she cried.

Mazy heard the faint roar of the sea waves as they rode ever closer. Others had described the sound to her as a constant rushing in one's ears, or like the beating of the wings of a large flock of birds, but now she was hearing it for herself. Her heart raced as she tried to imagine how vast it would be.

She'd thought the land would be rocky, but all was lush and green farmland, with some marshland mixed in. And then there it was, the vast sea, shining blue and bluer as it spanned the east and touched the sky in the distance.

They rode along the sandy path that followed the shoreline, a short cliff on their right that fell straight down to the narrow shore below, and always the vast sea was there beside them.

"I think I see it." Berenger pointed. A tower was visible above the tops of trees. Then the road curved around and they lost sight of it.

"Do you think it will need a lot of work?" Mazy asked. She had already decided she could help repair the roof if necessary. After all, she had helped build her own booth at the market and had helped Ro make repairs on the Swan when her father was sick.

"I don't think so." Berenger gazed at her with a content expression. "Lord Marcheford, the previous owner, would have kept it in good condition, and he only just died a few months ago."

Lord Marcheford was a viscount who had died without an heir, but Mazy had never paid much attention to nobles or what they did or where they lived. Ro had been more curious about such things than Mazy. She certainly had no idea how responsible or fastidious Lord Marcheford had been.

"It looks as if it has a good view of the sea."

"We shall soon find out." Berenger winked at her.

How could he be so calm?

Juliana was crying now, as she was overly tired and needing sleep. The nurse was trying to calm her, offering her a drink of water or a bit of cheese and a roll of bread. She grew quiet, and Mazy saw that she had fallen asleep against her nurse's arm.

As they rode along, Mazy saw a flake of snow, then another and another. It was snowing in earnest while they were climbing the castle mount, the castle gradually coming into view. As they rounded the last bend, Mazy gasped.

"It's more magnificent than I imagined," Mazy breathed.

Thankfully it was not snowing hard enough to obscure their view of the castle. There were three towers of varying sizes, one square and two round, with the main body of the castle having two rows of windows showing two levels, and every tower and roof was ringed with crenelations of masonry and gray stone.

"It's larger than I thought," Berenger said.

"It's huge," Mazy said softly, not wanting to wake Juliana. "I don't think I've ever seen a castle I liked more."

Berenger smiled. "I'm glad to hear that."

No doubt he was amused at her enthusiasm, but she was too happy to care. It was a magnificent castle, and she was in awe.

They were greeted by the servants, who all welcomed them. Berenger met the reeve and steward, and the three of them stepped into the former owner's study, where he kept his records. The nurse and Juliana went into the kitchen with the cook. Meanwhile, Mazy walked with the head house servant through the castle as she showed her all the rooms.

"Let me know which bedroom you and Lord Saynborne would like for yourselves."

It took Mazy a moment to realize she meant Berenger, her husband, when she said "Lord Saynborne." She would have to accustom herself to that name and title, as well as her own, for she was now Lady Saynborne.

After surveying much of the castle, she lingered in the bed-chambers on the upper level while the servant hurried off, saying, "I will make sure the servants are attending to their duties. But if you need anything, Lady Saynborne, ring the bell."

"Thank you very much," Mazy said.

She would have to get used to having servants available to her. She had grown up with servants, but she'd always thought of them as her father's servants, and they were as apt to scold her as to show her deference. This would be a new experience altogether.

She wandered from room to room, testing each of the beds, looking at the view from each window, weighing which room would suit her and Berenger best. She was staring out a window, watching the flurries of tiny snowflakes, when Berenger came in.

He put his arms around her from behind and she rested the back of her head against his shoulder.

"Is this not the most glorious view? The snow makes it look almost magical."

"Yes. And when you get tired of hearing the noise of the sea and the sight of it, I shall take you to see England's finest lakes and hills, then the mountains of Scotland."

"I can hardly imagine I would ever tire of it, but I shall want to see the lakes and mountains someday." She raised her brows at him, smiling playfully. "And there is plenty of room here to teach Juliana archery, knife-throwing, and horsemanship."

"What if she doesn't want to learn those things?"

"Then I can teach her to play the lute, and you can teach her to play the pipe. Remember the time when we played those songs for Roger at Strachleigh? I enjoyed that so much." She sighed.

He kissed the top of her head and hugged her tighter. "Then we shall have to play together again, as often as you like."

She turned around in his arms and kissed him.

"I am such a fortunate man."

"Yes, you are. You might have thrown all this away if you'd married Lady Bristow."

He was silent. Finally he said, "I know you are teasing me, but I feel sick when I think about it. You were there, right in front of me, and I almost turned my back on you. I would have hated myself if I had. I'm sorry I ever thought about marrying anyone else."

"I shouldn't tease you. I will thank God instead that He brought us together. And I'm sorry I was angry with you and felt abandoned by you. I had no right to feel that way."

"Yes, you did."

"No, I didn't. You did not owe me anything, and you were not responsible for me."

"But after your brothers abandoned you, I understand why you felt the way you did."

Mazy's happiness was a warm, glowing contentment that filled her and made her want to bless Berenger the way his love had blessed her.

They went through the rooms together and chose the bedchamber that would belong to the Lord and Lady of Saynborne. Then they went to find Juliana, to take her for their first walk on the ocean shore beside their new home, a home that would be the shelter they all needed from the hurts and attacks they had endured. This castle was a fortress, but also a home, where love would be the highest and best ideal, and where they would never again have to feel like they were alone or fending for themselves.

Here they were a family, safe and free to be themselves, to love and be loved. Here they would be their best selves, together, celebrating and supporting each other.

Together they would be a fortress as constant as the waves of the sea.

ACKNOWLEDGMENTS

I WANT TO THANK MY PUBLISHER, THOMAS NELSON, FOR everything they do and for making this series possible. I'm so grateful for all the great people who do so much excellent work for my books, from marketing to editing to cover design. Thank you so much!

Thanks to my daughters and husband for always being willing to listen to me rehash my story and help me brainstorm. I love you! And any friends who have listened to me talk endlessly about a story as I try to come up with the rest of the plot, thank you for being long-suffering. I'm thinking of you, Regina Carbulon!

I always want to thank my delightful friend and agent, Natasha Kern, who goes above and beyond in so many ways. There are a million stressful things that can happen, and yet you never seem stressed! Thank you for always having my back.

I feel like this book is special, as if it brought me full circle somehow. To me it represents that the painful transition in my life was over and I could put my true romantic self into my books again. I pray everyone falls in love with Mazy and Berenger as much as I did!

And I'm so thankful to God for allowing me to pursue my dream of writing and publishing. I pray He is glorified through my stories.

Thanks to my readers, for whom I am so grateful. May God bless you with every good thing.

DISCUSSION QUESTIONS

1. What was Mazy's dream when she was growing up? Why did her dream not come true the way she had hoped? Do you think she eventually got what she dreamed of?

2. Why did Mazy run away from home after her father died? Again, things did not initially turn out the way she'd hoped when she went to visit her brother at Strachleigh, but how did her life work out in the end?

3. Why did Berenger go to Prussia to fight? Did he get what he hoped he would from this venture?

4. How did Mazy support herself in London? How was this fulfilling? In what ways was it not fulfilling for Mazy?

5. How did Mazy defend herself? Do you think she enjoyed defending herself? Why or why not? How would you cope if you were forced to physically defend yourself, to the point of harming another person?

6. In what ways were Mazy's two brothers similar? How

were they different? Do you think Sir John redeemed himself in the end?

7. What traits did Sir Berenger possess that appealed to Mazy, and why? What was it about Mazy that appealed to Berenger? Why did he not marry her when he came back from fighting in Prussia?

8. Knights had to make a vow to uphold certain values and do what was right, but some knights broke their vows. How are knights similar to people in authority today?

9. Why did Mazy not want to marry Martin?

10. Why did Mazy wish to warn Sir Berenger about Lady Bristow? Would you have done the same thing? Or would you have decided he deserved what he got?

11. What do you make of Sir John's character and personality? Was Mazy wrong to hope that her brothers would protect her?

12. Why did Sir Berenger feel responsible for Mazy's well-being? And why was Mazy so angry with him when he wanted to hire someone to protect her?

13. What did Sir Berenger and Mazy learn about accepting help from others? What did they learn about helping others?

From the Publisher

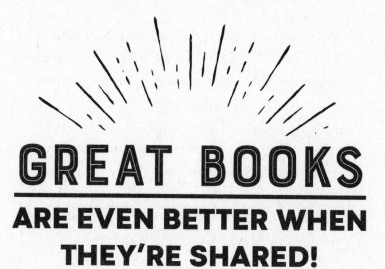

GREAT BOOKS

ARE EVEN BETTER WHEN THEY'RE SHARED!

Help other readers find this one:

- Post a review at your favorite online bookseller

- Post a picture on a social media account and share why you enjoyed it

- Send a note to a friend who would also love it—or better yet, give them a copy

Thanks for reading!

Don't miss any of Melanie Dickerson's
Dericott Tales

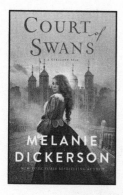

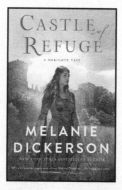

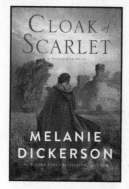

Available June 2023

Available in print, e-book, and audio

THOMAS NELSON
Since 1798

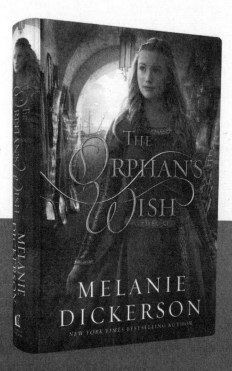

ABOUT THE AUTHOR

Jodie Westfall Photography

MELANIE DICKERSON IS A *NEW York Times* bestselling author and two-time Christy Award winner. Melanie spends her time daydreaming, researching the most fascinating historical time periods, and writing and editing her happily-ever-afters.

Visit her online at MelanieDickerson.com
Facebook: @MelanieDickersonBooks
Twitter: @MelanieAuthor
Instagram: @melaniedickerson123